"Then you will take me home."

He gave a quick nod and moved closer.

His imposing size made her wish she could fade into the corner, but that would be retreating. Aliss leaned forward, her face meeting his, leaving her captor weaponless.

A glint surfaced in his eyes. "How do you know you can trust me?"

"I can ask the same of you."

His icy stare froze her. "Do not think to play games with my people's lives."

"How dare you even suggest that!"

"I dare anything when it comes to the protection of my people."

"Like kidnapping a helpless healer."

He glared at her. "You are far from helpless."

His compliment startled her.

"You will heal my people," he said sternly.

"You will return me home." Her words were meant to seal their bargain and she could only pray that he was a warrior true to his word . . .

Other **AVON ROMANCES**

DONNA FLETCHER

THE BEWITCHING TWIN

AVON BOOKS
An Imprint of HarperCollinsPublishers

AVON BOOKS
An Imprint of HarperCollins*Publishers*
10 East 53rd Street
New York, New York 10022-5299

Copyright © 2006 by Donna Fletcher
ISBN-13: 978-0-06-075783-0
ISBN-10: 0-06-075783-3
www.avonromance.com

First Avon Books paperback printing: March 2006

Avon Trademark Reg. U.S. Pat. Off. and in Other Countries, Marca Registrada, Hecho en U.S.A.
HarperCollins® is a registered trademark of HarperCollins Publishers Inc.

Printed in the U.S.A.

10 9 8 7 6 5 4 3 2 1

Chapter 1

He is dying.

Aliss hurriedly dressed, slipping into her dark green skirt and pale yellow blouse, while concern over the cleric's claim of his imminent death weighed on her mind. The cleric had been fine just this morning when she spoke with him. How could he be dying?

As a healer, she did not take any illness lightly, and being woken in the dark of night by a distraught clan member made one assume the worst.

Aliss quickly scooped her long red hair on top of her head, fastened it with a couple of bone combs, slipped into her doeskin boots, grabbed her healing basket sitting beside the door, and hurried out of her cottage.

A chill filled the late night air, reminding her

1

that although spring had arrived a few weeks ago winter was reluctant to depart. She should have grabbed her shawl but it did not matter. The cleric's cottage was but a short distance.

A dark cloud blocked the light of the near full moon, causing Aliss to be more cautious of her steps. The night seemed more quiet than usual, not a soul stirred, the only sound a mere whispered breeze.

She arrived at the cleric's cottage and was disturbed to find the ill man alone. It was unusual that someone would not have remained at his side while she was summoned. The clan Hellewyk always looked after each other and although the young cleric had only been with them a month, he was considered family and treated as such.

Aliss hurried to his bedside, dropping her basket beside her.

"Aliss, is that you?"

"Aye, Cleric John." She reached out to touch the man's forehead, worried that fever might be the culprit.

He grabbed her wrist. "You brought your healing basket with you."

"Worry not, I have what I need to tend you."

"It holds *all* you need?"

She hoped to ease his concern. "My cottage is not far if I should need more."

"Nay, I do not want you to leave me. Does your basket not hold enough healing herbs?"

"It is filled with more than just herbs. I am certain that no matter what ails you, I have something to soothe it and make you well."

"You are a very good healer."

"So I have been told. Now let me tend you, for I do not think you are dying."

"I am sorry."

"You have nothing to be sorry for," Aliss said. Thinking he meant that he had disturbed her sleep, she sought to soothe him. "Illness and births do not wait for the light of day. I am often summoned in the middle of the night."

"Something I counted on." He leaped off the bed, grabbed her other wrist, forcing both behind her back, and had her trussed like a captive animal before she could blink.

Her scream barely reached her throat when a cloth was shoved into her mouth. A strip of cloth was wound around her mouth and head and tied at the back.

The room suddenly turned upside down when he hefted her over his shoulder, grabbed her healing basket and scurried to the door. He paused cautiously and once satisfied they were alone, he left the cottage without bothering to close the door behind him.

Panic rushed up and sent a wave of nausea coursing through her. Who was this man since he obviously was not a cleric? Why was he abducting her? Where was he taking her?

Fear struck her heart. The culprit who had abducted her and her twin sister Fiona when they were newborns had been caught and punished. They had been reunited with their parents and their brother Raynor.

Could this abduction somehow be connected?

She was jostled as her abductor lost his balance but he quickly regained his footing.

His trail would be easy for Fiona to follow. She was an excellent hunter and horseman and skilled in weaponry. Protective of Aliss, she would let nothing stop her from hunting the kidnapper down, not her pregnancy or her husband Tarr, chieftain of the clan Hellewyk.

Fiona would come after her, she had no doubt. But it disturbed her that her abductor was leaving a trail someone could easily track, because it meant he was either a fool or he had a plan that made it unimportant if he was followed.

She jerked her head up.

Had she heard voices? Were they behind her?

Distant footsteps kept pace with the cleric. She strained to see in the dark. Had someone discovered her absence already? Was her rescue close at hand? She continued to stare into the darkness, but not a single shadow intruded on the night.

She prayed for courage and prayed her sister followed. She heard the footsteps again, but again they faded.

Were Tarr's men surrounding them this very moment? Would she soon be returned home to family and friends?

Please let this nightmare end soon.

A sudden thought struck and she did not know whether to be fearful or relieved. This abduction could have to do with recent events that had not only upset her but her parents' clan Blackshaw as well as clan Hellewyk.

It had all started with a prediction made by the prophetess Giann before the twins were born. It was also the reason for their kidnapping those many years ago. Destruction to the clan was predicted if one twin did not wed. However, recently it was learned that destruction would befall the clan if *both* twins did not wed. When the Blackshaw and Hellewyk clans learned of this, clan members began demanding that Aliss wed soon since the prediction did not specify which clan would be affected.

Tarr was then forced to deliver the unpleasant news to Aliss, though he emphasized that she could choose her own husband, just as long as she did so quickly.

She did not wish to wed. Healing was her life and she had no time to pamper or care for a husband.

Could this abduction be a man intent on wedding her? The clan Hellewyk was known for its strength and wealth. Any number of men would find it advantageous to wed her.

The man come to a halt and stilled.

Had he heard the footfalls too? Did they concern him?

She hoped they did, for then it would mean rescue was imminent.

He moved again, but more cautiously.

Aliss tried to calm herself. She had to remain alert and ready for anything, whether it was a rescue or a chance to escape. Fearful or not, she had to do what she could to free herself, or to survive.

They came upon a small clearing and he

stopped. Suddenly footsteps rushed at them and four men quickly surrounded them. She recognized not a one of them.

"No one has followed," one said.

Fear gripped her as her abductor eased her off his shoulder and onto her feet.

"Her absence remains unknown," said another.

Her stomach clenched. No one would know of her disappearance until morning. She was on her own.

"We must get moving. The others wait for us," one said.

There were more of them? Why were so many men needed to capture one lone woman?

They said no more. Her abductor gave her a slight shove, a silent order for her to walk, and she did.

The clouds refused to release the moon, making it difficult to see the path they traveled. Aliss focused her attention on the trail, which gave her little time to study the men surrounding her.

But a quick assessment revealed they wore no plaids, and though the men had spoken her language, their tongues had not flowed easily. They were also very tall except for the cleric; his head only reached their shoulders.

She shivered as she realized she walked with foreigners.

Aliss stumbled several times along the way and was righted by the strong hand of one of the four men. Their concern had her wondering if they meant her no harm, until the imposter cleric spoke up.

"Keep her safe. He will have our heads if she is harmed before he has hold of her."

Who wanted hold of her and for what reason?

"Hurry, we must break shore by sunrise."

His words rang repeatedly in her ears as they hurried her along. They were taking her to a boat. They intended to sail off with her. Panic gripped her heart and penetrated her soul. She wanted to scream. How would Fiona follow? She was not a skilled sailor and the Hellewyk clan fished from the shores of the lochs and rivers, using a small rowboat or two now and again. They possessed no sailing ships large enough to carry a troop of warriors.

The more she fretted over her situation the more she realized she had to attempt an escape. If they sailed off with her, she would probably never set foot on Scottish soil again.

She had to be courageous and take a chance. No matter how fearful she was, she had to make certain they did not get her on the boat.

It was a couple of hours' walk to the coastline, but with a hurried pace they were sure to arrive sooner. If she were going to attempt an escape, it would need to be soon or else she would not have the cover of the woods for protection.

Once they hit open land, there would be no place for her to hide. It was now or never. She had to take the chance and run. She could not wait.

Run!

Aliss obeyed the scream in her head and twisted to her left, startling the men around her and giving her enough time to scoot past them into the dark woods. It was unfamiliar territory to her and she counted on it being the same for the men.

She gained a distance on them and paused behind a thick tree, listening for footsteps. She heard them and they were headed straight for her. If she ran, they would certainly catch her. If she remained where she was, melted against the tree, the moon still obscured by a cloud, then they just might not notice her and pass her by.

She could then wait until she heard their footfalls no more and backtrack and begin her journey home with caution.

A sudden strong breeze swept through the woods, sending the tree's huge drooping branches sweeping down to hug her like a protective mother.

The men shot past her and she watched their shadowy shapes fade in the distance. She waited several more minutes before she scurried around the tree and hurried off in the direction from which she had come.

Aliss had traveled only a few feet when the potent cry of a wolf halted her abruptly. She shivered, for it sounded close by. Caution had her taking careful steps, hoping not to alert the animal to her presence, yet knowing tardy steps could mean capture.

She now had two predators to worry about and no way of protecting herself with her hands tied behind her back. She twisted her wrists, loosening the ties as she walked.

A few feet more and hearing no other sounds,

she stopped and with haste used the side of a tree to work the cloth off her mouth. When free, she spat out the gag and took several deep breaths.

She hurried off again, praying she was headed in the right direction. When sunrise was near, she would seek shelter and remain hidden. Her absence in the village would be discovered when she did not arrive to share the morning meal with her sister. She always let Fiona know if she were unable to attend, so that she would not worry. Her sister would realize right away that something was wrong and go in search of her. Fiona and Tarr would then be on her trail in no time. She had to remain free for a few more hours and then she would be rescued; she was certain of it.

A sudden noise pierced through her thoughts.

She failed to identify it and that sent fear racing through her. She hastened her pace just as she recognized approaching footfalls.

Someone followed her.

Was it man or beast?

Chapter 2

A wolf's soulful howl ripped through the night.

Aliss finally shook her hands free of the ties and broke into a run. She doubted she could outrun a wolf but then she was not sure who stalked her.

She jolted to a halt when her captors burst out of the woods and surrounded her. They circled her with their arms extended, keeping her caged, allowing her no avenue of escape.

"We have her, Wolf," the cleric cried.

Dread hit her like a mighty wave. Wolf was the leader of the barbarian Wolf clan from the north. He had attacked the clan Hellewyk on two occasions, causing much damage yet taking no lives. It had been surmised that he had been searching for someone within the clan.

Had that someone been her?

The men moved away from her, leaving her unguarded and alone to face the Wolf. Fear made every limb tremble and wiped away what courage she had managed to maintain. A brief thought to drop to her knees in a show of submission to the terrifying Wolf crossed her mind. However, pride interceded, along with her sister's firm reminder that strength was a shield that deflected the mightiest of weapons.

The clouds shifted apart and drifted off, releasing the moonlight to penetrate the darkness.

He emerged from the darkness with the sleek grace of an animal confident in his skills and potency and with no fear of any foe. He was of a towering height, made even more intimidating by the black wolf head draped over his shoulder, the tail of the beast hanging at his side. A black leather tunic, leggings, and boots almost succeeded in obscuring him in the darkness.

Moonlight danced off reddish golden streaks that raged through chest-length dark blond hair, while harsh lines and solid curves of muscle, which would seem hard to some, ran smoothly together, startling the senses. Blazing green eyes that matched her own pinned her to where she already stood frozen.

He made his way to her and without a word grabbed her, flung her over his shoulder, and took off into the night like an animal all too familiar with the shadowy landscape.

It was not long before they reached the end of the woods and entered the stretch of rocky and ragged land that preceded the coastline. She knew that when they set foot on open ground there would be no options left to her.

Her fate was sealed.

Sunrise greeted them as they approached the rowboats that waited at the water's edge. In the distance, Aliss could see the outline of a large boat, Viking in style though different enough to make one wonder about its origins.

The Wolf dumped her into the rowboat, and when she attempted to scramble out in one last try for freedom, he grabbed her arm and yanked her back. She fell against him, hitting hard muscle. He held her firm, her face plastered to his solid chest and the wolf's face staring her right in the eyes.

It surprised her that he carried no dirk or sword at his side, but then the strength of his hands warned her that they were weapons enough to do severe damage to a man let alone a woman.

The rowboat rolled with the waves as it left the shore and Aliss cast sorrowful eyes on the Scottish coastline, fearing she might never set foot on her homeland again. She grew ill at the thought, and that, combined with the rough roll of the boat, made her feel ready to heave.

She raised pleading eyes to him, and before she could say a word, he turned her quickly, bending her over the side of the boat. With an arm around her waist, he held her head as she retched repeatedly.

When she finished, her body and determination spent, he cradled her against him but spoke not a word. She felt confused. Why was the Wolf being so considerate?

They were soon at the ship, and she was tossed over his shoulder, carried up a rope ladder, and deposited on the top of a barrel. He walked off, stopped, grabbed a fur cloak from a chest and tossed it to her. She caught it, gratefully wrapping herself in its warmth. Whether she shivered because of concern for her plight or the morning chill she was not certain; she only knew that the cold had seeped into her bones and she could not stop trembling.

The Wolf took quick charge of his men and soon the numerous oars cut the water like sharp knives and the striped sail caught a good wind. Before long, the shore became a small dot in the distance until with a blink of an eye it vanished.

"We will be home by nightfall, Rogan," the man who led the oarsmen called out, and the Wolf leader nodded.

Rogan.

Aliss now knew his given name and that they were returning to their home. If she remembered correctly, the Wolf clan inhabited an isolated island off the north coast of Scotland. A place that neither the Scotsmen nor the Norsemen claimed as home. As far as she knew, the Wolf clan was made up of nomads with allegiance to no one but themselves. They were in fact barbarians and the thought made her tremble. She burrowed deeper into the fur cloak, hoping to ease her worrisome chills.

"With their pitiful boats the Hellewyk clan will not be following us any time soon," laughed one of the men.

"You call those splints of wood boats?" chided another.

The men continued to poke fun at her clan as they sped through the water at an astonishing speed. Sadly, they were right about the boats. They were much too small to brave the ocean waters, or to carry a sufficient fighting force.

"Winter freeze will be the first we hear of them," joked another.

Aliss listened and digested the news like a bad piece of meat. It would be winter before Fiona and Tarr could reach her. She was on her own.

She needed a plan but her thoughts were scattered, her fear so great that her mind was too jumbled to think cohesively. Fiona would know what to do but she was not Fiona. Aliss was a learned healer; she defended lives against illnesses. She abhorred the fighting that senselessly took lives and left endless suffering in its wake.

She glanced at the leader of the Wolf clan talking with one of the men at the bow of the ship. He stood with confidence, his sturdy legs holding firm as the ship fought the choppy waters. His arms lay crossed over his wide chest and his head was held high, demanding respect. He would surely frighten his enemy to death before they could draw a sword, but perhaps she gave too much credence to his arresting appearance.

No matter how strong a man, he could be

struck down with a single blow or by a sickness. No man was impervious, though Rogan certainly gave the appearance of infallibility. He stood at the ship's bow with a confident arrogance. He was the master, the ship his mistress who obeyed his every command.

How did she deal with such a man?

He turned his head and his glance caught her stare. She quickly turned away and chided herself for letting him intimidate her. She would need to deal with this man sooner or later, but how?

How did she not let him frighten her?

Her adversaries were usually illnesses. After determining the cause, she could then supply the means with which to conquer it. If she knew why he had abducted her, perhaps then she could conquer her fright and he would appear less intimidating.

She jumped when another fur was dropped across her lap and Rogan squatted down on his haunches beside her.

She was caught by the dark green of his eyes. A faint scar fanned the corner of his right eye and she thought he must have been very young when he had received it. Faint lines around his mouth and weathered bronze skin had her wondering about his age.

"Many questions must run through your mind."

"As you would expect of someone who has just been abducted," she said, "and does not know why."

"I have need of you."

"Define this need," she said sharply, before losing confidence.

"Your skills. They are necessary to my clan."

"Tell me more," she said hesitantly, daring to hope that was all he wanted of her.

"Illness has ravaged my clan. Old and young alike are dying and some are not affected at all. It is as if the heavens pick and choose who will be spared. Your skill as a healer is known and I need it to help save my people."

"Then I wish to make a trade," Aliss said, knowing full well she would never deny the ill the benefit of her knowledge.

He smirked. "You think to bargain with me when you sit here on my ship, as my prisoner?"

The reason for her abduction could also be the solution. Excited, she spoke with haste. "I have something you want, my skills; you have something I want, my freedom. I will trade you one for the other. As soon as I heal your people, you will return me home. It is a fair and reasonable bargain."

"You must heal my people," he said as if confirming his acquiescence.

She nodded and repeated, "Then you will take me home."

He gave a quick nod and moved closer.

His imposing size and the fierce wolf head made her wish that she could fade into the corner behind her, but then that would be retreating, and she could almost hear her sister scolding her for cowering. Fiona's rebuke would be clear: show the enemy a weakness and you give him a weapon.

"Then we have a bargain," she said with bravado.

A glint surfaced in his eyes and for a moment, Aliss expected him to smile, but he did not. "How do you know you can trust me?"

"I can ask the same of you."

His icy stare froze her.

"Do not think to play games with my peoples' lives."

The mere suggestion that she would use her healing skills to do harm turned her fiery hot and melted away her fear. "How dare you even suggest that!"

He nearly plastered his nose to hers. "I dare anything when it comes to the protection of my people."

"Like kidnapping a helpless healer."

He glared at her. "You are far from helpless."

His compliment startled her.

"You will heal my people," he said sternly and stood.

"You will return me home." Her words were meant to seal their bargain and she could only pray that he was a warrior true to his word.

Chapter 3

The ship made land just as the sun descended into the horizon. Several men jumped out when they got close to shore, and with thick ropes cast to them, they pulled the vessel onto dry land.

Aliss stood, about to wrap a fur cloak around her to ward off the fine mist beginning to fall, when she was abruptly scooped up into Rogan's arms.

He walked to the side of the ship and it took a mere second for her to realize that he intended to jump off with her in his arms.

"You cannot mean to—"

He arched a brow and stepped forward.

She flung her arms around his neck and recited a silent prayer.

He leaped off and landed on his feet without

staggering. After walking a few feet, he put her down and yelled something to one of his men in a language she did not understand. His hand caught a fur cloak that was thrown to him and he wrapped it around her.

"It is a short walk to the village."

"Good, then I can see to the ill as soon as we arrive."

"You will eat first."

"Afterward."

"Before. You have eaten nothing all day."

"Neither have you," she reminded him.

"Then we will eat together."

He walked off, leaving her startled. She had not expected that response. She had assumed he would want her to tend to the ill immediately. She had hoped to, for the sooner she healed the ailing the sooner she would be going home.

She was already missing her sister and she could only imagine how Fiona was feeling. There had never been a time when Fiona and she had been separated. They had always depended on each other, had always been there for each other. Now she had only herself to rely on.

Aliss kept pace with Rogan and his men, walking just a short distance behind him. The shoreline faded into rocky terrain that soon turned hilly with a smattering of woods that grew denser as they headed north.

The land appeared harsh and unforgiving, more barren than fertile, and she wondered how Rogan and his people survived here. A sudden thought jolted her and she almost stumbled but righted herself quick enough. Could the Wolf have another reason for abducting her?

The Isle of Non.

Her brother Raynor had laid claim to it but then so had Tarr—and so had Rogan, though unsuccessfully. The isle would certainly provide a better home for the Wolf clan than this place. Was there more to her abduction than healing the ill? She would make certain to uncover the truth and be prepared for whatever befell her.

The village sat at the base of a hill. The dwellings, not a full dozen, looked more like huts than cottages. They were well maintained, however, with the roofs freshly thatched and sodded. Large open spaces divided each plot of farmland, the soil recently tilled and probably seeded.

The people themselves appeared cautious and curious, mumbling among themselves as she passed by. Did they know who she was? Had Rogan informed them of his intention to return with a healer?

The men had drifted off upon entering the village and she was left alone with Rogan. He had not glanced over his shoulder to see if she trailed him. Why should he? There was no fear of her escaping. She was here until he chose to return her and that depended on her fulfilling her part of the bargain.

His dwelling sat at the end of the village, at the foot of the hill. It was long, the turf roof shaped like an overturned boat with two smokestacks at each end. She followed him through the front door and passed down a corridor, the end splitting off to the left and right. Rogan turned right and they entered a large room.

A hearth comprised the back wall with one window covered with animal fur. A large wooden chest sat beneath it. A long table with benches on each side sat in front of the fireplace, wooden bowls were stacked in a neat row in the center, and tankards divided each stack.

The fire's flames licked a bubbling cauldron and several thick candles provided good lighting to the room.

"Sit, we will eat," Rogan said, dropping the wolf pelt he wore on the chest.

After leaving the fur cloak on a bench near the doorway, Aliss took the seat closest to the hearth. A pretty young woman entered with a smile and a basket on her arm. "I have food for you and your guest."

"Thank you, Anna," Rogan said. "Leave it, we will help ourselves. I am sure you are eager to spend time with John after his lengthy absence."

Her cheeks turned rosy and she was gone in a flash, but not before Aliss noticed the rash on her neck. "Is a rash one of the symptoms of the illness?"

"No. Anna is the only one afflicted with a rash and she has not been ill." Rogan moved the basket to the center of the table.

Aliss stood and began to unwrap the items, revealing warm bread, hunks of cheese, and dry salted fish. "Is her husband John the one who posed as a cleric?"

"By his own desire." Rogan frowned as he

took bowls and filled one with the hot stew from the cauldron. "Wagging tongues were directed toward Anna when the rash appeared and she did not grow ill. Soon there was talk that she bore the devil's mark of protection. To prove the gossipers wrong John volunteered to play the roll of the cleric."

"Did his sacrifice stop wagging tongues?"

"For now." Rogan set a steaming bowl of rabbit stew in front of her.

Aliss reached to tear a piece of bread from the loaf when Rogan's hand landed gently on hers.

"You will help us."

Aliss was stunned by the ferocity of his confidence and the tenderness of his touch. His warm, callused palm tickled her flesh and the strange sensation unnerved her. She was feasting as a guest instead of a captive; but she was here against her will and she would do well to remember that.

She tore at the bread to dislodge his hand. "I will do my best to heal your people."

Rogan filled his own bowl and sat opposite her at the table.

The meal was relatively quiet. She was hungrier than she had realized, but then she had not given food much thought. Her mind had been too busy.

Now with her stomach filling, the warmth of the fire easing her chill, and the bargain for her release settled, she was curious to know more about the man called the Wolf and to learn what other motives he had in mind.

She found it odd for a leader and warrior, considered harsh and fierce, to serve her food. He had not commanded one of his people to serve him or that she should wait on him. Was this truly his nature or was he attempting to win her confidence?

"You spend much time in your thoughts."

"I learn much there."

He braced his elbows on the table and cupped his hands. "What have you learned?"

She was about to admit that he puzzled her, when she thought better of it. "My thoughts are my own."

"You *fear* to share them?"

"I do not *wish* to share them."

He broke off a piece of cheese. "You do not trust me."

"That is not surprising."

He tore the piece in two and handed her one.

She took it, and the very tips of his fingers brushed hers, raising gooseflesh up her arm. She snatched her hand away. "I will need to see what herbs flourish in this area."

"I want your trust."

"Why?" she snapped, annoyed he would not leave the matter alone.

"Because I am all you have at the moment. There is no one but me to protect you."

"Protect me?" she asked with dubious humor.

"You are under my protection now and I ask that you *trust me*."

"You have brought me here to tend your people. What does it matter if I trust you or not?"

"When trust is shared, you know that you can always depend on each other—no matter what happens. I want you to know you can depend on me without question."

"Trust is earned."

"Are you telling me I must earn your trust?" he asked.

"Do you trust me?"

A hint of a smile touched the corners of his mouth. "You are a worthy opponent."

She laughed softly. "You wish my trust, yet you refer to me as your opponent. This matter needs more consideration on your part."

He tore a piece of bread in half and handed one to her. "I will win your trust."

This time in accepting the offered morsel was she actually accepting his trust?

She stood abruptly. "It is time for me to tend the ill."

He pointed to her bowl. "You have not finished eating."

"I have eaten enough."

"You have barely touched your food."

"I am no longer hungry," she said impatiently.

He stood slowly, the firelight dancing off him and causing his vast shadow to envelop her and devour her in a heartbeat. Aliss almost lost the last ounce of courage she had left. Her first instinct was to cringe and hide in the dark corner, but her sister's sharp tongue entered her mind and quickly changed that.

Show him no fear.

Her shoulders went back and her chin went up and she walked around the table to meet him.

Folding his arms across his chest, he said, "You are a stubborn one."

She nearly smiled for she felt as if Fiona was there helping to protect her.

"My healing basket?"

His green eyes wandered over her face, lingering for a moment, and she had the sudden feeling that he could read her deepest thoughts. She tore her glance away and looked around as if in search of her basket.

He grabbed her chin and forced her to look at him. "You can trust that I will keep you safe." He released her, walked over to the chest beneath the window and opened it. "Your basket is by the doorway."

Aliss spotted it and quickly snatched it up. She jumped when he unexpectedly draped a dark red wool cape over her shoulders.

His hands grasped her shoulders. "My touch alarms you?"

"Since we first met, which is not even a full day ago, you have hoisted me over your shoulder, scooped me up into your arms, held me to your chest, wrapped me in cloaks, and jumped off a ship with me in your arms. You take liberties and do not expect me to react uncomfortably?" She shook her head. "I think not." And hurried out the door.

Chapter 4

Rogan woke with a start from a dream that haunted him less frequently of late. He sat up and swung his legs out of bed, stretching his arms over his head. He missed his wife Kendra, gone two years now, and a son who had never taken a breath.

He ran his fingers through his tousled hair before shaking the sad memories from his head.

Aliss.

She was why he had dreamed of his family. Her presence had brought back memories. He and Kendra had spent many an hour talking at the table, she always challenging his opinion, making him see reason when anger blinded him. He had loved her very much, but she would have been the one to argue that life goes on. Kendra would have reminded him that no matter the hurt, the disappointment, the grief, life continued and so did love.

So he went on, knowing that was what Kendra would expect of him.

He dressed in black leggings and a tan shirt, and hooked a wide black leather belt around his waist. He was ready to speak with Aliss and see if she had determined anything pertinent concerning the persistent illness that plagued the village.

A bed had been set up for her in the other room, but as he entered, he was surprised to discover it empty. When had she left and why hadn't she woken him?

Perhaps Aliss had taken shelter in someone's home last night, too tired to return to his cottage. Otherwise, it meant that she had worked throughout the night.

He left in haste. The village was just waking for the day, the sun having dawned barely an hour ago. He spotted John and Anna strolling hand in hand and walked over to them.

"Have you seen Aliss?" he said instead of offering a greeting.

"She is with Ivan," John said. "He does not fare well."

Rogan nodded and headed to Ivan's home. His annoyance subsided as his walk turned brisk. Ivan was a man who had seen many battles and survived each one. He lived with his daughter and son-in-law and their four children. He had been ill on and off. Recently, he had been more ill than ever.

Aliss was spooning a liquid into Ivan's mouth when Rogan entered the cottage. She spoke softly to the old man, and when she finished, she rubbed his forehead and then patted his hand before holding it and continued to speak gently, though firmly, to him.

"You are not dying. I will not let you."

"It is my time," Ivan said.

"It is not and I will not hear you say that again."

Ivan took firm hold of her hand. "Are you an angel come to redeem me?"

"I am a healer who has come to make you well."

Ivan nodded, his eyes closing. "I trust you."

"Good, for it will make a difference," Aliss said, then placed his hand on his chest as Ivan had fallen asleep.

Rogan watched her roll her shoulders back as if attempting to ease the soreness from her joints. Then she yawned wide, her hand rushing to cover her mouth.

He walked over to her and she turned her head toward him as he approached.

"I need to talk with you," she said in a whisper and cast a glance toward Ivan.

He understood that she did not wish to disturb the patient and he grabbed her healing basket at her feet and stepped aside, indicating he would follow her.

She nodded with a smile that turned to another yawn as she quietly left the cottage. She stopped to speak with Myra, Ivan's daughter, and after a brief exchange, Aliss left the cottage.

Rogan had retrieved her cloak and once outside he draped it over her shoulders. "The early morning holds a chill."

She turned sleepy eyes on him. "It feels refreshing."

He had the intense urge to scoop her up in his arms and cart her off to bed—to sleep. She looked exhausted.

"We must talk."

He was anxious to hear any news regarding the illness. "Tell me over breakfast."

She yawned. "I am too tired to eat and I must get a few hours' rest before seeing to the other ailing villagers."

"You need—"

"For you to listen to me," she finished.

He remained silent, keeping pace with her slow strides.

"The villagers I have examined thus far all have the same complaints. They suffer intense stomach pain and they can hold no food down. What puzzles me is that they grow ill and then seem to improve only to grow ill again and again, while some succumb to the illness."

"Can you heal them?"

She sighed. "I hope so, though it may take time. I really do need to rest now."

"Are you sure you do not want to eat first?"

Aliss shook her head. "I am too tired."

She almost stumbled when they neared his cottage and his hand was quick to steady her. Her skin was warm and soft, the sleeves of her blouse having been rolled up. And for an instant he thought he felt her ready to drop into his arms, but then it seemed she caught herself and regained her composure.

"You need rest. You will be good to no one if you do not take care of yourself," he warned.

"Do not worry. I will do what you brought me here to do—but I will do it *my way.*"

He grabbed her arm, jolting her to a stop. "I rule here."

Her green eyes sparked. "I heal here."

"Rogan!"

The frantic shout had them both turning.

"Derek has fallen ill," John said.

Aliss looked to Rogan. "A friend?"

"A good friend."

"Let us hurry."

Rogan went straight to Derek's bedside upon entering the cottage. "You were always one for finding a way out of work."

"Someone needed to teach you to have fun," Derek said with effort.

Aliss nudged Rogan away from the bed.

"She is a good healer." Rogan said, remaining behind her and wanting to assure his friend that he would be all right. *He* wanted to know that Derek would be all right, though seeing him so deathly pale and weak when he was a man near to Rogan's own size worried him.

"I knew you would not fail the village." Derek

took a fortifying breath. "When others grumbled about your not returning, I argued that you would be back. I would—"

"You will be quiet," Aliss ordered with a gentle smile and a firm tone.

"You, my lovely lass, are a beauty and your touch angel soft. How lucky am I."

Rogan grinned, glad to hear Derek attempting as usual to charm a lady, which certainly indicated he was not at death's door.

He watched with interest the way Aliss tenderly cared for his friend. As she discussed his ailments with him, she gently pressed her palm to his forehead; her slim fingers probed the area around his eyes with a featherlike touch and then it appeared as if she stroked the flesh beneath his jaw.

Derek responded to her touch with a smile and to her questions with his usual charm. Rogan did not think there was a woman alive who did not fall under Derek's spell, even when he was sick.

Aliss smiled and laughed at Derek's responses. They appeared more a couple sharing an intimate talk than a woman attempting to heal an ailing man.

"It is good you keep a smile and do not surrender entirely to your illness," Aliss said.

"I cannot mend too fast when I have such a beautiful healer to look after me," Derek said with a grin, then suddenly gripped his stomach in pain.

Aliss placed her hand over his where he held his belly.

"I will give you something to ease the pain."

He sighed in relief. "You are an angel."

Aliss mixed a powder in hot water and stirred until it dissolved. "The potion will also make you sleep."

"Anything not to feel this pain."

"How long have you suffered with it?" she asked.

"A few hours, though discomfort preceded it."

Rogan listened as Aliss probed for more information. He had heard the same complaints from everyone for the last six months and his frustration returned. He could do nothing to help his people, nothing but find them a skilled healer.

After Derek was settled, his eyes nearly closed, Rogan and Aliss left the cottage.

"I will eat now and then rest," she said, rolling her shoulders back as she walked.

"Have you learned anything about this illness my people battle?"

"It is too soon to say. I need time to see if the potions I give them are effective."

He shook a fist to the heavens. "If I could see my enemy I would deal him a blow that would have him running." He threw his hands up. "But this enemy I cannot see. I know nothing about him. He attacks my people silently, without warning, and disposes of them one by one. How do I fight an invisible foe?"

Rogan did not expect an answer. He did not believe there was one.

They sat at the table already prepared with food and Rogan saw to it that Aliss's plate was filled. She looked too weary to tend to herself and yet she looked lovely. Her beauty had startled him when he first saw her and her exquisite features continued to intrigue him. Her creamy flawless skin was a perfect backdrop for her radiant green eyes and long red lashes. Her plump lips were rosy and her nose pert and they were framed by a mass of fiery red hair that refused to behave in an orderly fashion.

"Derek made mention that he defended your absence and assured the doubtful of your return," Aliss said.

The shattering of the silence startled him, and he gave a quick nod.

"You were gone long from the village?"

"Yes," he said.

"In search of?"

"You."

"Why me?" she asked. "There are other healers."

He had expected curiosity from her or was it defined answers she searched for? He had heard she was the quiet twin, less likely to argue or challenge, interested only in her healing. He had counted on her intense interest in her work to keep her from delving any further into the reasons for her abduction. But she was far more curious than he had anticipated and he would have to be very careful dealing with her.

"You are far more skilled."

"Who told you this?"

He shrugged. "Gossip, wagging tongues."

She did not look convinced.

"True or not, I had to take the chance."

"Had you tried other healers? What of your own healer? I have yet to meet her."

"She succumbed to the illness months ago."

"I am sorry," Aliss said and looked ready to continue her interrogation.

Rogan quickly leaned over the table, his face near hers. "You are our only hope."

Anna rushed into the room. "The healer is needed. Tara's babe has taken ill."

Aliss scurried off the bench, grabbed her basket by the door, and hurried after Anna.

Rogan sat where he was, elbow on the table, his head resting in his hand, staring at the flames in the hearth.

"You *will* heal my people, Aliss. The prophetess predicted it."

Chapter 5

⌒◯◯⌒

Aliss managed to grab a couple of hours' sleep before she woke to Anna shaking her shoulder. Ivan had grown worse and Myra, his daughter, feared death was imminent.

The old man was weak yet not at death's door and she would do her best to keep that door closed to him. She had ordered a special broth prepared and for him to be fed with it at regular intervals, like a newborn who needed constant nourishment.

She had visited with several other villagers; their symptoms mimicked the others'. She had realized soon enough that she needed to study the symptoms and see if she could make sense of them before she could find a way to conquer the malady.

After having seen to all those who were ailing and made sure they rested comfortably, Aliss needed to search the surrounding woods and fields to see what herbs and plants were available to her. The activity would also serve another purpose. She would seek the help of some of the women in her search and befriend them, thus giving her a chance to find out all she could about her abduction.

Aliss chose a good-sized basket from the ones stacked in the corner near the fireplace. She grabbed the dark red wool cloak from the peg near the door and flung it around her shoulders as she hurried outside.

The sky had become overcast in the last hour, causing a slight chill to the spring air and hinting at rain. She would forage for her plants until she felt the first raindrop.

"Where do you go?" John asked.

Aliss was not surprised by his presence, for she had noticed that he always lurked nearby. "To see if one of the women would join me in the woods to search for healing plants."

"That is not a good idea right now."

Though small in stature and with average features that drew little attention, John still demanded notice. His strong presence and sharp mind made people aware of him and had earned him the respect of the clan Hellewyk. Of course, they had thought him a cleric.

"Why is that?" Aliss asked as John approached her.

"Rogan prefers you remain near."

She almost laughed but thought better of it. "Does he fear I would try to escape? Where would I go?"

"It is not where you would go. It is who might take you."

This time she chuckled. "He worries that the healer he abducted will be abducted?"

John did not find her response humorous. "You are under the Wolf's protection now. You can hunt for plants another time."

She did not wish to argue. "No, I cannot. I need to make certain I have a sufficient supply of healing plants. Is there no one who could accompany me?"

John ran an apprehensive glance around the surrounding area. "I need to remain here right now."

"Is something wrong?"

He appeared uncertain, purposely holding his tongue.

"A sensible explanation might change my plans."

He yielded. "A band of marauders have sacked a farmland not far from here. Rogan set chase after them and has ordered everyone to remain in the village."

"A wise edict."

John seemed surprised by her response.

"I can be sensible when reason prevails. I will consult with Rogan to see when he feels it safe for me to enter the woods."

"Till then?"

"I have much to occupy me. You need not worry," she assured him.

He cast an anxious glance toward a small cottage tucked near the woods, smoke puffing from the single chimney.

"Anna waits for you?"

He sighed. "We have missed each other."

"Go to her then and make up for lost time."

"I am to look after you," he reluctantly admitted.

"I will be tilling the soil for a garden unless I am called to tend the sick."

His shoulders slumped. "I should help you."

"Nonsense," she said and shooed him away. "Go. I am particular how my garden is tilled and tended."

"Rogan would expect me to help," he said, slowly stepping away from her.

"I will deal with Rogan."

He grinned. "Are you sure of that?"

She crossed her arms. "You should be worried about Rogan dealing with *me*."

His grin faded. "Do not underestimate the Wolf. He can strike when least expected."

"I will keep that in mind," she said, and when John turned and walked away gooseflesh crept over her skin.

While Aliss preferred not to be acquainted with that side of Rogan, she knew she had no choice. Fiona would remind her that ignorance of an enemy would guarantee defeat. She would need to understand Rogan, whether she wanted to or not, whether she feared to or not.

She returned the basket to where she had found it, switched from her cloak to her shawl, and found a large tan cloth she fashioned into an apron to protect the only garments she possessed. Then she determined the best area for a garden, and after finding a pick, she began to till the soil.

She loved the scent of freshly dug earth. It stung the nostrils like an intoxicating perfume. She piled the rocks she unearthed for later use and continued to enjoy her laborious task. She wanted the rich soil ready to receive the few seeds she had in her healing basket and the plants she hoped to acquire on her foraging expedition.

Aliss stretched her back, easing her aching muscles, when finally she stood at the end of the large plot she had worked on for several hours. The first drop of rain had struck with the last turn of the soil. She was proud of her accomplishment and relieved that she would have a bed to receive the much-needed batch of healing plants.

She turned, ready to seek shelter, when out of the corner of her eye she caught a quick-moving shadow. Uncertain if it was her imagination playing tricks on her or someone actually loitered in the woods, she pretended to finish the already completed job while keeping an eye on the shadows that appeared to dance like demons among the trees.

Then like a flash of lightning she caught two glowing orbs burning bright green between the leaves of a low-hanging branch.

Wolf's eyes?

She could not be sure and the thought that it could be someone else, not Rogan, stalking her,

sent her into a fright. One abduction in two days
was enough; she needed no more, and besides,
she had struck a bargain with Rogan. She was
not going anyplace but home.

The urge to run grabbed hold of her, but common sense warned that if she took flight she
would alert the predator and he would give chase.
She gathered her few items, added a stone to use
as a defense weapon, and casually backed away.

Her eyes remained fixed on the woods, her
hand gripped the stone; she was ready for combat if necessary.

A clap of unexpected thunder caused her to
jump, her heart to leap, and her legs to take
flight. She turned on a run, her foot catching on a
large rock that caused her to lose her balance and
topple like a felled tree.

The dark soil rushed up to meet her face and
she braced for impact when suddenly she was
scooped up and swiftly spun around to land in
Rogan's powerful arms.

He glared at her with knitted brow. "Why do
you run?"

She cupped a hand over her fisted hand that
clenched the stone. "I saw something in the
woods."

His head did not immediately turn in that direction; instead, his eyes slowly perused the area
as he spoke. "What did you see?"

"Eyes like that of the beast you wear on your
shoulder." He wore no beast now, though.

His glance came back to rest on her. "Are you
certain?"

"I know what I saw," she said adamantly.

"It was probably the headdress of a clansman who dutifully protects our boundaries."

"The eyes were too bright, too—" She hesitated, finding her own thought disturbing. "Too unearthly."

"And the stone your hand grips? Did you think it a good defense against an unearthly creature?"

Aliss raised her fisted hand. "It is better than nothing."

Another thunderclap had her realizing that the misty rain had turned heavy and that she was getting wet.

Rogan appeared to think the same for he hurried them into his cottage, placing her on her feet once they were through the front door.

"My healing basket," she said, starting to go back out into the rain.

Rogan grabbed her arm and pulled her back inside. "I will get it."

She looked at his hand that gripped her, felt the heat of his touch seeping into her; the potency of his grasp reminded her how defenseless she actually was against this powerful man.

He left her there to fetch her basket.

Aliss shivered, her skin chilled—or was it concern that made her shiver? Did she trust the Wolf to keep his word? Would he return her home? Was she truly here only to heal his people? She hurried down the corridor, suddenly feeling ice-cold, but soon she was warming herself in front of the fire in the hearth. She rubbed her arms to chase away the gooseflesh but it stubbornly returned. Her wet clothes needed drying if she expected the shivering to stop.

Rogan entered and placed her basket on the bench next to the doorway. She envied him his dry clothes, his fur cloak, now hanging on a peg to dry, having protected him from the weather.

She turned back to the fire and hugged herself in an attempt to get warm.

Rogan disappeared for a few moments then reappeared with an armful of garments.

"Take these and use them. I cannot chance you getting ill." He dumped them on the table and walked out.

Aliss sifted through the garments; skirts, blouses, tunics in various colors and material from soft wool to worn linen, all clean and scented with heather.

With hasty movements, she shed her wet clothes and hurried into a forest-green skirt and sky-blue blouse. The garments were a size too large for her, but with a leather strap that served as a decent belt, she was able to tuck the extra fabric in at the waist and fashion the outfit to her size.

She removed her leather boots to dry by the fire and folded the other garments and placed them on the chest near the window. She then set to heating cider to further warm her bones.

"Are you finished?" called Rogan from the other room.

"Aye, come join me for hot cider."

"Hot cider sounds welcoming," he said, entering the room. He stopped abruptly.

Aliss wondered at his prolonged stare. As if regaining his senses, he hurried to take a seat at the table.

She filled two tankards and sliced bread and cheese for them to share.

"The clothes seem to fit."

"With a tuck here and there. You must tell me who they belong to so that I may thank them for their generosity."

"Not necessary," he said, cupping the hot tankard Aliss handed him.

"It is only proper I express my appreciation."

Rogan shook his head. "She is deceased."

"Oh," Aliss said, and plopped down on the bench opposite him at the table. "I am sorry. Who was she?"

"My wife."

The Wolf had had a wife? She would have never imagined him a husband to any woman. She thought of him only as a warrior and a fierce one at that. That he could have loved surprised her, though he could have wed out of necessity.

"I am so very sorry," she said sincerely.

"It has been two years."

"Still, it is a hurt some never get over."

"The pain has diminished and I am left with good memories."

"What happened to your wife?" she asked, eager to learn more. "If you do not mind my inquiry."

"She died in childbirth."

His grief was obvious and she sympathized. "Oh, how dreadful. The child also?"

He nodded. "My son perished with her."

Death did not discriminate. It claimed the young and the old alike and she had shed many a tear and grieved with those left behind.

"Death makes no sense," she said, hugging her tankard of cider.

He shrugged. "It is a part of life that cannot be avoided."

"But a part no one wishes to embrace."

"Kendra, my wife, embraced all of life."

She was surprised by his smile and sense of acceptance.

"Life is to be lived, she would tell me. Then challenged me to live it."

Aliss had not imagined a man who wore a wolf's head and skin as a husband who had loved deeply or father who grieved for an unborn son. There was much more to this man than she had first thought and she was anxious to learn more.

"You tilled the earth?"

She nodded, accepting that he no longer wished to discuss his deceased wife. "I need an herb garden. The soil is ripe for planting and nourishing seeds."

"You tended the soil alone?"

"My choice," she said firmly. "John wished to help but I needed none."

"Sent him to Anna, did you?" He smiled. "For a man who deceived you, you are generous with him."

"What point is there for me to harbor anger and resentment? You need my skill, and although I do not agree with how you obtained my help, after seeing how ill your people are, I can understand your reasoning. John did what he had to do. I cannot fault him for that or hold it against him."

"You forgive easily."

"My healing work has taught me that forgiveness benefits more than revenge. Of course, knowing that I will be returned to my family helps."

"You would protest more if you thought you were not returning home?"

"I would escape," Aliss said.

Rogan chuckled. "How would you escape?"

"I am not sure, but in time I would find a way and return home."

"You could never escape me."

His resolute tone sounded more like a snarl and his green eyes turned dark, like the color of winter pine trees. Here was the wolf side of him, the predator who stalked, captured, and devoured his prey.

How could she trust a wolf?

"I do not need to escape," she said confidently. "You will return me home."

He did not reply; he drank his cider.

Chapter 6

◦~∽⧗∿~◦

One day flowed into another, spring took firm hold of the weather, and life rolled by, but not idyllically. The people of Rogan's clan continued to grow ill while some healed and others suffered relapses. The only thing Aliss had prevented thus far was more deaths.

Occasionally, she would grow melancholy with thoughts of home and her sister, but mostly she worked relentlessly, eating little and sleeping even less, growing ever more frustrated when another person took ill.

The illness struck randomly; she could make no sense of it. And she pushed aside the thought that any day it might attack her.

It was late and Aliss was exhausted. She smiled when she saw the narrow bed by the fireplace. Her limbs ached with weariness and she threw herself down on the lumpy mattress with a grateful sigh.

She nestled her head in the pillow, her eyes drifting shut, ready to surrender to sleep and hoping no one disturbed her at least for a few hours.

"Aliss. Aliss."

She heard her name in the distance. She should respond; instead she snuggled deeper into sleep.

Someone grabbed her shoulder and shook her until she had no choice but to wake.

"What is it you want?" she grumbled, forcing her eyes open.

"Someone is badly hurt," Anna said, hovering over her.

Aliss sprang out of bed forcing Anna to jump back. "Who? What happened?"

"James, a mere lad, wounded in battle."

"Battle?" Aliss shook the sleep from her mind and rushed around gathering items that she might need. "What battle?"

"The marauders struck again. We must hurry. He does not do well."

Aliss grabbed her basket and followed a teary Anna out the door.

Women kneeled in prayer outside the cottage and the men, dirty and weary from battle, followed her every step with pleading eyes. She could almost hear them begging her to save their fallen comrade.

Aliss entered the cottage, the stench of blood

thick in the warm air. Rogan stood off in the corner, stoic in stature and expression. John stood next to him, his eyes heavy with tears yet to be spilled. Crying softly, an older woman kneeled beside the bed and a man stood alongside her, his gnarled fingers resting on her shoulder.

Aliss walked to the bed.

Tears ran down the man's face. "Please, he is our only grandson." He raised his twisted fingers. "I cannot fight. He claimed he was a man and would fight in my stead." He choked on the pain and cleared his voice. "Please save him."

"I will do what I can." She wished she could give them more hope, but she had learned that she could not keep death from claiming his victims.

Anna along with John ushered the couple out of the cottage.

Aliss went directly to the lad, and almost cried herself. He was a mere boy, perhaps thirteen years. His face was sweet and lovely, so like an innocent child's, but he was no child. He had tasted battle; he was a man.

"I am dying," James cried out in pain.

Aliss took his hand and he gripped it tightly. "Death has yet to claim you," she said.

"I see him," he whispered harshly and stretched his neck to stare in the corner. "He waits for me in the shadows."

"And there he shall remain."

"Do not let him take me. Please, I beg of you," he said and tried to pull himself up.

Aliss tried to hold him down but he was frantic to escape death and sprang up in bed. The sudden movement was too much for the fresh wound and the pain struck James fast and furiously. He turned deathly pale and screamed as if he was being ripped asunder. Then in an instant he dropped back on the bed and was quickly plunged into the blessed peace of unconsciousness.

Now was the time to examine him, when he would feel no pain. With urgent fingers, Aliss gently moved the bloody blanket off him. "A stomach wound."

"The worst kind," Rogan said behind her.

He stood close to her. She could feel his breath on her neck and hear the helplessness in his voice.

"Leave me with him," she ordered.

He placed a firm hand on her shoulder and squeezed before leaving her alone with the young lad.

Aliss realized soon enough that there was little hope for saving the boy and yet she felt compelled to fight death as hard as she could.

"Can I help?"

Aliss looked up to see Anna. "Blood does not make you squeamish?"

She shook her head. "Tell me what to do."

Aliss obliged her and together they worked on young James.

Aliss felt healing was a privilege and she worked hard to give it the respect and attention it deserved. She spoke with learned healers and worked alongside women who through trial and error had learned the way.

One woman in particular had impressed her.

She lived alone in the woods, her fair skin wrinkled with time but her mind as sharp as a young lass's. Gretell was her name and she had taught Aliss things about healing that some might deem heretical.

She had sworn Aliss to secrecy and made her understand that she was not to pass the knowledge to another until she felt certain she could trust the woman with the wisdom.

Aliss called upon that knowledge now to help her save James. Gretell had dissected dead animals and had shown Aliss parts of the inner body. One thing she had taught her was that if no damage was done to the organs then she should stitch the wound and pray.

Her examination had shown her that James's organs had not been wounded. While he had been slashed open, the sword had done no other damage. If she stitched him up, treated the wound with the salve Gretell had taught her to mix, and prayed no fever set in, then perhaps James would live.

It was a slim chance but one Aliss had to take.

"I am going to stitch him," Aliss said.

Anna looked puzzled. "He is dying. His innards are exposed. No one survives that." She pointed to the sword slash that had laid his stomach open. "It is too big to stitch. It will not stay closed and the pain will be too great for him."

"True enough, but he is unconscious and will feel nothing." Aliss rinsed her bloody hands in the bowl on the chest next to the bed. "Besides, I will not stand here helpless and watch him die a slow and horribly painful death. If you feel unable to assist me, I understand."

Anna shook her head. "No, I will help. I have just never heard of a healer doing such a thing before."

"I do all I can to heal," Aliss said proudly. "I cannot stand by and simply let someone die without trying to save them, even if the situation appears hopeless."

"I am glad you have come to heal us."

"Something I have yet to do."

"You will," Anna said with certainty.

"Thank you for your confidence in me. It will help when we work on James."

The two women worked side by side, Anna following Aliss's every direction. It was well past dawn when Aliss finally finished and Anna ushered James's grandparents back into the house.

"He sleeps," Aliss said to the couple, who could not take their eyes off their grandson.

"He will live?" asked the grandmother.

"I cannot say for sure," Aliss answered honestly. "Right now sleep, rest, and light nourishment is what he needs to heal completely. There is also swelling, redness, and fever to worry about. I will keep a close watch on him, as will Anna. Hopefully he will be victorious in this battle."

"He is strong," his grandmother said optimistically.

"Tell him that often," Aliss said. "It will give him the courage to fight for his life."

"How can we thank you?" the grandfather asked.

Aliss looked to their grandson. "I will have my thanks when I see him walking, smiling, and flirting with the young girls of the village."

The elderly couple smiled, nodded, and turned their attention to their grandson.

Aliss had instructed Anna in James's care and they divided the time that each would spend with him. Aliss now had other ill people to look after and a slew of other things to do and not enough time to do them all.

Derek had improved then suddenly had had a relapse. Ivan was doing much better. Tara's two-year-old had improved greatly and was up to mischief already.

Aliss headed back to Rogan's home. Why did some ailing people improve and others did not? Why were they suffering relapses? How had she managed to prevent deaths since her arrival? The answers were there. She just was not certain where to find them.

Aliss was surprised that she had not seen Rogan the rest of the day. He usually managed to keep company with her throughout part of the day. He kept out of her way, but he was there observing.

At first, she had thought he did not trust her, but she had come to realize that he not only felt a responsibility to his people but he actually cared about them, and they in turn cared for the Wolf. There was camaraderie among them all, a close-ness that was palpable, and her curiosity about the clan was quickly turning to admiration.

She had learned that the Wolf clan had inhab-ited this island not far off the coast of Scotland for many years. Its peoples were a motley mix of various heritages. Shunned, for various reasons, by their clans, they had formed their own. A fierce band of warriors with no allegiance to king or country, they were feared by many and yet Aliss found them a loving and generous people, not at all the barbarians she once thought them.

Normally by late afternoon, she would be feeling the effects of a hectic day, but today she felt empowered instead of tired. The surgery she had performed on James had gone better than she had hoped, right down to the neat little stitches, all fifty of them.

When she last checked on him he was sleeping comfortably, having woken briefly. Anna had made certain to give him the sleeping brew so he would rest. So far, all was well, but it was still too early to tell if he would survive.

Before she did anything else, she needed to make more salve and brew more potions for the ailing. She hurried into the cottage, eager to get started, and came to an abrupt halt when she saw John bent over the table, knife in hand, ready to cut into Rogan's hand.

"Stop!" she screeched.

"I told him to let you look at it," John said defensively and backed away from the table.

Aliss walked right up to Rogan. "You have an injury and you do not summon me?"

"You are busy with more important matters," he said firmly.

"You think that is a good explanation for foolishness?"

John sneaked out the door before the couple could notice his departure.

"You call me a fool?"

Aliss turned to examine his hand and he pulled it away. "You need healing, you go to the healer."

"My wound is nothing more than a sliver of wood embedded in my finger. It hardly needs a healer to extract it. Besides, you exhaust yourself day and night tending the truly ill."

"That is why you abducted me. To heal your people." She was beginning to believe that he spoke the truth about his reason for her abduction. Everyone she had spoken with verified Rogan's intention to bring a skilled healer home to cure his people.

"*My people,* not me," he said, standing to tower over her.

Again, he put his clan before himself. However, when it came to healing, she fought with as much gusto as he did for his people. She stood her ground and did not back away, though his size easily intimidated.

"So if you were sick you would not let me heal you."

"That is different."

"It is not. Now give me your hand," she demanded, holding hers out to him.

"You are busy enough without needing to tend me. You have not been home once today and you probably have not eaten all day."

"I was not hungry," she said, and poked at his

chest. "And who are you to talk. You have not even washed the dirt and stench of battle off you."

He grabbed her wrist. "I was too busy burying the dead."

She gasped. "I am so sorry. I did not know you lost men."

"I did not. I helped bury the enemy." He released her and dropped back in his seat. "They will hurt us no more."

She reached for his hand and he did not stop her.

"That is how you got the splinter?"

"The wooden handle broke." He turned his head and stared at the flames. "I buried a lad younger than James today. I hoped I would not have to bury James." He turned back to her. "Has he died yet?"

"You expect him to?" she asked.

"I have seen no man survive a gut wound." He jumped when she touched his swollen finger.

"You should have come to me immediately with this."

"I had no time to give it thought."

"There is time now."

He took hold of her hand when she released his. "We will eat after you are done. You need nourishment."

She smiled. "You need a bath; then we will eat."

"Do you tell me I stink?" He grinned.

She held her nose and laughed.

"Tend my finger, healer, so that I may wash and appease your senses."

It was more than a sliver of wood embedded in

his finger, but with gentle prodding Aliss managed to remove it without much difficulty. She cleansed it with a warm potion and patted it dry.

"After you wash, I will put salve on it and bandage it. Tell me immediately if it should discolor or pain you." She looked at his finger then at him. "You will show me the wound each morning and night."

"Will I now?"

Her finger gently probed the skin; she was glad to see that the swelling was already subsiding. "Yes, you will."

"Why would I do that?" he asked, slipping an arm around her waist and spreading his legs to tug her closer to him.

Panic gripped her, and with a gentle pushing of her hands, she eased away from him and started sorting the dried herbs on the table.

He stood and walked up behind her, standing close but not touching her. "Why, Aliss?"

"I want to make certain no poison sets in the wound." He stood too close, his heat seeping into her, titillating her skin, giving her gooseflesh.

"Thank you for caring."

She turned, quickly bracing her hands on the edge of the table behind her. "I care for all the ill."

"And who cares for you?"

Chapter 7

Rogan entered the room quietly, freshly washed from his dunk in the stream, his hair damp and his chest bare. He watched Aliss from the doorway. In between crushing herbs to a fine powder, she tended the stew bubbling in a cauldron over the hot fire.

She had impressed him when they first met. Her escape had been unexpected but it had been a display of her courageous nature, something he had not foreseen. He had heard rumors about the twins, the strength of one, the gentleness of the other.

He had been surprised to learn that the gentle twin possessed strength of a different kind. Once she had learned of the illness that plagued his clan she forged like a warrior into battle, relentless and untiring in pursuit and destruction of the enemy.

However, when he stepped near her, touched her, her courage faded and she retreated like a young lass uncomfortable with her emerging womanhood. Her dual natures made her an enticing woman, as did her beauty.

He would not deny he found her attractive or that her presence chased away the loneliness he had suffered since his wife's passing. Then there was that healing touch of hers that his people gossiped about. He had thought them delirious—but then it had happened to him.

He had felt the warmth and tenderness of her touch when she tended his finger. He did not recall a twinge of pain. All he remembered was her loving touch and the desire to feel it again.

"The stew smells good," he said, entering the room.

"It is almost ready." Aliss glanced over at him.

He smiled as her eyes rounded and fixed on his naked chest; with a shake of her head, she quickly turned her back on him to fuss over the cooked stew.

He glanced with appreciation at the perfect image of her narrow waist, curving hips, and round backside. His hands itched to reach out and run his fingers ever so intimately over her naked flesh, getting to know every delightful inch of her.

He silently cursed his lascivious thoughts. His mission was more important than satisfying his lust.

Rogan slipped on a shirt and plopped down at the table. After a few awkward minutes, they began to talk and a relative comfort fell over them. They had grown accustomed to sharing daily news at the evening meal, just as he and his wife had done. And lately he looked more and more forward to this time together. Aliss never failed to find a bright spot in her day or to make him laugh at something she had heard or experienced. He found her soothing nature extremely attractive.

When supper was finished Rogan asked, "Do you plan to see James? If so, I will go with you. I would like to see how he fares."

"Prayers are forever on my lips for him," Aliss said while refilling her basket.

"Do you really think he has a chance?"

"Time will tell."

They both reached for her basket at the same time, Rogan's hand slipping over hers. He could not help but squeeze her soft flesh ever so lightly and he could have sworn he felt her tremble.

"I will carry it for you," he said.

She looked about to refuse him then suddenly she nodded and hurriedly withdrew her hand from beneath his. This time her shiver was noticeable, cautioning him that she was not impervious to his touch, and that knowledge fired his loins all the more.

A smile and a shake of his head as he followed behind her expressed perfectly his own confused thoughts on the matter.

*   *   *

Aliss remained behind to watch over James. Anna had insisted that she would return later in the night so that Aliss could get some sleep.

Rogan had spoken with James's grandparents before taking his leave and the older couple retired hours ago to a sleeping pallet on the floor.

She now sat alone with James. His color looked good, his sleep quiet; she prayed both were a good sign.

Aliss leaned back in the chair, the first time all day she could sit and do absolutely nothing. But while her fingers might be idle, her mind refused to stop. Healing forever occupied her thoughts; tonight, however, Rogan had taken its place.

"Who cares for you?"

His question had lingered in her mind since he had uttered it.

She had not answered him. She had not known how to answer him. Her sister cared for her, but she had the feeling that was not what Rogan had implied. His question had pertained to a man caring for her.

Why should it matter to him? And why had the sight of his naked chest so unnerved her? She had seen many men's naked chests before and never had they affected her as Rogan's had.

His taut muscles rippled one into another, producing an upper torso that was lyrical in form and flesh. Old scars dotted his chest here and there, reminding her that he had suffered his fair share of battles. And how appropriate that he carry a significant scar over his heart, as if physically scarred by his wife's passing.

She shook her head vigorously. Her exhaustion was obviously making her delirious with nonsensical thoughts. The Wolf had abducted her from her home and here she sat admiring his naked chest.

He was a man—no, a warrior—intent on having his way at all costs and she would do well to remember that. She was here to serve a purpose and once it was done, she would return home—thank God.

No more sharing meals with him, no more conversations and no more bare chests. She suddenly felt upset and shook off her distress with a shiver. She reminded herself that she would soon be free, a prospect she was looking forward to. She loved her freedom, answering to no one but herself, coming and going as she pleased, studying her healing, no one to bother her—that was her life. But was it what she truly wanted?

"Water."

James's mumbled request pulled Aliss from her musings and she gently lifted his head as she pressed a water-filled cup to his lips.

"Thank you," he said with a heavy sigh and struggled to keep his eyes open.

"You are in pain?"

He gritted his teeth and took a deep breath. "I am grateful for the pain." He caught another painful breath then released it. "It tells me I am alive."

"Sleep helps heal you," she said.

His eyes suddenly widened and Aliss was

struck by their vivid blue color, like a spring morning after a rain, bright and full of promise.

"Will I live?"

It was a plea more than a question and one she had heard endless times before.

She had found that no good came of lying to the ill. "I cannot say for sure, though I am encouraged by your courage."

"I want to live," he said with conviction.

She took his hand in hers and squeezed gently. "Then fight along with me."

"I will never stop fighting."

"Neither will I."

His eyes closed and his faint smile faded and Aliss continued to hold his hand.

Anna showed up shortly after midnight. "Go rest, the sick will be expecting your visits tomorrow."

Aliss nodded. "Instruct his grandmother what to do then get some rest yourself. I prefer he not be alone during the night and you taking turns with me helps relieve me of the sole burden of his evening care."

"I enjoy helping," Anna said and took the seat beside the bed.

"Again, if fever or—"

"I know," Anna interrupted. "You are to be summoned directly if fever or fester sets in."

"I see that I leave him in capable hands."

Anna turned to refill the water cup and the fire's light glared off the rash on her neck.

Aliss could not help but examine it.

Anna jumped when Aliss's finger touched her.

"I am sorry," Aliss apologized. "I have been meaning to have a look at your rash. How long have you had it?"

"It started just around the time people began falling ill."

Aliss studied the persistent skin irritation. "I think I may be able to rid you of it."

"Really?"

She rummaged in her basket and opened a small crock. With a gentle touch, Aliss covered the rash with the thick salve.

She handed the crock to Anna. "It may take several applications before we see results."

Anna hugged it to her chest. "I will faithfully apply it as often as is necessary."

"Morning and night to start," Aliss said and yawned.

"Go and rest, morning will be here soon enough."

Anna was right. Morning arrived with a shock; another new case of the mysterious illness had surfaced and fear grew in the healthy.

In late afternoon Aliss returned to the cottage to replenish her basket, and realized that she needed to take time and search the surrounding woods for herbs. A few of her staple herbs were nearly depleted and she could not afford to run out of any of them.

When she left the cottage, she gave a quick glance to the woods behind it. She halted. Had there been a stirring in the woods? A figure? A pair of eyes? Green ones like the ones before?

Or had she imagined them? Yet again?

A strong hand grasped her shoulder.

Aliss jumped and yelped.

"I am sorry," Rogan said, stepping in front of her. "I did not mean to frighten you."

Aliss took hold of his forearm. "I was deep in thought and did not hear you approach."

"You were staring at the woods."

She nodded and grasped his arm more tightly. "I think my tired mind sees things that are not there."

"The woods are safe now."

"That is good to know." Still she clung to his arm.

"Aliss! Aliss!"

She let go of Rogan and turned to see a frenzied John running toward her.

"Hurry, James's grandmother is screaming that Anna is a witch."

A crowd had gathered around James's cottage listening to the hysterical woman inside screaming accusations of witchcraft and the devil's cohort at Anna.

Rogan quickly dispersed them with a firm voice. "Go tend to your business."

Aliss hurried into the house followed by John and Rogan.

Anna turned to Aliss. "I stopped by to see how he was and he suddenly began burning with fever."

The old woman rushed to Rogan's side, grasping at his shirt. "Keep the devil's own from my grandson. She brought this fever on him. He was fine before she entered and laid hands on him."

"Anna did no such thing," Aliss said sternly, while hurrying to examine James. "She is a new healer with good instincts. She would cause no one intentional harm."

"She bears the devil's mark," the woman said, backing away from Rogan and pointing to Anna. "It grows bright."

The salve had soaked into Anna's skin, causing the rash to look as if it burned her skin; an effect of the salve Aliss had not considered a problem. She had no time to explain this to the woman, her concern being for James.

He had a fever and the wound festered.

Aliss turned to the woman who cowered in her husband's arms. Her fear of losing her grandson caused her foolish accusations; Aliss did not wish to cause her any more pain, but she needed Anna's help.

"Do you trust me?" she asked the woman.

The woman nodded without hesitation.

"Then believe me when I tell you that Anna is no threat to your grandson, and leave us both to try to save him."

Rogan and John assisted in getting the distraught couple out of the cottage while Aliss and Anna went to work on James.

Shortly after midnight, Rogan attempted to get Aliss to return to the cottage and rest but she refused. James's fever had risen and fallen throughout the evening and she could not leave his side. It was imperative that she continue to rub him down with a damp cloth that had been soaked in a mixture of herbs. She also had to keep the blankets stripped off him in hopes of ridding him completely of the fever. Only then would he have a fighting chance.

Just before dawn the fever finally broke, releasing James to rest comfortably. She sent a protesting Anna home, the young woman insisting that she should remain and look after him. Aliss felt that James's grandmother could do what was necessary until morning and would probably want to help, relieved that her grandson still lived.

Rogan was standing by the fireplace when she returned home and she eased his concerned expression. "James is still with us."

"Your hard toil is much appreciated."

"It is what I am here to do—heal. Then I go home," she reminded him, and intended to keep on reminding him.

He stared at her a moment, then bid her good night and went off to his room.

His lack of response worried her.

Would he be true to his word?

Chapter 8

"**W**here is Aliss?" Rogan asked of Anna, as he caught her leaving her cottage.

"Last I saw her she was speaking with Derek." She smiled. "He feels so much better. He is almost his old self."

"I know." He nodded then shook his head. "Aliss is not with him, I just saw Derek."

"James?" she questioned, and her smile grew brighter. "He is healing so nicely, sitting up, finally eating well this past week, and Aliss says the stitches will come out soon."

"Yes, I heard," Rogan said, having heard nothing else in the last few days. The people were excited; if the healer could save James from death, surely she could cure the persistent illness. "She is not there, either."

"Perhaps she rests—"

"Aliss rest?" Rogan snapped sarcastically, and Anna took a step back. "She has been up since before dawn and suppertime is near and I can find neither hide nor hair of her."

Anna's brow shot up. "Laurel. She is due to deliver in a couple of weeks—"

Rogan shook his head and marched off, mumbling to himself. Aliss had worked herself senseless since arriving here; little sleep, little food, endless healings, and not a thought for her own well-being.

Her day started before anyone else's in the village and never seemed to end. He had grown tired of watching her hectic pace, but no amount of threats deterred her from her course.

Last night she had really tested his mettle when, after he had insisted that she get some needed rest, she persisted in working with her herbs and potions, although she had promised she would retire soon.

He left her only to return in the morning to find her sound asleep, her head resting on the table. She had never gone to bed, though exhaustion had claimed her as she had worked. When he had woken her, thinking to see that she slept in her bed for at least a couple of hours, she immediately started her day.

He had had enough. Now *she* would listen to *him*.

Rogan entered Laurel and Peter's cottage without knocking. The young couple's eyes turned wide when without a word he scooped Aliss up and flung her over his shoulder, grabbed her basket and walked out the door.

"What do you think you are doing?" Aliss asked, pounding on his hard back.

"Looking after you since you are too stubborn to do it yourself."

She forced a laugh. "You call this looking after me?"

"What would you call it?"

"Another abduction," she snapped. "Now put me down!"

"When we get home," he snapped in return.

"This place is not my home."

Rogan entered his cottage and turned into his room, where he was certain no one would disturb her, and dropped her on his bed. "For now, this is your home."

Aliss scrambled to the edge of the bed.

"Do not dare set foot out of that bed. You will rest." He could hear the warning snarl in his voice. It did the trick; she did not move.

She raised herself on her knees. "I am not tired and there is work—"

"That can wait."

"It cannot." Her shoulders slumped. "You must let me heal as I see fit."

"And what if you get sick? What do I do then?"

"Why don't I, or you, or Anna and others not get sick while some do? That is the true question."

She plopped down, crossing her legs, and Rogan caught a hint of a firm, slender calf before she tucked her skirt over it. She had beautiful cream-colored, touchable skin and a heart that never stopped caring.

He joined her on the bed.

"I intend to find the answer. It is here right in front of me. *I know it*," she said.

"What is your life like back home? Is there a man who cares for you?"

"What does that matter?" she asked, annoyed.

"Healing, healing, healing. That is all you ever talk about. I have wondered if you have anything else in your life."

"I love my work."

"I understand that," he said, and reached out to tug gently on a strand of her fiery red hair. "But you are a beautiful woman, surely you have many men chasing after you."

"I have no time for a man in my life."

He wrapped the red curl around his finger. "No time or no interest?"

She swatted his hand away. "I do not wish to sit here talking about nonsense when time could be better spent in finding ways to combat this malady."

He leaned closer and he could feel her body shiver like a trembling breath washing over him. "Talk of intimacy frightens you."

"It does not!"

A catch in her voice told him otherwise.

"Do you not want a man to love you?"

He reached out and grabbed her arm as she scooted to the end of the bed.

"I need no man."

It sounded more a challenge to him than a fact.

"Why is that?" he asked, tugging her back to the middle of the bed.

She hesitated.

An abrupt, "Tell me," got him his answer.

"I have no time for a man. Men demand as you do now." She glanced at his grip on her arm. "You hold me here. You say I must rest and I say no. Is the choice not mine?"

"I look out for you," he argued, releasing her.

"For no other reason but that I am needed to tend your people."

He moved his face close to hers. "So say you."

She stammered her response. "Wh-what o-other reason—"

"Could there be?" he finished, and stroked her cheek with his finger. "That you are a good and generous woman whom a man could easily love."

"I need no man," she reiterated sharply and made a dash for the edge of the bed.

Rogan was quicker and had her on her back in a flash.

"Sometimes we deny what we want the most," he said, staring down at her.

"That is nonsense."

He loved the way her eyes fired a blazing green; a passion lay burning in them. A passion he was certain she had yet to discover. He leaned closer. His lips so near to hers that it appeared they kissed, but they did not, though when he spoke his warm breath stroked her pink lips like a kiss waiting for an invitation.

"Is it nonsense? Think about it." He stood and walked to the door. "Do not dare get off that bed at least until supper."

"If I do?" she challenged.

He laughed deeply and walked out the door.

Aliss listened to his fading laughter. He had left her to rest, but it was her thoughts that he really left her to. Thoughts of him kissing her. Not that he had; was she disappointed?

His lips had been close enough for her to almost feel them on her own. She licked her tingling lips, recalling the warm sweetness of his breath and the way it had tickled and tempted. She had for a brief moment actually thought of kissing him.

She jolted up and pressed her fingers to her mouth.

Was she crazy?

Had she actually thought of kissing the Wolf?

She felt her head, certain she suffered from fever.

Nothing.

She scurried off the bed and heard his laughter in her mind. Should she challenge him?

With a heavy sigh, she dropped back on the straw mattress.

He had upset her—or was she upset with herself? Their talk had reminded her of the problem she had left behind in Hellewyk and would face upon her return.

Marriage.

Unwanted marriage, though her brother-in-law Tarr had offered her a chance to choose her own husband. No amount of protesting had changed the circumstances. Tarr had decreed that the prophecy Giann had predicted be satisfied, which meant that the twins, she and Fiona, had to wed if the clans were to avoid destruction. Fiona had fulfilled her part; now it was Aliss's turn.

She had yet to find anyone suitable. Though there had been many willing prospects, none had impressed her. Actually, none would have tolerated her propensity for healing.

She hesitantly touched her lips and thought of the intimacy expected of her once she wed. How could she be so intimate with a stranger?

A peck or two on the cheek was all the experience she had with kissing, though Fiona, her sister, claimed it was fantastic and urged her to try it. She had insisted it would help her to decide on a husband. If a man could not kiss then Aliss should not even consider wedding him.

What else, though, did she look for in a husband?

Kindness. Strength. Patience.

Rogan possessed all three qualities. He had demonstrated them often with his clan and with her.

What of love?

She jumped, startled by the question that popped into her head. She had not even considered it. She had no time for it. She was not certain she would recognize it if it hit her in the face.

Would a kiss help acquaint her with it?

Kissing, Fiona had said, was a pleasure to be

shared repeatedly and often between husband and wife. If a man's kiss left her feeling nothing, then he was not the one for Aliss.

She rested her fingers to her lips.

How would Rogan's kisses leave her feeling?

Aliss drifted off to sleep, her mind chaotic with kisses.

"Sweet, you taste so very sweet."

Aliss sighed with pleasure. His lips caressed every inch of her face, her closed eyes, the tip of her nose, her cheeks, her chin, her forehead.

"Sweet."

He kissed along her neck. It tickled and she laughed softly, hunching her shoulders to prevent him access. She relinquished them and his kisses resumed, bringing her a pleasure she had not known possible.

Her lips began to ache for him. He had not kissed her lips. She wanted him to kiss her lips. He had to; how else would she know if he was the one?

She turned her head toward his mouth. "Kiss me."

He kept his lips a breath from hers.

"Kiss me!"

"Do you know what you ask?"

"Kiss me."

"Do you know who I am?"

"Kiss me and I shall know."

"Are you sure?"

"Yes," she insisted, her eyes springing open.

She stared into the eyes of a snarling wolf and screamed.

"You are all right. You are safe."

Aliss ceased her struggling once she realized

that Rogan held her protectively in his arms. She rested her head on his chest, grateful to have escaped her nightmare.

"It was nothing more than a bad dream," he said.

She refused to close her eyes, fearing she would return to the snarling wolf. All she wanted to do, at least for a moment, was remain safe and warm in Rogan's arms.

She glanced up at him.

"Want to tell me about it?"

She shook her head, while realization startled her. She woke to escape one wolf only to land in the arms of another. Or were they one and the same? She eased herself out of his embrace and casually moved to the edge of the bed.

"Your actions answer."

She stood away from the bed. "And that would be?"

"You dreamed of me and now you run."

"Since I woke screaming, I would not think that a compliment."

He stood abruptly. Aliss was in no mood to continue their debate. She turned away and walked to the door. "I am hungry."

"Are you, or do you run away, Aliss?"

She raised her hands to her cheeks when she entered the other room. Even with warm hands, she could feel the heat that had rushed to her face when he accused her of retreat. She hurriedly busied herself at the hearth. The fire's heat was a good excuse for rosy red cheeks.

"Sit and eat since you claim hunger."

She turned to notice the table laden with food.

"The women of the village wished to show their appreciation for your help thus far," Rogan said, and was about to take a seat when Anna rushed into the room.

"James complains of severe stomach pains."

Aliss hurried out with Anna. Rogan followed close behind.

A quick examination and a few facts proved James had eaten too much. A brew to ease his discomfort and a lecture to the grandparents about his meals was all that was needed.

Unfortunately, Aliss, after finishing with James, was summoned again then again and again until she was finally finished around midnight.

Rogan waited outside the last cottage and held out his hand to her.

She thought to take it, grasp it tightly and not let go. He anchored her when she felt herself adrift and lonely, especially after hours of tending the ill. The sudden thought of dependence startled her and she quickly handed him her healing basket.

He took the basket then reached out and grasped her hand firmly in his.

She did not object; after all, it was what she had wanted but feared reaching out for. It felt so good to be connected to him by a simple grasp of hands, though if she allowed her tired mind to rationalize it, she would understand that their clasped hands meant much more.

She forced her mind silent, too tired to make sense of her musings. But before long her thoughts wandered to her work, or was it that she felt in safer territory there? "I thought by now I would have prevented any new illnesses." She shook her head, disappointed. "Three more tonight."

"But none have died since you arrived," he reminded her.

"And none have mended permanently, except—" She stopped. "Tara's son Daniel has suffered no relapses."

"True enough." Rogan laughed. "He runs around like a little banshee."

She started walking again. "What is different about him?"

"His age," Rogan offered.

"What else?" Her stomach rumbled.

"You need food."

"I need answers," she insisted.

"I will help you search for your answers," he offered. "I want this culprit caught and done away with, never to bother my people again."

"You are all different and yet—"

"We care for each other, for if not, no one else will."

"What brought you all together?"

"A common trait," Rogan answered. "No one else wanted us. We are not pure breeds. Our blood is mixed. No specific birthright means no specific allegiance to any clan, or so it is believed. My father had settled us in the far north of Scotland, nearer to Oslo, where the Norse left their mark."

"What brought you here?"

"Love."

Chapter 9

They entered the cottage and were soon settled at the table to eat the meal that had been delayed several hours.

"You cannot tell me that love brought you here and then say no more," Aliss urged. "Tell me the story."

"It breaks the heart," he warned.

"Most love stories do. Now tell me."

He watched eagerness break through her weary-filled eyes and turn them bright green. Rogan rested his arms on the table and began his tale.

"My father had to make it on his own since he was eight. His father refused to claim him and his mother died from sickness. He found that few were interested in a lad with blood of Scot,

English, and Norse mixed in his veins. He wandered for a good many years accumulating others just like him.

"Together they forged a clan, and since my father had always admired the nature of the wolf, he took its name. The Wolf clan was born and my father was its leader. He along with his men would hire out as mercenaries. It was while in the service of a powerful chieftain that he met my mother."

"They fell in love." Aliss smiled with excitement.

"Almost instantly, though they dared not admit it to anyone, even themselves. You see, her father had plans for her to wed another, a uniting of two powerful clans."

"That was to be my sister's fate, an arranged marriage, though it worked out well for her."

"Not so my mother. They knew their only chance to be together was for my mother to run away with my father."

Rogan grew silent. His father had recited the tale often to him and the memories he had imparted were harsh and bitter for Rogan to recall, yet endearing in their own special way.

"Memories hurt."

He heard compassion in her voice and knew that she had to have suffered a similar loss. Only someone who had known loss could truly understand its unique pain.

He continued. "My parents returned to my father's land. They soon discovered that my mother's father intended to come after her and they decided to leave, not wanting to place the Wolf clan in jeopardy. The clan would not hear of losing their leader. They all agreed to join him."

Rogan's glance drifted down to his hands, clenched on the table in front of him.

He was not surprised when Aliss squeezed his hands reassuringly.

He looked up at her, her beauty startling, her concern obvious, her tender touch palpable, and a sense of loving warmth flooded him. He had realized of late just how very comfortable he felt when with her. She was so very easy to talk with, even to share the silence with. Theirs was a natural companionship—or was it more?

"What happened?"

"My mother was taken away from me before I saw my first year. He came for her, her father, with more men than my father could battle, though battle he would have if my mother had not stopped him.

"My father told me that she refused to see the Wolf clan slaughtered because of her and—" He bit back the anger and bitterness. "Her father warned that he would slice her son's throat in front of her and let her watch me bleed to death if she did not return willingly with him."

"Did you ever see your mother again?"

Rogan shook his head. "Mother made my father promise to take me away. She did not trust her own father. She feared he would see me dead regardless of what she had agreed to and Father agreed with her. We never saw my mother again."

"How very sad for you all."

Rogan reached up and wiped away the lone teardrop that lingered in the corner of Aliss's eye. "Love can be sad and it can be happy, but love is forever beautiful—just like you."

He watched her body tense and she took her hand off his. He did not want her to shy away from him. He wanted to learn more about her, come to better understand her, this woman who lovingly healed yet evaded loving.

"What of your parents?" he asked.

Her smile was slow in coming, as if she had to think on the question, then it suddenly burst wide and generous.

"I have two sets of parents."

"Two?"

"There were the parents that raised Fiona and me, a kind and loving couple, and then there are our birth parents, Oleg and Anya. They are also kind and loving. We were taken from them when we were newborn babes. Fiona and I have only recently reunited with them and with a brother, Raynor."

"How did you feel when you learned about them?"

"It was strange to suddenly discover that the loving parents who raised you are not truly your parents. Upon meeting my real parents, I found myself feeling terribly sorry for my mother as I do for your mother. Neither of them were able to watch their children grow, hug us, laugh with us, cry with us, though they always continued to love us."

"You would make a good mother." He almost laughed when her eyes sprang wide, her mouth dropped open, and she sat speechless.

She was quick to rein in her shock. "I do not have time for children."

"No?" he questioned. "That is odd. You deal so well with ill children. Even the devilish little Daniel behaves around you."

She jumped as if his name sparked a thought. "We need to discuss Daniel."

"Now?" he asked, knowing she was uncomfortable with where their conversation had drifted and looked to avoid it.

"You told me you would help to unravel the mystery of this illness, and I believe Daniel is the best place to start." She shook off a yawn.

"Tomorrow," he said. "You need to sleep."

"There is too much on my mind. Sleep will elude me tonight."

"Try anyway. We will discuss this in the morning." He stood and waited for her to stand, leaving her no choice but to follow his lead.

She did not budge. She dismissed him with, "I will see you in the morning."

"Not this time."

Her wide-eyed innocent gaze made him laugh. "I have no intention of leaving you at this table to fall asleep like last time. You will get in that bed now." He pointed to her bed.

He smiled as her protest was swallowed by a yawn.

Rogan walked around the table, took her hand and gently eased her to her feet. He tucked a curly red strand behind her ear, tugged at her earlobe then ran a finger along her chin. It was impossible not to, she was so soft and touchable.

"You are tired. Why fight it? Sleep and we will discuss Daniel in the morning."

"But—"

He pressed a finger to her lips and wished instead it was his lips that silenced her. A taste, that was all he wanted; a taste of her sweetness.

He lowered his head.

Rogan jumped, startled, then she ducked out of his arms like a frightened animal fleeing capture and hurried into bed.

"We will talk in the morning," she said and pulled the covers over her head.

She lay curled in a ball and he would have loved to have gone to her, join her under the covers and simply hold her in his arms. She needed to be held and loved gently.

He shook off his foolish thoughts, turned and went to seek the solace of sleep. His mind had been filled with Aliss of late and in ways he had not intended.

He knew someday he would find love again, but with Aliss?

It was not in his plans, but then plans changed all the time.

Aliss watched the sun rise. It rose like a majestic fiery ball; its rays stretching over the land to nourish all it touched. The seedlings she had planted had sprung and the tiny plants turned eager leaves toward the sun.

She mimicked them, lifting her face up for a kiss.

The small village was just coming to life and she was reminded of her own clan and of her sister. She missed her. A day did not go by that she did not think of Fiona and returning home. A day also did not go by without Rogan popping into her thoughts.

He would be there suddenly in her head when she least expected it. It was usually a recollection of something he had said to her or the thought of his hand on hers, warm and strong and welcoming.

It had disturbed her to realize she had welcomed his touch, innocent as it was, though was it? Lately she was beginning to notice his hand reached out to her more and more and she did not mind. His touch seemed natural and somehow right.

Aliss walked along the outskirts of her garden, meaning to tend it. Instead, she weeded her way through her chaotic thoughts.

She could not continue to deny her attraction to the warrior wolf, nor could she make sense of it. It was as if it had happened without thought or reason. It was simply born naturally.

As love was so often born.

She shook the nonsensical thought from her head. Love had nothing to do with it. Circumstance was what had produced her strange musings. Her abduction had forced their closeness. She lived in Rogan's cottage, shared meals with him. He had even given her his deceased wife's clothes to use.

She stroked the soft, dark green wool skirt and fingered the pale yellow blouse she wore. Had her wearing his wife's garments rekindled memories in him? Had he suddenly felt the emptiness of his loss and looked to her to ease his grief?

Aliss sighed in frustration. Why did she waste time on such nonsense? This was the very reason she had not wanted to wed. She had not wanted her mind distracted from her work.

There was a time she had thought that there could be a balance between her work and love. After observing couples and their daily lives, she realized that had been just a dream. Marriage took work, understanding, and patience. She spent her patience on her healing. She feared she would have none left for a man.

"Heavy thoughts this morning?"

Aliss grabbed her chest and spun around to face Rogan. "You frightened me."

"I called out to you."

"I did not hear you."

He approached her, a plaid of mixed dark colors wrapped around him, his chest bare, his hair rumpled from a night's sleep and his green eyes sharp and steady on her.

"Then you *were* lost in heavy thoughts," he said and stopped in front of her.

"A common trait of mine," she admitted.

"Something you wish to discuss?"

Aliss attempted to ignore the firm muscles in his wide chest and the thickness of his arms. There was strength there and power. She had felt it time and again when he had lifted her so effortlessly. He could fight barehanded without a problem.

She suddenly recalled how Rogan had attacked Hellewyk land and pierced Tarr's arm with one mighty blow of a hand-held arrow. She had tended the wound, amazed at the strength it would take to accomplish such a feat.

Now she saw for herself the strength in the man who had injured her brother-in-law and shivered.

He reached out to her and she stumbled away from him.

"What is wrong?"

"You attacked Hellewyk land in search of me? Why? You could have just requested my help."

"Tarr would never have allowed you to leave with me."

She did not argue the truth. Tarr would have never permitted her to go with Rogan.

"Your silence tells me we are in agreement."

She gave a reluctant nod then suddenly asked a question that had lingered in the recesses of her mind since arriving there. "What of the Isle of Non?"

He hesitated before answering, "What of it?"

She shrugged. "I recall my brother Raynor mentioning that he chased you and your men off the isle. Why were—"

He didn't let her finish. "I thought the isle belonged to Tarr."

His troubled expression caught her curiosity. Why would the ownership of the isle concern him? "A dispute that has been settled with the joining of the two clans. But what interest do you—"

"I hope someday you will understand the reasons behind my actions."

"I hope so too, but what of the isle—" She stopped and stared into the woods. "Did you see that?"

"See what?" he asked, and followed her glance.

She shook her head. "I must be seeing things. I could have sworn I saw a pair of green eyes."

"My men patrol the woods regularly. More than likely it was one of them you saw."

She continued to stare into the woods. "The eyes looked like they breathed life."

"A trick of the light," he suggested.

She did not agree. "I think not."

"I will search the woods myself," he assured her.

She reached out and grasped his arm. "No, you must not go yourself. Promise me."

He laughed. "You fear for me?"

She released his arm quickly and stepped away from him, feeling more foolish than ever. "Do what you will. It matters not to me."

He approached her again, but she walked away.

"I wish to tend my garden." She bent down and yanked a small weed, squeezing it in her hand.

He grabbed her arm and hauled her to her feet. "Is it so hard to admit you care what happens to me?"

"I care what happens to everyone."

"I am no different?" he asked, releasing her.

She stared at him, her heart pounding.

"Aye or nay will do," he said.

"It is not that simple."

"Why not? Open your eyes, see for yourself, and you'll have your answer."

"My eyes are open."

"My mistake," he said caustically. "It is your heart that you need to open."

She gasped. "My heart is more open than yours will ever be."

Rogan laughed. "Your heart is locked away."

"I dare—"

"Speak the truth?"

"I will listen to no more." She marched past him. He grabbed her, yanking her against his chest. "Not even to what your own heart and mind tell you?"

"They tell me not to be foolish."

"Mine tells me to take a chance."

"On what?"

"On you."

Aliss yanked her arm free and she ran into the cottage, knowing she was running more from herself than from him.

Chapter 10

A liss slammed her fist on the table and cursed her own anger. Her eyes were open wide, very wide. She knew exactly what she saw. Did she not?

She rubbed the spot between her eyes. The area that always ached when she thought too much. It was a dull ache, not a throb, and more annoying than painful.

How to get rid of it?

Stop pondering?

She laughed at herself. That was not likely, especially now since she felt the fool for treating Rogan so rudely. He had been nothing but kind to her since her capture. At first, she had feared her treatment at his hands, for rumors had presented the Wolf as a fierce warrior to be feared.

Gradually, she had learned differently. Rogan was nothing as she had imagined him, and in a strange way, his kindness had proven difficult for her. The Wolf was no longer the predator she first thought him to be. He did not bite, though sometimes he snarled, but he always protected her.

Then why had she grown angry with him?

Because he spoke the truth?

Did she refuse to open her heart and take a chance?

Being a healer, she had always embraced sound reasoning. It allowed her to examine and dissect illnesses so that she could logically find a treatable solution. She had not reacted logically to Rogan's remark, but why? Because she did not want to think that perhaps he was right and there was an issue she needed to explore. She had enough on her mind right now; she needed no more problems to ponder.

She sighed, feeling she owed him an apology. She needed more time to consider his words. She turned and hurried out of the cottage.

She stopped abruptly just outside the door, confronted by half a dozen warriors on horses. Rogan was in the middle of them atop his pure white mare. His intense features were in sharp contrast to how they had looked only moments before.

His green eyes looked ablaze with fury, his mouth closed tightly as if he forcibly kept his words from erupting, and every muscle in his chest and arms was taut as a fine-strung bow.

Rogan looked ready to do battle.

He turned his head her way and his eyes seared her like a fiery hot arrow. She placed her hand on her chest, covering her heart.

Rogan looked to John, who stood to the side. "Keep her in sight."

With that, he took off, his men following.

Aliss turned her attention to John. "What is wrong?"

"I cannot say." He turned away from her.

She stepped in front of him. "You must know something."

"I know nothing." John insisted.

"Should I be concerned?"

John shook his head vehemently. "Rogan would never let anything happen to you."

"You must get tired of being the one who guards me."

John's youthful eyes turned wide. "No, no. It is an honor, Rogan choosing me to guard you." He grinned. "Besides, this way I get to see Anna."

"Then let us not keep her waiting," Aliss said. "I only need to get my basket."

"I will get it," John said, and hurried into the cottage.

Aliss looked to the distance and sent a silent prayer for Rogan's safe return. Suddenly the skin on the back of her neck prickled.

"Aliss, come to me."

Aliss turned at the whispered summons of a woman.

Green eyes glared at her from the woods and the soft voice continued to summon her until finally she obeyed and walked into the woods.

* * *

"You were not to let her out of your sight," Rogan said, having returned an hour later to find his village in uproar and a search for Aliss in progress.

John's hands trembled as he offered an explanation. "A minute. I only left her a minute, to fetch her basket. I returned and she was gone. I searched and searched." He shook his head. "I could not find her anywhere."

Anna stilled his shivering hands with her confident ones. "We all began searching as soon as we realized she was missing. Anyone who was able helped."

Rogan dismounted and threw his reins to a waiting young lad. Anna and John did not wait for their leader's command and quickly left to rejoin the search.

Derek approached Rogan. "She could have attempted an escape."

"Do you believe that?" Rogan snapped.

"No, Aliss would not leave the ill, but it was your first thought."

"It crossed my mind," Rogan said with a near growl.

"She will leave sooner or later, will she not?"

"Mind your business, Derek. It is safer for you that way."

"I know you too well," Derek said. "Be careful, my friend, do not let the misery of the past rob you of a happy future."

"I can have no happy future until I have settled the past. Now do you help search for Aliss or stand here and lecture me?"

"We found her! We found her!"

Rogan turned in the direction of the shout and took off.

He stopped suddenly when he saw Aliss on the forest floor, green grass, rotted bark, and brush cushioning and partially covering her prone body. Nature had concealed her well in her bosom.

Anna and John kneeled beside her, Anna gently patting her pale cheeks in an attempt to wake her.

Rogan dropped to his knees beside her, leaned down near her ear, and whispered, "Wake up, Aliss."

He locked his strong hand protectively around her chilled one and squeezed, letting her know that he was there with her and he would let nothing happen to her.

"You are safe." The words reverberated in a whisper near her ear in hopes that they would penetrate her deep sleep and free her.

"What are you doing on your knees?"

His head snapped up and he stared into her shining green eyes that opened wide, closed, and fought to open again.

Aliss moved her head slowly from side to side. "I am on the ground."

"That you are," Rogan said with a wide smile, relieved that she had woken.

"How did I get here?"

"I thought you would answer that question."

"Anna, John?" She stared at the couple. " What are you doing here?"

"They searched for you and found you," Rogan explained.

"I was lost?"

"You disappeared when I went to fetch your healing basket," John said.

"No, I waited for you." Aliss was adamant.

"And?" Rogan asked, concerned to hear what followed.

Aliss glared at him for a moment, wrinkled her brow and shook her head. "I do not remember."

"You do not know how you came to be in the woods?" Rogan asked.

Aliss was startled. "I am in the woods?"

Rogan slipped his arm beneath her back and helped her to sit up. "See for yourself."

She looked about her. "Motherwort," Aliss said, pointing to a reddish-violet plant. "I must pick some." She attempted to stand.

"Stay where you are," Rogan ordered.

"I often gather motherwort for the women," Anna said. "I will get some for you."

Aliss stared at Anna for a moment.

"Is something wrong?" the young woman asked.

Aliss shook her head. "Something about—" She shook her head again. "My mind is foggy."

"You will rest. Anna will see to the plant," Rogan said and waited, prepared for her to disagree.

"That is a good idea. Will you help me up?"

He almost fell back, so surprised was he by how easily she had agreed. She grabbed his arm and he lifted her to her feet. She seemed uncertain of her footing and kept her hand gripped to his arm. He slipped his other arm around her waist to steady her until he was certain her legs would hold her.

When her steps were finally stable, she continued to cling to him, pressing her body close to his. He drew her into the nook of his arm, wanting her to know she was safe, wanting to keep her safe.

During the short walk to the cottage, Rogan gave thought to Aliss's disappearance and discovery. She had not been that far into the woods or her body that concealed that it should have taken so long to find her. Which led him to wonder if the prophetess, Giann, had a hand in this.

"It is odd that I do not remember how I came to be in the woods," Aliss said when they entered his cottage.

He reluctantly released her to sit on the edge of her bed while he stoked the fire to ward off the chill that pervaded the room. He wanted her warm and comfortable, safely tucked away in his home where no harm could befall her, if only for the day.

"I do not recall entering the woods," she said. She tugged off her boots, crossed her legs and tucked her feet beneath her, her elbow on her knee and her chin resting in her hand.

Rogan sat beside her, her covered foot pressed against his thigh. Her foot was small, her toes playing against his muscled thigh, stretching and kneading the ache away.

"What do you recall?" he asked and reached

beneath her skirt to take hold of her foot and massage the tender flesh.

She sighed long and softly, and it tingled his insides.

"Waiting for John as he had told me to do."

"I had thought you fearful of the woods and never would have expected to find you there." His fingers worked on the sole of her foot, kneading and rubbing and feeling her relax to his touch.

"The eyes—" She paused, and her brow creased. "Hmmm, that feels so good."

"What about the eyes?" Curious himself.

She shook her head slowly. "I cannot . . . hmmm, your hands work magic."

His hand drifted up her ankle to knead her silky flesh and she leaned her head back, closing her eyes and sighing her pleasure.

"Magic, pure magic," she said with a smile. "I know there is much that I should be thinking on but right now I do not want to think on anything."

"You deserve to rest."

"No, there is something I should remember. Something important."

"It can wait—"

"Why can I not remember?"

"Do not concern yourself with that now," he said, feeling that he had surmised correctly. Giann definitely had had a hand in Aliss's disappearance. Her skills were great and could make one forget she had ever been in her presence.

She rubbed her head and slouched against him as though she had fallen into the comfortable position a thousand times before.

"This confuses me."

"Do not worry over it. It will do you no good."
She raised her head. "I am missing something."

Her faint pink lips were soft and moist like the
petals of a freshly bloomed flower kissed by the
morning dew and much too near his own. He
ached to taste their flavor, yet knew one taste
would not suffice. He would want more, much
more.

"What do you miss?" he asked.

He watched her eyes settle on him as he ran his
tongue over his dry lips, leaving them damp.
Her breathing grew labored as her eyes remained on his mouth and there was no doubt to
her thoughts.

He leaned in close, afraid to speak and chase
her away.

She stared at him, licking her own lips, prepar-
ing for a kiss? He hoped so.

He wanted to kiss her. No, he needed to kiss
her. When had a kiss become a need? At least a
kiss from Aliss.

He moved his hand from beneath her skirt,
running it up her leg over her breast and to her
neck. He would help her along, let her initiate the
kiss, feel comfortable with it.

He stroked her neck. "So soft, such beautiful
skin."

Aliss jumped back as if she had been burned.
"That is it."

"What?" he demanded, annoyed that he had
been suddenly robbed of a kiss.

"I know what caused Anna's rash," she said, excited. "*Motherwort*. She mentioned that she picked the herb often for the women in the village. Some healers break out in rashes when handling it. That explains the continuity of her skin malady."

"This is important?"

"Of course," she said, jumping out of bed and pacing the floor in front of him.

"The rash persisted since Anna continued to gather motherwort."

"If she had not it would have gone away," Rogan said with a nod then shook his head. "I still do not understand your excitement."

"I have discovered the reason for her rash, which allows for a permanent cure."

"And?"

"It has given me insight into the reason for the illness that has plagued your village."

That got his attention. "You think you may have discovered the enemy?"

"There is a good chance that your people are digesting something that continues to make them ill. It would explain why some grow healthy only to grow ill all over again"

"You do not know what it is?"

"That will take time, patience, and many questions to determine."

"I can help," he offered, and held his hand out to her.

She took it eagerly. "The more help, the more quickly we find the solution."

He tugged her toward him, but she panicked and backed away.

"Do not be afraid. Come to me, Aliss."

She jolted, yanked her hand free and ran from the room.

Chapter 11

~~~ ⌒∞∞⌒ ~~~

Aliss knew work was the only cure for her troubled mind. She could not understand how she had gotten into the woods. Why had she lain unconscious on the ground and why had Rogan's touch thrilled and frightened her at the same time?

It certainly was not sensible to entertain the idea that Rogan could have feelings for her or she for him. Her time here was limited anyway so why make it more difficult for herself than it had to be.

He did, though, have qualities she would favor in a husband.

Husband?

Tarr had decreed that she must marry, leaving the choice of a husband to her. So like it or not she would wed. Did she not want to choose a suitable husband, one she could at least tolerate?

Rogan treated her kindly and respected her work. He made few demands on her and offered his help when necessary.

Aliss slowed her hurried pace and her racing thoughts. She had left the cottage in haste to go where? To run? But from whom, Rogan or herself?

She smiled and waved her appreciation to those who acknowledged their relief over her safe return before delving back into her musings.

Rogan was also a fine clan leader. He treated his people well and he was respected in return. He had many fine traits that would suit a woman contemplating marriage.

Kiss him.

The voice was so clear and loud in her head that she came to an abrupt halt and almost tripped. She could have sworn she had heard her sister's impatient tone. It was, after all, advice Fiona would give her.

Aliss had to admit she had been tempted more than once to see how it would feel to kiss Rogan, but she had always panicked and run. What did she fear?

"A kiss would prove what?" she mumbled, but heard no answer. Where was her sister when she needed her?

Guilt made Aliss shiver. She should be thinking about her sister and returning home, not how it would feel to kiss Rogan. Fiona would be rounding with child by now and worried that Aliss would not return in time to deliver the babe. What was the matter with her? She had no time for such nonsense as a kiss, and besides, Tarr would never approve of a union between Rogan and her.

She hastened her steps.

She would find the reason behind this illness and finally return home.

To what?

Wedding a stranger? Someone she had no feelings for? Someone who would interfere in her healing work? Or someone who would care not at all one way or the other?

Rogan had plucked her out of a hopeless situation, one with no solution, at least not a suitable solution. The time spent here had reminded her how much she enjoyed her freedom and independence. But even though Rogan had abducted her, he had not treated her like a prisoner. She was allowed freedom in the village and she had cherished that.

Still, Fiona and Tarr were her family, and she had yet to get to know her mother and father or her brother Raynor. What would they think if they knew she thought of kissing the Wolf?

She giggled softly. Fiona would encourage her.

Aliss sighed. She really did miss her sister. They talked often, took walks together, shared secrets, and helped each other through difficult times.

She was alone now with no one but herself to help her.

Not so. She corrected herself and knew it to be true.

Rogan had been helpful and protective since first they met. He could have set her to tending his people and ignored her all this time. Instead, he had taken her into his home and made certain she had what she needed and that she got sufficient food and rest.

The Wolf was a good man.

"Aliss."

She spun around at the sound of Rogan's voice. He had slipped on a shirt and his green eyes had softened in color.

"I thought you might need your basket."

He held it up though he made no attempt to give it to her and Aliss made no attempt to take it from him. Her heart raced a little faster than it normally did and a sudden breathlessness attacked her.

Her smile came slowly. "Thank you."

"I will carry it for you," he said eagerly.

She nodded and he walked alongside her.

No mention was made of her rushed exit. They strolled together in companionable silence.

Aliss was soon busy talking with those who were ill or had been ill. They went from cottage to cottage. Rogan asked a question or two of his own that proved helpful until finally they both agreed they were famished and returned to their cottage.

"You search for a common cause," Rogan said once they had eaten.

She nodded. "Something that links them all together. It makes sense. Like Anna's rash. I knew something caused it but what—" She shook her head. "I only realized it when she spoke of gathering motherwort. It is one plant that can be risky for some to handle."

"I understand now what makes you such a fine healer."

She grinned. "My stubborn nature?"

"Your propensity for digging until you get to the truth of the situation."

"Truth can cure many ills," she said, "as long as it is acknowledged."

Their eyes settled gently on each other and for a silent moment lingered there as if caught in a trance or an embrace that neither wished to relinquish and neither acknowledged.

Aliss tore her glance away and suddenly feeling the need to know asked, "Once this is settled, you will take me home as promised?"

"Once all is settled—" He paused and shifted his glance to the tankard in his hand. "You will go home."

Aliss had not realized she had held her breath nor had she expected his answer to disturb her. "I am eager to return and not so eager to return."

Rogan raised a curious brow. "Tell me."

"I must find a husband when I go back," she admitted, though why she shared her problem with him she could not say. Perhaps it was her need to talk of it and that he was a generous listener.

"Why is that?"

"It has to do with a long-ago prophecy—" She knitted her brow. "Odd, that I cannot recall the exact prediction. I had heard it repeatedly and the only thing I can remember is, on a full moon twin babes are born, with their birth sounds the horn." She shook her head. "I cannot remember the rest."

"What has it to do with you having to wed?"

Aliss heard genuine curiosity in his voice. "It is something about the clans being in danger if my sister and I do not wed—I think." She shrugged. "All I know is that according to the prophecy I must wed, the clans demand it."

"Clans?"

"Hellewyk and my parents' clan, Blackshaw."

"Who will you wed?"

"I have no idea, though Tarr has left the decision to me."

"I am sure you have not lacked for prospective bridegrooms."

"Not at all," she admitted.

"Any you favored?"

She shook her head. "Not a one."

"What will you do?"

"Hope to find a man I can tolerate," she said with a laugh.

"This really troubles you."

A knot tightened in Aliss's chest along with the urge to cry. Rogan's heartfelt remark had caused it. He actually understood how much the situation disturbed her and it sounded as if he was as troubled about it as she was.

She nodded and swallowed to keep the knot from rising to her throat.

"If we can find the solution to this illness that ravishes my people then it should be simple to discover a way to keep you free of an unwanted husband."

"You are kind to offer me help and hope. I am pleased that you are my friend." Her voice quivered.

The knot tightened and almost reached her throat. She had friends, but they were really more acquaintances; her work left her little time to cultivate friendships. Her one true friend had been her sister. Now she had Rogan, but for how long?

"I am honored that you accept me as a friend. I know how difficult it must be for you reconciling the man who abducted you with the man who wished your help."

"You are two, Wolf and Rogan."

"It is necessary sometimes."

"Not confusing?" she asked.

"Not at all. The wolf calculates and waits and when needed attacks."

"And Rogan?"

"Rogan is simply a man."

Aliss stared at him and shook her head slowly. "You are not simply a man."

"Who am I, then?"

A good question and one she could not answer. It was more what she felt when around him, while watching him with his people, acting as a leader, as a warrior, as a friend. How did she explain his empathy for the suffering of his people? How did she detail his honor in protecting his clan at all cost? How did she make clear how a mother's unselfish love produced an unselfish son? How did she admit her admiration for a man who had loved and lost and yet was not afraid to love again?

No, he was not simply a man; he was much more.

"Have to think about the answer, do you?" he teased.

Laughter spilled easily from her lips though she blinked back the single tear caught in her eye. "It is difficult to define a man like yourself."

"A compliment?"

"Yes." She nodded. "Perhaps one day I will find the words to explain."

He smiled. "I look forward to that time."

Aliss did too, for perhaps then they would meet again after parting. She did not like to think that once she left the Wolf clan she would never see Rogan again.

"Kiss him."

She jumped, startled by Fiona's voice in her head.

Rogan stood and rushed around the table to her side. "What is wrong?"

"Nothing," she said with a forced smile.

"You are not a good liar."

"I am—" Her mouth dropped open. Was she just about to admit to being a good liar?

"Yes?"

His one word challenged her to finish.

"Not!"

He roared with laughter, and when it subsided, he scooted in beside her on the bench.

He smelled of fresh earth like the fields after

planting, pungent and delicious. The need to savor his taste overwhelmed her and she was
close to reaching out and grabbing hold of him
to kiss him.

Stop!

She warned herself, though it did little good,
so she had no choice but to put distance between
them.

Rogan, she realized, had a different idea, and
as she slipped off the bench, he stood and
blocked her escape.

He motioned her to come to him, a simple jerk
of his hand as if he summoned her. She
remained . . .

Defiant? Fearful?

Why did she not approach him?

He stretched his hand out to her. "Come to me,
Aliss."

He tempted her, his voice so soft and soothing.
And she was so doubtful. What did she fear? Did
she refuse to love? Fear to love? Fear interference
from love? What always stopped her from accepting the attention of any man?

And why? Why did she want so desperately to
kiss Rogan?

"I would never hurt you," he said, keeping his
hand stretched out to her.

"What do you want of me?"

"To taste you."

She shivered and he hurried over to her, wrapping her in his warm, strong embrace.

"You are cold."

She stared up into his eyes filled with a fiery

brilliance that stirred her soul and enflamed her flesh.

"A taste," he whispered. "Just a taste."

He bent his head and claimed her lips before she could protest.

Chapter 12

A liss melted at the first taste of him. Warm, delicious, and succulent like a favorite food you could not get enough of and wanted to savor forever and ever.

His lips melded with hers, encouraging a response, sparking her passion, urging a reaction, and she responded with all the fervor of an innocent who longed to experience more.

He obliged her, his tongue teasing her lips apart then darting into her mouth then out then slowly reintroducing himself, until she eagerly accepted him and dueled with his tongue like a young maiden new to the dance.

She relished the comfort of him and how he allowed her to play and experiment, yet taking charge and teaching her how a kiss was shared and enjoyed. He taught and pleasured her at the same time.

She moaned softly, wanting the kiss to last longer and he did not disappoint her. He kissed her long and hard and slow and soft. And just when she thought him finished he would begin again until she shivered in his arms.

His hand slipped under her blouse to her breast, his fingers gently kneading her flesh, his thumb repeatedly rubbing her nipple until it hardened to his touch.

He pressed against her and she felt him hard and strong, aching for her.

The thought jolted her like a shot of lightning from the sky. What was she doing? Was she crazy?

She tore herself away from him and he was left standing with empty arms.

"I cannot do this," she cried and hurried out of the cottage.

Rogan did not follow. He plopped down on the bench, dropping his head into his hands and attempting to calm the passion that raged through him.

He throbbed with wanting her. He had not expected a desire that intense. A kiss had been his first thought, but then . . .

He stood and paced the room, passion flooding him like a rising river.

He wanted Aliss. He could taste his need for her. It was as strong as the salty taste of battle that had to be faced regardless of the outcome. He felt that now. No matter what the outcome of their joining, he had to have her, share with her, pleasure her.

His own body ached with need, crying for fulfillment. He had not expected this; never gave it thought. He wanted Aliss as he had not wanted a woman in a very long time—or perhaps he had never wanted one as vehemently as he did now.

The taste of Aliss was pungently sweet and hot, a stark contrast that intoxicated the senses and made him hunger for more.

Reality pierced him like a mighty sword and he stopped pacing. Her abduction was a means to an end, no more. He had never intended to hurt her. She was there to serve a purpose and when that purpose was done, she would return home.

He had no right to alter that plan. He had no right to allow his emotions to interfere. What must be done must be done. He had no choice, just as she had no choice but to wed.

He glanced down at his fisted hand, not realizing he had made a fist. He stared at it, felt the strength that ran through it and the force with which he could deliver a man unconscious.

The man who would kiss Aliss.

His knuckles whitened and his mind went wild with thought of any man other than himself kissing her. He would tear the man's heart out with his bare hands and . . .

"Damn." He pounded the table, but it did little good. He would have much preferred it to be a face, the face of the faceless man who would wed Aliss.

He ran his fingers through his hair and returned to pacing the floor. This was crazy. How had a simple kiss stirred such fierce jealousy in him? And why?

A rumbled growl surfaced slowly along with the urge to pummel something. He turned and left the cottage and headed straight for the woods.

The woods were quiet, the setting sun dappling the forest with its last precious rays of light. This was his sanctuary, his fortress of solitude, where he could bask in its healing peace.

Peace.

Peace of mind and heart. He would have that if he followed through with his plan.

But at what expense?

"You seek nature to heal your troubled mind and soul."

Rogan turned, folding his arms across his chest. "You summoned Aliss to the woods."

"An accusation?"

"You tell me, Giann." Rogan challenged the prophetess, not caring whether it was a wise choice or not. His concern was to protect Aliss.

"Your plan to claim the Isle of Non is not as simple as you thought, my friend."

He had to agree, though he refused to admit it. He held his ground, like a warrior prepared for battle. Giann had proven her powers time and again. She knew things of the past and foretold the future and she had never been wrong.

"So you warned me, and the answer to my query?" he demanded.

"I summoned her."

He remained calm though inside he raged. It was pointless to argue with Giann, and besides, he knew that soon enough her presence would calm him completely. She had that effect on people. He wondered if it was her flawless beauty or her regal form drenched in the colors of the forest.

It mattered little. She held the power and thankfully she did not abuse it.

"Why?" His one word echoed through the forest like a thunderbolt.

She smiled and Rogan was reminded of a radiant star in the heavens.

"She needed reminding."

"Of a prophecy you failed to mention to me?"

"To fulfill it is her duty. Her purpose. Her destiny."

"So you tell me nothing of this monumental prophecy, merely that she will heal my people. You summon her and then render her unconscious?"

"You need not know of it, and she but napped."

"Napped?" Rogan nearly shouted. "We could not revive her."

"It was a deep sleep, which did her much good."

"How?"

Giann smiled once again, and Rogan thought the sun had burst in front of him.

"You will see."

He rubbed his eyes. He could barely see anything, and when he finally could, Giann was gone. She was like that, appearing unexpectedly and vanishing just as unexpectedly.

She had, however, left him feeling at peace. How? He could not explain it. His circumstances had not changed and yet he felt less concerned, as if the situation would resolve itself and he need not worry.

He took a deep breath, breathing in the strength of the forest. Fresh earth, pungent pine, sweet berries, familiar and comforting scents that fortified him.

He would do as he must and let nothing stand in his way. He had waited many years to set things right and he could let nothing deter him from his intentions. He turned and saw Aliss sitting on a stump weeping softly.

Her gentle cries were like a knife to his heart and he felt guilty, as if he were the cause of them.

He walked over to her and squatted down on his haunches in front of her. He tenderly took her hands in his, moving them away from her face and to his lips. He kissed her fingers, once, twice, three times.

"Tell me why you weep?"

Aliss sniffled. "I do not know."

"Does the crying help?"

"I think so." She shook her head. "Though I am not certain." She cried some more.

Her tears once again stabbed at his heart and he felt as helpless as a warrior without his weapon or shield.

"I rarely cry." She sniffled back her tears.

"Everyone cries."

"Have you?"

He almost felt as if he could drown in the tears

that pooled in her wide eyes, their green color reminding him of the surface of a loch sprinkled with nature's summer dust.

He kissed her fingers again, taking time to think over her question. He remembered shedding tears now and again as a young lad, the episodes fading as he matured. He, like Aliss, rarely shed tears except . . .

"I wept when my wife, Kendra, died in my arms and again when I held my stillborn son."

"I am so sorry," she said, freeing her hands to grasp his in hers. "My tears are frivolous compared to yours."

"All tears are relevant to those who shed them."

She stared at him a moment. "I had not expected wisdom from the Wolf."

He moved in closer. "Never underestimate a wolf. They are cunning and wise in ways man does not realize."

"Do you warn me?"

"Yes."

He was not surprised when she released his hands. It was better this way, better to keep a distance between them. His plan had been set in motion. There was no changing it. He *could not* change it. He had waited too long to settle this debt of honor. He could let nothing stop him.

Nothing.

Damn, but he wanted to kiss her again, yank her into his arms and ravish her mouth until they finally lay copulating on the ground.

He jumped up and stepped away from her, but

the vision had already been burned into his mind. He could not stop seeing them both naked, her creamy skin so stark in contrast to the bed of earth beneath her. And her red hair flamed as if it had been ignited with the passion that raged through them both.

He could feel his hands spreading her thighs, hear her welcoming moans, feel her flesh wet with desire, and he was rock hard with wanting for her.

Rogan turned narrowed eyes on her, his breathing heavy and his salacious thoughts soaring. With a growl and a snarl, he escaped the woods, leaving his prey intact.

Aliss remained on the stump, stunned. In one breath, he soothed her, and in another, he warned her before fleeing like a scowling beast. She did not understand him or her tears.

This was the very reason she had not entertained the thought of marriage. She did not want love interfering with her work. And love did that; it interfered to the point where all thought revolved around that special someone.

In the last few hours her mind had been sidetracked from her healing work to thoughts of kissing Rogan. The kiss itself had nearly devastated her. It was more than she had imagined and the emotions it had stirred in her had brought her to tears.

For what reason?

She had no answer.

What she did have was clear proof that kissing and anything that went with it would greatly interfere with her healing work, and that she could not tolerate. She could not have her mind occupied with nonsense while she dealt with the sick.

She stood and wiped the last vestiges of tears off her face with her fingers. She threw back her shoulders and stuck out her chin.

Nothing would stop her from treating the ill, finding ways to prevent illness and cures for recurring maladies. She was a healer first and foremost, nothing else mattered, especially a kiss.

Even if it did feel too good to be true.

Even if she did enjoy it immensely.

Even if she had thought about kissing Rogan again.

Even if she desperately wanted to.

Even if . . .

She shook her head and refused to think any more on the matter. It wasted precious time that she could be spending on her healing work.

She was a healer; she would heal.

"A woman loves."

Damn her sister's voice. She would be the one to remind her that she was a woman as well as a healer and that a woman had needs, just like a healer had needs. Fiona would warn her to reconcile the two, just as the Wolf had to do with Rogan, who was simply a man.

She always thought of herself as a healer, nothing more.

She was, however, a healer and a woman. How did she meld them together when the healer was the stronger of the two?

Chapter 13

❧◦◦◦❧

Rogan wanted to scoop Aliss up and carry her off to bed, but he was certain she would protest, argue, and dig her feet in. She would not be budged from Ivan's bedside.

The only thing he could do was to keep vigil with her from time to time throughout the day.

She had remained by the old man's side for over a full day. Ivan had been doing well when suddenly he had grown severely ill. He could keep nothing in his stomach, not even the broth Aliss had specially prepared. He could barely lift his head or move his arm. Everyone thought that this time was the end for him. His daughter Myra wept softly next to his bed until Aliss chased her away.

Aliss refused to give up and tended Ivan like a

small child, spooning liquid into his mouth and checking constantly for fever.

"He was fine two days ago," Myra whispered to Rogan as she drifted over to stand beside him. "He was eating like his old self. Margaret indulged him with that dark bread he favors, though I cannot stomach its bitter taste. He ate every bit of it along with my rabbit stew."

"He turned ill soon afterward?" Rogan asked.

"The next day."

Aliss held out an empty crock. "I need more boiled water."

Myra hurried to fetch it.

Rogan stepped back from the edge of the mantel he had been leaning against. He had noticed that Aliss's shoulders had slumped. He had learned from watching her time and again that it was a sure sign of fatigue combined with the burden of deep concern. When she reached this point, she often doubted herself, questioning her skills.

The only recourse was for her to step away, rest, and return renewed, refreshed, and ready to battle. In his eyes, Aliss was a relentless warrior, battling a foe that lurked in plain sight yet could not be seen.

He admired and respected her courage and resolve, but she could also be stubborn. A warrior knew when to retreat and replenish his reserves for another attack.

Aliss needed replenishing, soon, or defeat would surely claim her.

He walked over and placed a hand on Aliss's

shoulder, and felt the knotted muscle jab at his palm. "You are tired." He kneaded the stubborn muscle with strong fingers and she slumped back against him.

"I cannot leave Ivan's side until he improves."

Her green eyes told him differently. They were fraught with despair that this time she might not be able to save him.

"You have done all you can."

She grabbed his hand on her shoulder. "There must be something I am missing. Why can I not see it?"

"My father is grateful, as is my family, for all you have done for him," Myra said, handing her the crock of water.

"It is not enough," Aliss said and took the crock to infuse with a blend of crushed leaves.

"Is so," came the feeble reply.

Three pairs of eyes widened in surprise as the old man's eyes fluttered open.

"Let me go, my time," he managed to say.

"No!" Aliss snapped. "It is not your time or you would not be fighting so hard to live. I know death. He comes when it is time and not before. He is not here for you. You will fight and you will live."

"Stubborn," Ivan mumbled.

"Absolutely," Aliss said, and spooned the fresh liquid into his mouth.

It was after midnight when Ivan's purging finally subsided and Aliss no longer feared leaving his side. She was grateful for Rogan's arm around her waist as they walked to the cottage. She was so very tired, bone tired, every step an effort, every muscle taut with tension. Yet, there was no time to worry about her physical complaints.

"Ivan cannot survive another relapse. I must find the culprit and fast."

"After you rest we will combine our findings and see what we can make of the puzzle."

"No time for rest," she argued.

"No time not to," he said, and scooped her up into his arms. "You cannot do your best if you are not at your best."

"There you go with words of wisdom again." She yawned.

"There you go proving me right."

She attempted a laugh but was too tired and rested her head on his shoulder. "Have you any thoughts as to the culprit?"

"You never stop, do you?"

"No, I cannot." She sighed. "And it worries me."

"Why?"

"I see how you tolerate my endless madness for healing out of necessity. I cannot imagine any husband enduring it willingly, and yet I must search for a husband who will. I had hoped I would not be forced into such a difficult situation."

"You will not."

She popped her head up, surprised.

"I told you that if we can find this culprit that attacks my people, then we can find a solution to your problem."

"And if we do not find the culprit?"

Rogan stopped in front of the door to the cottage. "Do you really believe you will let the culprit escape you?"

"Absolutely not."

"Then your situation will also be resolved, worry not."

Aliss laid her head on his shoulder with a sense of relief. She did not know how it would all work out, but Rogan's reassurance lifted the burden for now.

She was grateful when he laid her on the bed. She rolled onto her stomach, cringing at the pain that stabbed her neck and shoulders.

His hands were instantly at her neck kneading and rubbing until she wanted to die from the pure relief of his touch.

"That feels good," she said, sighing.

"Your neck and shoulders tighten like a warrior who has drawn his bow or wielded his sword in an all-day battle."

"Some warrior I am, needing to be carried off the battlefield."

Rogan snickered.

"Was that a laugh?" she asked, raising her head.

His fingers kneaded along the center of her neck up into her head until she surrendered and lowered her head to the mattress.

"You walked with dignity off the battlefield."

"Really? You believe that?"

"I witnessed it for myself," he reassured her. "More importantly, you refused to leave until you knew all was well. Only a brave warrior would posses such spirit."

"I am not brave. My sister is but I am not."

He laughed. "You could fool me, considering the way you jumped off that large boulder onto the man below to protect your sister."

Aliss sat up with a bounce. "How do you know about that incident?"

"I am the man you fell on."

"You! I jumped on you and knocked you out?"

"Almost knocked me out," he corrected. "You dazed me well enough that I could not move right away and I watched as you ran off to help your sister. It took courage to enter an unknown fighting arena with no thought of your own life, only that of saving your sister."

"She is my sister and I love her. I could never leave her to die without . . ." Aliss attempted to choke back her tears, but fatigue left her without an ounce of strength and she began to cry.

Rogan reached out for her and she went willingly into his arms.

"I do not cry this much."

"It is only the second time I have seen you cry, and you are tired."

She continued crying. "Yes, I am."

"And you miss your sister."

"I do." She nodded. "And I know how helpless she must feel not being able to help me."

"She will see you soon enough."

Aliss looked at him and burst into a torrent of tears. Seeing her sister would mean leaving Rogan and never seeing him again. The idea ripped at her heart.

"It is all right, Aliss," he said, attempting to

comfort her. "Very soon you will be reunited with Fiona."

She continued to cry, her mind filled with joyous thoughts of hugging her sister, as well as a heart-wrenching vision of watching Rogan sail away forever on his ship. He would never hold her again, touch her again, kiss her again. The thought was too much and with teary eyes, she reached out to claim his lips.

He tasted so good and so very familiar, as if the taste of him belonged to her and her alone. She loved the firmness of his kiss. It made her feel that he wanted to drink deeply of her as if he could not get enough of her. The feeling was certainly mutual for she could not get enough of him and that thought enflamed her already fueled passion.

They fell back on the bed together, arms locked around each other and lips sealed in a thirst-quenching kiss that refused to end.

Aliss protested each time Rogan attempted to end their kiss, nipping at his lips, running her tongue across his mouth and wreaking havoc with their senses.

Rogan finally grabbed hold of her chin. "This must stop now."

"Why?"

He pressed himself firmly against her.

Her shocked gasp was not for the hard feel of him but how she had reacted to it. She had moistened instantly and a tiny throbbing sensation had begun to build.

"You are right," she said, and shoved gently at his chest to move him away.

He did move, though he did not get off the bed. "I like when we kiss."

"So do I," she admitted with a sheepish smile.

"Why do you hesitate to love?"

His query startled her speechless until she thought on his question. She was about to deny her resistance to love when she answered, "I do not know."

He reached out and stroked her cheek with his fingers. "You honor me with the truth and your trust."

"You have proven yourself trustworthy." She thought she caught him flinch, then scowl, then smile. The myriad of expressions confused her until she realized it was a trick of the eye caused by the hearth's flickering flames.

"Have you thought about loving?" he asked.

Aliss had hoped he would not pursue his query; exhaustion made her much too vulnerable now. Or perhaps she didn't want to admit that she was growing comfortable with the Wolf?

"Perhaps now and again."

"And you dismiss the thought," he confirmed.

"I know not what else to do with it."

"Let yourself think on it," he encouraged.

She yawned. "I do not have . . ." Another yawn swallowed her words and her eyes drifted shut. "Wake me with the sun," she said before another yawn attacked.

"Rest, you need it," he urged gently.

In minutes, she was snoring lightly and Rogan reached around her to pull a light wool blanket over her.

He lay beside her studying her lovely face. Hers was a natural beauty, her creamy skin flawless, her lashes as fiery as her mane of red curls, her slim nose in perfect symmetry with her features, and her rosy lips much too inviting.

She was bewitching and he had fallen easily under her spell. It could not be helped, fight as he did against it, it seemed inevitable. They were drawn to each other. She wanted his kisses as much as he wanted to kiss her.

Was this the prelude to love?

The signs were all there as they had been when he had fallen in love with Kendra. He had wanted to spend all the time he could with her, hold her, touch her, kiss her, and damn, how he had ached to make love to her.

He felt all those things now about Aliss, and he felt grateful, grateful to be experiencing such powerful feelings once again. He had forgotten the intensity of love; sorrow had replaced it with his wife's death. He wanted to savor the feelings that had finally revisited him, explore them with Aliss and let the sensations take them where they might.

He reached out and stroked her silky skin, her cheek cool to his touch. She was such a special woman. He could not imagine that any man would not want her, healing propensity and all. And he could not imagine any man but him touching her, a thought that had haunted him of late.

Rogan rested his hand on her hip and watched her sleep and listened to her snore, a light purring sound. He would not mind hearing her purr in his ear each night. He would cuddle close with her; perhaps join in with his own snores to form a distinct melody of their own.

He shook his head and rolled quietly off the bed, reluctantly going to his room.

Was he crazy?

How did he think this could possibly work between them?

She had deemed him trustworthy, confiding in him.

He dropped down on the bed, pillowing his head with his arms and stretching his feet out.

He was a wolf in every sense of the word, cunning, fearless, and fiercely loyal, that loyalty being the very reason Aliss was here with him. She, however, would not view it that way, and how could he ever get her to understand?

Strange, he felt he was on the precipice of finding love once again, excited and eager and fearful that once Aliss learned the truth he would plunge over the edge alone.

Chapter 14

~~~

"**Y**our neck healed nicely," Aliss said, slipping her yellow blouse on and tucking it in her waistband.

Anna beamed. "I am so very happy the rash is gone. And for good as long as I do not touch motherwort with my bare hands. I cannot thank you enough for helping me."

Aliss sat down beside Anna on the grassy knoll not far from the stream's edge. The sun was bright, the air warm for early morning and she felt refreshed having just washed from top to bottom in the stream.

She squeezed the excess water from her red hair and used the thick towel she had dried off with to soak up the rest before she attempted to comb it.

"You have thanked me many times over with all your help."

"I enjoy healing work—" Anna paused a moment before rushing to finish her words. "I would love to be a healer."

"You would make a very good one."

"I would?" Anna asked, surprised.

Aliss began to comb the tangles from her hair. "The clan will need a healer once I am gone. I will teach you all I can until then and you can continue to learn on your own as I once did."

"You really are going to leave us?"

"Once I determine the cause for the persistent illness and provide a cure, yes, I will leave." Aliss shook her head. "You knew that. Everyone here does."

"True enough," Anna said sadly. "Lately, a few of us have thought differently."

"Why is that?"

Anna shrugged and averted her eyes.

Aliss would have none of it. "Tell me, Anna, what wagging tongues say about me."

"Nothing bad," Anna reassured. "Many rather hoped that you would choose to remain here with us."

"Why?" Aliss tugged at the last knotted strand of hair.

Anna grinned and leaned closer. "Many of us hoped that you and the Wolf would fall in love."

Aliss's mouth fell open and the comb dropped from her hand. "Fall in love?"

"We all had hoped he would find love again. The Wolf is such a good man. He deserves someone special and we all agree you are very special and just right for him."

Aliss sputtered in shock. "H-he ab-abducted me. How can I be right for him or he for me?" She may have given the prospect thought, but to hear another voice, it startled her.

"His intentions were good. He meant you no harm; we desperately needed a skilled healer. Being the protective chieftain that he is, Rogan saw to our needs."

"And nothing more?" Aliss asked, trying to assuage the nagging doubt that would creep up on occasion and tempt her sanity.

"What more could there be?" Anna asked curiously. "You see for yourself the illness that brought you here. We are a simple people who love and laugh and break bread together."

Aliss's brow wrinkled. "You break bread together." She grabbed hold of Anna's arm. "All bread?"

"What do you mean?"

"Does everyone eat the same type of bread?

"More eat the light than the dark bread," Anna answered.

"Which do you and John eat?"

"The light, sweeter bread." Anna shook her head. "The black bread is tasteless to me."

"Not bitter?"

Anna had no more than given her head one shake when Aliss jumped up and hurried off. A surprised Anna followed quickly behind her.

Aliss hurried to find Rogan. She had to speak with him now. It was important. She heard the clash of swords and knew he practiced with his men. It was a daily ritual meant to keep their skills sharpened.

She pushed past the circle of men and stopped a safe distance from the mock battle.

"Stop!" she yelled at a high pitch that had everyone cringing.

Rogan turned a shaking head at her.

"It is important. I need to talk with you right now," she said.

His opponent wandered off, as did the circle of men, giving the couple a modicum of privacy.

She marched right up to him. "Did Myra tell you something about black bread that Ivan had eaten before he had gotten sick?"

"Yes, she—"

"Has Derek eaten black bread?"

Rogan nodded.

"Young Daniel?"

"I am not sure."

Aliss turned with a flourish but was stopped when Rogan grabbed her arm. "I will go with you."

"Put down your sword, then, for this enemy must be vanquished with the mind as the weapon."

He did and they hurried off together, Anna rushing to keep up.

In no time, Aliss discovered a trail of sickness that followed the black bread and it led to Margaret, the old woman who had originated the recipe.

Margaret was not at her cottage when they

stopped and the three divided up to locate her. Anna found her and quickly fetched Aliss and Rogan.

"I saw Margaret enter James's home, a basket on her arm," Anna said, breathless from running.

Aliss bolted past the two, her skirt hiked up in her hands and her feet pounding the earth. She came to an abrupt halt once past the opened door and quickly searched the room.

James was sitting by the fireplace, his grand-parents were at the table, and Margaret was spreading honey on chunks of black bread. They all greeted her with a smile and invited her to join them.

Aliss went over to Margaret and took the of-fered bread from her hand. "Thank you, but I need to speak with you first."

Anna and Rogan entered.

"Anna, please see that everyone waits for us to share the delicious bread," Aliss said, her hand gently guiding Margaret out the door. She nod-ded for Rogan to follow.

The old woman's steps were slow and Rogan helped her to sit on a bench near the door, which Aliss closed so no one could hear their conversa-tion.

"How long have you been baking black bread, Margaret?" Aliss asked, sitting beside her.

"As long as I can remember." She smiled. "Not everyone has a taste for its distinct flavor."

"So I have learned."

Margaret pointed a finger at Rogan. "He never

liked it." She patted Aliss's arm. "You should try it."

"I will. Have you made it the same way all these years?"

The old woman seemed reluctant to answer.

"It is important," Rogan said firmly.

Margaret leaned away from Aliss and cast an anxious look to Rogan. "Have I done something wrong?"

"No, Margaret, not at all," Rogan assured her.

Margaret sighed. "To be truthful, it is not I who have baked the black bread these last few months." She held up gnarled fingers. "I cannot knead the bread as I once did so Tara has been kind enough to mix the ingredients and knead the dough and leave the loaves for me to bake."

Aliss placed her hand on the old woman's arm. "Have you eaten any of the bread she has prepared for you?"

Margaret cast her eyes to the ground, gave her head a shake then looked up at Aliss. "I never favored the black bread, I only make it for those who do."

"I need the loaf you brought to James."

"I thought he might enjoy it," she said, and stood with Aliss's help.

"I'm sure he will but this loaf is mine if you don't mind," Aliss said.

Aliss soon had the black bread safely in her hands and she and Rogan went directly to Tara's cottage.

The young woman was busy mixing another

batch of bread and welcomed them with a smile and an enthusiastic greeting.

"We are here to see if you can help us with something," Aliss explained.

"Of course," Tara said, and wiped her hands on the cloth tucked by a corner in her waistband.

"You have been baking bread for Margaret, but you don't eat any yourself?" Aliss asked.

"She confided her secret finally, did she?" Tara asked with a laugh and shook her head. "And no, I don't like the black bread though Daniel does."

Aliss asked, "Have you followed her recipe exactly?"

Tara hesitated. "Has she complained of my bread?"

"No, she has praised your baking skills."

Tara sighed, relieved, and plopped down on a chair at the table. "Good, I didn't want her to find out that I accidentally changed her recipe."

"How so?" Aliss asked.

"I'm not very good at identifying herbs, most look the same to me, and only recently did I realize I had been using the wrong herb in Margaret's black bread and returned to her original ingredient."

"That would explain why the illness suddenly stopped," Aliss said to Rogan.

"Illness?" Tara said, grabbing at her chest. "I caused everyone to get ill?"

"Do not worry yourself," Aliss said. "Have you any of the herb you had used?"

"A little, I think." Tara looked in her crocks and soon presented a single leaf to Aliss.

One whiff of the sickly-sweet dried leaf and Aliss knew she had caught the culprit. The old healer whom she had learned from had taught her to distinguish scents. She had warned that a knowledgeable nose could save lives.

"This is poisonous," Aliss said.

"You are sure?" Tara asked, tears welling in her eyes.

"I am sure."

Tara looked to Rogan. "I am sorry. I did not know. You will not make me leave here, will you? Daniel and I have no place to go. This is the only home he has ever known and the only place I have ever felt wanted and safe."

"You are not going anywhere, Tara. This is your home and here is where you will stay. I told you when you first arrived here years ago that you became part of this clan and will remain so until you take your last breath."

"But I have hurt my family."

"Not on purpose," Aliss reminded.

"No one will trust me ever again," Tara said sadly.

"No one need ever know of this," Rogan said firmly.

"You will tell no one?" Tara asked with surprised relief.

"It is not necessary for anyone to know. The problem has been solved and no more will grow ill. That is what matters."

"You are a good man, Rogan," Tara said through tears. "I am in your debt."

Aliss was certain there would be no more illnesses. She also made sure to teach Anna how to determine which plants were poisonous. That she held the teaching session out under the bright afternoon sun where the women wandered by and sat to join them was no accident.

Aliss visited with those who were still recovering, confident now that they would be well in no time. James was growing stronger every day and would soon be completely healed. The herb garden flourished and she taught Anna the properties of the different plants and mixtures to aid in specific healings.

The days rolled by, and one by one, the people healed nicely. No more grew ill and Margaret's black bread continued to be in demand.

Summer was in full bloom. Children ran in play, healthy babies were delivered, gardens flourished along with the people. The Wolf clan was doing well.

It was time for Aliss to return home.

Chapter 15

Rogan knew the time approached. Soon Aliss would ask him to take her home. She had fulfilled her part of the bargain and now it was time for him to fulfill his. That, however, he was not going to be able to do, and when she discovered why, he wondered if she would forgive him.

He sat at the table in front of the hearth wondering what he would do. He had not counted on Aliss and her bewitching ways.

He had waited as the days passed and the people grew well. Waited for the time she demanded to be returned home.

He had also noticed that she kept her distance from him after discovering the cause of the illness. She no longer stood close to him, reached out to take his hand, seek out a kiss, or rest her head on his shoulder. She distanced herself from him day after day, moving further and further away until it felt as if she had already departed.

He rubbed his head. This was not going as he had planned. It had seemed so easy when he had first made preparations—and now? Now Aliss was no longer a means to an end. She was a woman who intrigued him, excited him and soothed him.

Damn, but he was in trouble. He leaned his head back and groaned.

"What is wrong? Do you not feel well?" Aliss asked, dropping her basket by the door and anxiously hurrying over to him to feel his forehead. "You are warm."

"I am fine," he argued.

"I will fix you a brew."

She walked away from him and he reached out and snagged her around the waist, drawing her to him to rest his head on her chest.

"You keep your distance from me. Why?"

He could hear her heart beat slow then fast then slow and fast again, and he hugged her waist.

"I am not sure."

Honesty again. It speared his heart for he was not being honest with her.

"I miss touching you, kissing you." Honest words from him and spoken from the heart. When he looked up at her, her green eyes had softened and her arms drifted around him.

"I am confused."

"Have I done that to you?" he asked, concerned, reaching out to grasp her arm and slip his hand down until his fingers locked with hers. He brought them to his lips and kissed them.

"You make me feel—"

"Cared for?"

He felt her shiver and he stood, wrapping his arms around her.

She pushed him away and took a step back. "You know I leave soon."

"So was our bargain."

"It is still so."

"If you still want it so," he said.

"It can be no other way."

"Why?"

"My work—"

"Is an excuse," he said.

"It is important."

"Above all else?"

"I thought you understood."

"I understand more than you realize."

She shook her head. "Do not make this hard for me."

"Kiss me," he demanded.

"No!"

"Why?"

She turned her head and he pounced on her, grabbing her by the shoulders. "Tell me why."

She closed her eyes. "Because I am afraid I will not want to stop. Please. Please let me go."

"You will simply walk away?" he asked as if he did not believe her.

"What choice do I have?" She stepped around him and hurried out of the cottage.

That she would soon leave Rogan had weighed heavily on her mind. She had never expected to admire the Wolf. He was a courageous warrior, but even more, he was a man who cared deeply for his people and protected them however he could. He was also a man who had loved a woman, lost her, and was not afraid to love again.

She drifted along the edge of the woods, the sun near to setting and the warm night air whispering across her face like a lover's kiss.

Her hand went to her lips and she thought about the kisses she had shared with Rogan.

"How do you feel when you kiss him?"

She smiled at her sister's familiar voice in her head. Leave it to Fiona to remind her of how important a kiss was. How could she ignore how she felt when Rogan kissed her? It was like he weaved a magical spell around her and entranced her.

She liked the feeling and would think about it throughout the day. Would those memories be all she had? Would she never know a kiss like that again?

Did she want to?

Not from anyone but Rogan.

Her answer came sharp and swift and made her realize that she could never kiss another man. What was she thinking? She would only be disappointed, and besides, she did not want to kiss another man.

She began to pace. She had not thought this through. She would return home only to face the prospect of finding a suitable husband. How could she find one after sharing kisses with Rogan?

Other men would pale in comparison. She would never be satisfied with another man. Would she pine for Rogan the rest of her days? Would she wonder if there was a chance for them to love each other?

She kicked at the dirt, frustrated with her situation, when she was struck by a thought. If she felt this strongly about leaving Rogan and his kisses, why not marry him? It would be a good solution to her problem. She would not be saddled with a man she did not favor. She could wed a man whom she actually cared about, maybe a man she could eventually love.

He also did not mind her healing work. He had been an encouragement to her through the ordeal of healing his people. He would not demand she tend to him and forsake her passion to heal.

Of course, there was the problem of convincing Tarr of her decision. After all, Rogan had speared his arm with an arrow and he had attacked Tarr's land on two occasions.

However, Tarr had stipulated that the decision was hers to make.

She pushed her doubts aside and concentrated on her situation. Tarr might capitulate if he believed her in love and allow her to wed Rogan. Or . . .

She shook her head, rejecting the sudden notion. It might not be a wise choice, though it would prove the most effective. No one could stop her from wedding Rogan if the marriage took place here. The deed would be done, their vows consummated.

No one could object. It would be over and done and they would be bound to each other for life. Did she want that? Did she want marriage to Rogan?

She had not wanted to marry at all, but she would wed regardless of her own desires. Why not wed Rogan?

The debate raged in her head and try as she might, a solid answer was not forthcoming. She found reasons to wed him and reasons not to. The point of the whole matter, though, was that she was going to wed, one way or the other.

What choice did she really have?

"Aliss!"

The shout spun her around and she rushed forward to meet a harried Anna. "What is wrong?"

"Laurel is in labor and calls for you."

Aliss smiled. "Good, a happy occasion for a healer."

"I have delivered only one babe," said an anxious Anna.

"Deliver one, deliver them all. Worry not. I will teach you what to expect, what to watch out for, and what a privilege it is to bring a babe into this world."

Rogan stepped out of the cottage as they passed the door.

"We need to talk," she said and stopped for a moment. Anna rushed past her. "But first I must birth Laurel's babe."

Rogan grabbed hold of her arm. "Tell me now."

"I have no time."

"Now!" he insisted.

"I wish to marry you," she said, and yanked her arm free to hurry off.

Rogan stood staring after her then suddenly broke into a grin. It faded rapidly with John and Derek's frenzied approach.

"We have a problem," Derek said.

The sky was filled with thousands of tinkling stars and Aliss was certain they twinkled in happiness for her and Rogan. It was after midnight when she returned to the cottage.

She had left Anna to tend Laurel and her newborn son. The delivery had gone smoothly. The proud father, Peter, kept tight hold of his tiny son, repeatedly telling him how much he loved him, while the new mother rested comfortably.

Aliss was anxious to talk with Rogan and see what he thought of her proposal. She had had no time to give her swift decision thought, and now, as she considered it several hours later, she wondered over her own sanity. But what was done was done.

She was disappointed to see John waiting outside the cottage.

"A problem two fields and a hill beyond," John said, letting her know that Rogan would not be returning soon.

"He is safe?"

John nodded though he averted his eyes.

"You are sure?"

"Rogan will return," John said, his head held high and his eyes on Aliss.

His response relieved her and she entered the cottage, turning briefly to say, "I am safe here in the village. There is no need for you to stand guard."

"Rogan commands, I listen."

There was no point in arguing with the young man. He would obey his chieftain, as he should.

As she snuggled beneath the covers, a strange thought came to her. Was John protecting her or making certain she did not leave?

Chapter 16

~~~OO~~~

Rogan returned home to an empty cottage the next morning, his mind in turmoil. The news he had received had been unexpected and to make certain it had been correct he had gone to see for himself.

To his regret, the message had proved true. He had perhaps four maybe five days left with Aliss before hell descended on them. Aliss had given him the perfect opportunity with her proposal to settle the matter to his advantage. But what would happen when she learned the truth?

Dusty and dirty from his tiresome journey and plagued with a weighty mind, he decided a dunk in the river would refresh him. Then he would find Aliss, accept her proposal, and pray he had made a wise choice—for them both.

He grabbed clean garments from his room and a towel and headed to the river.

Rogan washed the grime from his body, dunking himself repeatedly in the cool water and scrubbing every inch of his flesh. He wished he could cleanse his mind and heart as easily.

He had waited a long time to lay claim to what was rightfully his and had thought it would be an easy task. He had not counted on the healer stirring his blood or haunting his thoughts. Most of all, he had not expected a marriage proposal, the easiest of solutions to his problem.

Rogan stretched his way out of the water, raising his arms up to the heavens, expanding his chest to ease his aching muscles then swinging his head to shake off the water that soaked his long hair.

He gave one final stretch, extending his arms out to his sides and dropping his head back, and released a howl that trembled the woods.

Refreshed and revived, Rogan smiled and walked toward the river's edge, stopping when he caught sight of Aliss standing not far off on the grassy knoll.

Her eyes were wide, her mouth hung open, and her cheeks were tinged red.

She had been watching him and he had no qualms about letting her continue to watch him. He walked slowly out of the river, the water level dipping lower and lower, exposing his navel and gradually drifting farther and farther down.

He was not surprised to see her turn her back

to him in a flash when the water had dipped close to exposing all of him.

He kept his laughter silent and hurried to dress, noticing Aliss shift from foot to foot, plop her hands on her hips then drop them to her side, then cross them over her chest, then sigh heavily enough for him to hear her.

She was anxious, all right, enough that she chanced turning around on his possible nakedness.

"Have you given thought to my proposal?" she said, her fingers twisting the material of her skirt.

He approached her, tucking his brown and black kilt in at his waist and feeling her jitters as he got closer. "I have."

"I think it is a fine solution to my problem. You had said that when the malady was discovered, we could focus on finding a solution to my situation."

"I did—"

"It is a crazy thought, I know," she said with a shake of her head. "Though the more I thought about it the more it seemed to make sense. At least I hope it does—to you. It took me a while to rationalize it, but once I did, it struck me as the perfect choice. It made all the sense in the world."

Rogan remained silent since Aliss seemed unable to stop talking.

"I require a husband who will respect my penchant for healing and not deprive me of it but encourage me, which you do. Of course, I would like to reside near my sister and hope that there is a way we can resolve that issue. It certainly is a practical solution for me, and a beneficial one for you. Your clan will gain strength and respect being united with the Hellewyk and Blackshaw clans."

She finally stopped, took a breath and stared at him. "You must think me foolish or perhaps desperate and perhaps I am. But I realized that I give everything I have to my healing work—my mind, heart, and soul. I wonder if there is anything left to give to someone. Therefore, I am not certain that I can love someone the way your wife loved you. And I do not know if you would settle for less. However, I felt compelled to be honest with you about the reason for my proposal."

She spoke the truth to him, yet he could not do the same with her?

"It is not necessary you answer me at this moment. I understand if you are hesitant. The choice will alter our lives greatly and rushing into—"

"I will marry you."

She stared at him. "Why?"

He laughed and shook his head. "I thought that was what you wanted."

"I do. I do," she assured him. "It is just that I want to make certain you realize how much this union benefits both of us."

"I am well aware of the benefits and I accept your marriage proposal most willingly."

Aliss sighed with relief. "We will marry—"

"Immediately."

"I had thought to have my sister and family present but . . ."

"You know that is not possible. Tarr will never allow you to marry me," he said, and walked away from her to fetch his shirt on the ground nearby.

"Tarr assured me the choice of a husband was mine."

Rogan shook his head. "Tarr would never have imagined you choosing the Wolf."

Aliss's shoulders sagged. "You are right. He thinks of you as his enemy."

"Then it is wise that I am your husband before I meet him. We must be wed properly so that Tarr cannot claim the marriage invalid, and that means our vows must be consummated."

Her cheeks blossomed like a fresh red rose. "Is there anyone who can perform a valid ceremony?"

"Yes," he said, walking over to her. "We will be wed by nightfall tomorrow."

"Tomorrow?"

"There is no reason to wait. Besides, our bargain was for me to return you home once you healed my people."

"I go home?" she asked incredulously.

"Give me a week or two to prepare the ship and men and then we leave." He almost choked on his false words.

Aliss clapped her hands in glee. "I can't believe I am going home." She laughed. "And returning home a married woman.

"I have much to do before tomorrow. There is a celebration to prepare." She ran off laughing. "I will tell everyone that the healer weds the Wolf."

Rogan watched her run, skip, and laugh with joy. She was happy, but for how long?

He sat by the river's edge lost in his thoughts.

Was what he was doing fair to Aliss?

Should he have told her the truth before accepting her marriage proposal?

He would chance losing her that way, but either option could mean loss.

He would be bound to her once he wed her and no one could separate them. There was a chance that with time she would come to understand and forgive him for deceiving her.

What else could he really do?

He had a debt to settle and nothing would stop him from settling it. He had waited too many years for this moment.

"So you wed her."

Rogan turned slowly, not surprised that Derek sounded as if he accused him.

"She is a good woman," Derek said, his arms crossed. "She enlightens the people of the sudden nuptials with sheer happiness."

Rogan walked up to him. "Spit out what you have to say, Derek."

"She has been unselfish with her skills and has healed us. Is it fair to use her like this?"

"I have no choice."

"Don't you? Or have you convinced yourself you don't so that you don't feel like such a bastard for lying to her?"

"Wedding her was never part of my plan," Rogan said.

"Then why is it now?"

"Why do you defend her so?"

"She healed me when I thought for sure I would die."

"You never told me you thought you would die," Rogan said.

"There were nights I thought that if I closed my eyes I would never open them again. Aliss held my hand and convinced me that I would live to love many women." Derek laughed. "She understood each and every one of our fears and helped us combat them while she fought the enemy within us. She never gave up on any of us. She did everything to ease our suffering. I wish to do the same for her."

"I would never hurt Aliss."

"You do by marrying her," Derek argued.

"She must wed, you know that. Should I let her wed someone who would forbid her to heal?"

Derek shook his head. "I would not wish that fate on her."

"Then trust my decision."

"Do you?" Derek asked.

"It is the decision I arrived at and the one I will see through to the end."

"I hope it is a wise one, for Aliss's sake and for yours," Derek admitted.

"Finally, words I want to hear," Rogan said with a slap to Derek's back. "And ones that I wholeheartedly agree with."

"As does most of the village. You should know a large celebration is already being planned."

"I am pleased," Rogan said. "I want the day to be special for Aliss. One she will always remember."

Derek looked about to protest once again.

"You have always stood by me. Do I need ask if you will continue to stand by me?"

"No," Derek said firmly. "That is a question you need never ask me."

Rogan nodded, pleased that his friend remained his comrade. "Let us go share some ale, and while preparations are made for the celebration, we shall also prepare."

The two men walked off, not noticing the pair of green eyes in the shadow of the woods that watched them depart.

Chapter 17

~~~~~

"I cannot believe we are wed," Aliss said, staring at her hand locked firmly in Rogan's.

"How can you not?" Rogan laughed. "Just look at this celebration."

Aliss smiled and glanced around the village. Tables and benches had been moved outside, a summer's bright blue sky provided the perfect canopy, and everyone had supplied enough food for double the people.

Music, chatter, and laughter mingled as the whole village celebrated the joining of the Wolf and the healer. Gifts were even given to the couple, to Aliss's surprise—especially since many of the gifts were for her in particular.

Laurel and Peter had presented them with a beautifully crafted twig basket. James had carved her a small jar with a lid for her herbs, Anna had sewed a wool pouch, and a robust Ivan, with tears shining in his eyes, had presented her with a stunningly carved cross.

She knew the gifts were meant for more than just her wedding and she was grateful for each and every one of them.

What nagged at her, however, was the fact that the villagers assumed she would now be residing with the clan. It was not that she disliked the idea. It was that she desperately missed her sister.

Aliss had always assumed that Fiona would witness her wedding and enjoy the celebration to follow. She had never dreamed of getting married without her sister present. She had felt their forced separation more than ever preceding her vows, wanting so much for her sister to be there with her. She had half expected to see Fiona appear, so strong was the thought of her.

Aliss hoped that Fiona would understand the need for her to wed so quickly. She also hoped that her sister would accept Rogan as family with little difficulty. If she did then Tarr would also accept him.

"You wrinkle your brow. Troubled thoughts?" Rogan asked, squeezing her hand.

"I think of my sister. I wish she could have been here."

"She is in your thoughts so therefore she is with you."

"That is another thing I like about my husband. He is wise."

"Shhh, do not tell anyone. Most think me fierce."

"Wolves are both," Aliss said.

"They are also fiercely loyal," he whispered near her ear.

Gooseflesh caused her to shiver.

"You can always rely on me, Aliss. I will always be there by your side, holding you when necessary, freeing you when need be, and always supportive."

Aliss did not know what to say. She had not expected or requested he give so much of himself. She merely wished for a husband to fulfill the prophecy and free her, or was she afraid to admit that she wanted more?

Rogan kissed her cheek. "We will do well together."

"You are sure of this?" she asked, puzzled.

"I have not a doubt."

Aliss beamed and her cheeks flushed red. "I knew I was making the right choice in marrying you."

"That you did, my bewitching healer," he whispered and kissed her gently.

They drifted apart to see Anna running toward them.

"Daniel has had an accident."

Aliss scrambled off the bench. "Is he hurt badly?"

"I have not seen him. I was sent to fetch you."

"Let me get my healing—"

"I have it," Rogan interrupted from behind her, holding up her basket. "We best hurry."

Aliss touched his arm. "Thank you."

"I told you I would always be there for you." He looked to Anna. "Where is he?"

"Derek carried him to their cottage."

The child's cries could be heard before they reached the cottage and they tore at Aliss's heart and relieved her. At least he felt his pain and wasn't unconscious. She hurried into the house and went directly to his bedside.

One glance at his skinny little leg told her it was serious. A wide gash ran from beneath his knee to an inch or so above his ankle. Blood was everywhere and that had to be her first line of defense. She needed to stop the steady flow of blood or he would not survive.

"Please, help him," his mother, Tara, pleaded, kneeling beside the bed, holding his small hand and fighting tears.

Daniel cried louder when Aliss's hands neared the wound.

"A warrior must be strong," Rogan said, gently nudging the young mother out of his way to bend down by the side of the bed.

Daniel's eyes widened in awe and Aliss assumed it was because of fear. Here was the mighty Wolf, the leader of his clan speaking.

"You are a strong warrior, are you not?" Rogan asked, taking hold of the lad's hand.

The lad sniffled and nodded.

Aliss wanted to hug Rogan. Keeping Daniel occupied would allow her to determine her course of action. She set Anna to mixing herbs that would be needed and Tara to ripping cloths to bind the wound.

Aliss concluded fast enough that the leg would need stitching. She would worry about fever and festering later. Right now, she needed to get the wound closed.

If it were not for Rogan's help, the ordeal could have turned into a nightmare. He held the lad and talked to him though he cried and screamed. Anna and Tara held his leg while Aliss stitched as fast as she could.

Aliss was grateful when Daniel had cried himself to sleep from exhaustion. After making certain the lad was settled, she left him to his mother's care. Anna insisted on remaining to help, chasing the newlyweds out to continue their celebration.

"Will he be all right?" Rogan asked when they stepped outside the cottage.

"There is festering and fever to worry about. I cannot say for sure. Only time will tell."

Rogan took her hand as they walked. "What made you become a healer?"

"I can't say for sure. It seemed a natural thing for me to do. My mother taught me a little about healing, the things most instinctive to women. When she grew ill there was little I could do to help ease her pain and it upset me. I wanted to learn more, understand more about healing. The more knowledge I gained the more I hungered for even more, and I have never stopped wanting to learn."

"You can keep on learning as much as you want. Perhaps one day you will teach our daughter."

Aliss stopped and glared wide-eyed at him.

"You have not given *our* children thought?" he asked.

"I—I—" She shook her head.

He took both of her hands in his and smiled. "Have you not thought of the consequences of our making love?"

She sighed while continuing to shake her head. "This is why I will not make a good wife. I do not think as a wife should think. I think only of my work and myself."

"You never think of yourself, though thinking of your husband now and again would be good."

"I think of you all the time." She cringed as soon as her secret slipped out.

Rogan laughed. "Do you now?"

She shook her head. He was her husband now and she did not feel the need to hide the truth from him. She could share anything with him and not worry that he would judge her.

"I admit I do think of you."

"Good, then I admit that I wish I could carry you off to my bed and make love to you for the rest of the day and throughout the night."

His declaration tingled her flesh and she shivered in his arms.

He laughed softly as he hugged her tightly. "You will do more than shiver in my arms tonight."

She raised her head and whispered, "I have known no man."

"And will know no other but me," he murmured and kissed her.

"Hey, hey, none of that until later," Derek yelled as he approached them. "We have more celebrating to do before you two get to be alone."

"I will do the same for you on your wedding day," Rogan said.

Derek laughed loudly. "I worry not, since I have no plans to wed."

"Careful," Aliss warned with a shake of her finger. "I said the same myself and look at me now."

The three laughed as they drifted back to join in the festivities. Every now and again Aliss slipped away to see how Daniel was doing and she was grateful to find he was crying and complaining. If he were unresponsive to his discomfort, it would worry Aliss more.

With the lad left in Anna's capable hands and Anna herself convincing Aliss she was not needed for the rest of the night, Aliss left the cottage to find her husband waiting outside for her.

Dusk was fading to darkness, the celebration had ended and the final remnants of the festivities were being cleared away, and parents carried exhausted and overfed children to their beds.

Bed.

That is where Rogan intended to take her.

She liked the way he approached her with an outstretched hand, requesting her to join with him. She didn't hesitate, she took his warm strong hand in hers, and when his fingers wrapped around hers she felt safe, as if she had finally come home.

They strolled in compatible silence to the cottage. No one disturbed them. This was their time to seal their vows and begin life as husband and wife.

Aliss entered his bedroom in his arms, he having scooped her up moments before. He carried her to the bed and gentle lowered her to the mattress.

The scent of lavender drifted off the bedding and she smiled at the thoughtfulness of the women who had freshened the linens for them. The only light in the room was a single flickering candle beside the bed; the hearth was not needed with summer's warmth.

The lone window over the bed provided a night breeze along with a symphony of harmonious night sounds.

Her heart grew joyful and she cupped her husband's face in her hands. "My body trembles with bliss."

He turned his face to kiss the palm of her hand. "Never fear me. I would never intentionally hurt you."

Aliss smiled. "At least you admit you would not *intentionally* hurt me. Mother says that men swear they will not hurt the woman they love but that it is inevitable for they are men after all."

"A wise woman, your mother, and remember her words, Aliss. If a day comes that you feel I have wronged you, remember that it was not intentional. I am just a man who knows no better."

"You will not get away with such nonsense so easily," she scolded lightly. "I have witnessed how wise a man you are so therefore you are unlike other men. I expect more from you and I know you would never do me wrong."

"I am a man—"

"Like no other," she finished. "I will hear no more. It is more likely that I in my selfish ways will hurt you and know now that I am sorry for my selfish ignorance."

Rogan rolled over on his back to lie beside her. "You need never apologize to me."

"I fear I may do it often and if I fail to, at least you have this apology to recount and use if necessary."

"Then I claim the same," he said. "I apologize for hurting you and ask your forgiveness. Please use this when necessary or—" He turned quickly, his body nudging her on to her back. "*I* will use it when necessary."

She laughed. "I will honor it, though I doubt it will be necessary."

"But honor it you will?" he asked, nibbling at her neck.

She giggled a confirming, "Yes."

"Good, with that finally settled, dear wife—"

"Aliss! Aliss!"

Rogan moved off her, her hand having pushed at his chest at the sound of Anna frantically crying out her name.

"Back here," Aliss shouted and ran to the door and almost collided with the young woman.

"Daniel has a fever."

The words chilled her to the bone. "We must hurry," she said and pushed at Anna to follow her out.

Chapter 18

Rogan could not sleep nor did he want to. He had been tired, his head nodding and his eyes drifting shut before a quick jerk of his head had him opening them again. It was when he started snoring lightly that Aliss had insisted, had actually ordered him home to bed.

What good would it do to have both of them exhausted, was her theory. She was right. There was no real reason that he should remain with her while she tended the feverish Daniel. He could contribute no knowledge, only support, by remaining by her side.

Now lying alone in his bed he wished he had not left her. This was their wedding night and they should be together, whether here in his bed or he beside her as she did her healing.

He pillowed his hands beneath his head and kicked the light blanket off his one leg all the while mumbling complaints until finally he spit out an oath.

He knew what really troubled him and didn't want to admit it. Their vows needed to be sealed with haste if he didn't want to risk losing her for good. Time was ticking by and soon there would not be a minute left.

What then?

He groaned and turned on his side, splaying his hand on the pillow where Aliss had rested her head. Many nights he had thought about Aliss lying there beside him, her naked body pressed against his, his arm draped over her and the two of them breathing as one.

He had yearned for that dream to become reality, and now just as it was about to happen, it was snatched away from him. Was Aliss his destiny?

The question had him springing out of bed and wrapping his plaid around him in haste. With sandals on, he slipped out into the night and disappeared into the dark woods.

He knew who could give him the answers he sought.

Giann.

She had accurately predicted many events for his clan, including Aliss curing his people. Now he wanted to know if Aliss would remain his wife and if they would live a happy and long life together.

He walked to the small clearing where he usually met with Giann, his familiarity with the area making it easy for him to travel in the dark. He stood there and softly called her name, giving no thought to the late hour. When he needed to speak with her or she with him, they always heard the other's summons and answered.

"What is it you want from me, Rogan?"

He turned to the sound of her voice but caught only a shadow that hovered between the trees.

He was direct. "Is Aliss my destiny?"

"Her destiny was written before her birth."

"Explain," he said, concern gripping his heart.

"A prophecy foretold the twins' future."

"Which is?"

"On a full moon twin babes are born; with their birth sounds the horn; eyes of green, hair of red; destruction comes if without love they wed; for true love will bind their souls together and eternal love will be theirs forever."

"Aliss must love the man she weds for it to last?"

"And the man must love Aliss."

Rogan shook his head. "We've spoken no words of love."

"The heart knows before words are ever spoken. What does your heart tell you?"

"My heart aches for what I am about to do to her," he admitted with sorrow.

"Does that not tell you something?"

"It tells me that the taste of revenge is strong in my heart."

"Yet you make no effort to tell her the truth and see what is in her heart."

"I would lose her," Rogan said.

"Would you?"

"I cannot take the chance," he said adamantly.

"Cannot take the chance or fear taking the chance?"

"I will not lose her," he reaffirmed through gritted teeth.

"You may not have a choice." Giann's shadow drifted off, blending with the night.

Rogan lingered alone in the woods, Giann's remark heavy on his mind and heart. With his thoughts too chaotic to make sense of them, he finally returned to his cottage to find Aliss sound asleep in his bed.

He undressed and slipped beneath the blanket to find her naked. His heart swelled with joy, not to mention his manhood. She actually had felt at ease enough with him to climb into his bed naked to wait for him.

She was uncomplicated, giving, thoughtful, and she belonged to him as he belonged to her.

He hesitated to touch her. She slept so peacefully curled on her side, her body warm and content in its slumber.

He could wait until morning when she woke instead of disturbing her now.

What if tomorrow is too late?

He answered his own question by reaching out to touch Aliss.

He ran his hand slowly over her, wanting to familiarize himself with every inch of her flesh. She was warm and soft like fine-spun wool. Her bottom curved nicely as did her waist, which was neither thick nor narrow but just right for his hand to explore.

She stirred though did not wake and he continued to touch her.

The weight of her full breast in his hand brought a smile to his face and he tenderly squeezed the supple flesh and ran his thumb gently over her nipple. It hardened to his touch and he rolled his fingers around the stiff orb.

She stirred again, pressing against him until settling quietly once more.

His hand drifted along her flat midriff before descending over the slight mound of her stomach. It was barely detectable, but so much a part of her, like her wide hips that swayed seductively when she walked. He could not get them out of his mind. He had often daydreamed of her hips swaying beneath him as they made love. Now here she was in his bed and forever in his heart.

He inched his way down, his fingers tangling in the thatch of red hair between her legs, to finally touch her intimately as only a husband could.

"That feels so good."

Her whisper fanned his cheek and she turned into his arms.

"You are beautiful," he said.

"You make me feel that way."

They kissed, lingering in the taste of each other while his hands explored her.

Her erotic moan rippled his flesh and he pursued his exploration, delving into the intimacy that marked her womanhood.

She gasped and grabbed hold of his shoulders.

"I like the feel of you," he whispered and nibbled at her ear.

"I never imagined feeling so safe, so at ease, so crazed"—she sighed heavily and rubbed against him—"with wanting you."

He took her hand and placed it over the throbbing length of him. "I feel the same."

She grabbed hold of him. "Do not stop touching me."

"Never."

"Promise?" She squeezed him.

"Promise," he repeated.

She released him.

He kissed her before drifting to suckle at her breast like a man needing nourishment from a loving woman. He lingered there enjoying her taste and the sensation of her fingers running repeatedly through his hair, digging into his scalp, urging him to feast on her.

His hand drifted between her legs, his fingers working magic and gently entering her to entice her with thrust after thrust until she felt wet enough to accept him.

She reached down to grasp hold of him. "I want you."

He gasped. "Guide me."

He slipped over her, and with a gentle tug, she brought him to her.

"I want you," she begged, rubbing the length of him against her.

"I want the same," he whispered, rising over her, stealing a kiss and settling himself between her legs.

"Love me," she said on an aching breath.

"Always," Rogan chimed, and inched his way into her.

She groaned and he pulled back.

"No," she cried. "Do not deny me."

"You cried out in—"

"Pleasure." She smiled.

He kissed her softly. "Remember this moment and how very much I love you."

She purred. "I will never forget how graciously, how gently, how provocatively you loved me."

She arched her body as he plunged forward, and in an instant they joined as one. They moved in unison, their bodies swaying, their skin perspiring, their flesh aching, their lips tasting, and their passion soaring.

Rogan watched her toss her head back, felt her moan deep from inside, felt her hands grip his arms tightly, felt her tighten around him, heard her cry out her climax and felt himself explode like a star bursting in the universe.

He joined with her until they both were spent.

He pressed his forehead to hers, grazed her lips with his, and rolled off her to lie on his back beside her, hands joined, never wanting to let go of her.

He heard her sigh, felt her body relax beside him, and then she yawned.

"You are tired," he said, turning on his side,

and with his finger he brushed her hair off her damp face.

"I want very much to remain awake and—" She yawned again.

"You need to rest," he said, pulling the light blanket over her.

"But it is our wedding night."

"We have the rest of our lives together," he reminded with a kiss.

"I feel I have deprived you of—"

He pressed a finger to her lips. "We sealed our vows. We are one under God and no one can come between us."

"Are you sure?" Sleep slurred her words.

"I would want no other for a wife."

She smiled, a yawn following. "I have chosen a good husband."

"Then sleep and worry not for I am here beside you."

Aliss snuggled against him. "I had never imagined such comfort with a man."

"It will always be so."

"Promise?"

"Promise," he said, kissing her cheek and tucking the covers beneath her chin.

The morning dawned bright and Rogan was not surprised to find his bed empty. Aliss would not be able to start her day without checking on the ill, Daniel in particular, and he could not blame her. He wondered how the little lad fared himself.

She would be finished soon enough and then they would spend the day together uninterrupted, he hoped.

He had plans for the two of them and just the two of them. They would take a packed basket to the river and spend the day on the river's bank. They would have time to talk or lie in each other's arms, make love, nap, eat, and just be together.

He dressed in his plaid, a tan linen shirt, and his sandals. He combed his hair and let it fall as it would and then went to see to filling a basket. He smiled when he saw the spread of food the women had left on the table. It would be easy to pack a full basket and then go collect his wife and be off for the day.

That is, if Daniel was all right. He would not force her to go if Daniel needed her.

Rogan left the cottage to look for Aliss. He spotted her walking toward him.

She smiled and waved and hurried her steps.

He held out his arms; she ran into them and he swung her around.

"I missed you, wife."

She laughed and clung to his neck. "I thought I would be back before you woke."

"Is Daniel well?" he asked, a silent prayer on his lips.

Aliss beamed. "He does very well. He has some discomfort, but he handles it surprisingly well and is begging to get out of bed. I think he will heal remarkably fast."

"I am glad to hear that," he said, more relieved than she would ever know.

"Is that a basket of food I spy near the door?" she asked, stretching her neck to look at the cloth-covered basket.

"A surprise—"

"No more." Aliss laughed and wiggled free of his arms.

Rogan let her go to run to the basket.

"I planned a day of food and rest, just for the two of us, near the river," he confessed.

"Perfect," Aliss said, grabbed the basket and then hooked his arm with hers. "Let's go."

Chapter 19

A liss twisted her red hair and fastened it to her head with a comb. Her neck perspired not only from the weight of her long hair, but also from the heat of the day. The morning sun had grown considerably stronger by midday and she had no doubt the temperature would continue to climb.

Of course, the stroll she and Rogan had taken along the river's edge had not helped and now she would like nothing more than to shed her clothes and jump into the refreshing water.

She watched him spread a blanket on the ground under the shade of a huge oak tree and marveled more at his well-defined body than his considerate actions.

Last night when she had returned to the cottage to find Rogan gone, she had not hesitated to undress and climb into his bed. They were after all husband and wife, and she had actually looked forward to their joining.

She grinned. She had really enjoyed copulating with him, or had they made love? She liked to think it was love; she hoped someday they *would* love.

It had to be her own inadequacies that prevented her from accepting that love was possible without it being demanding. Hadn't Rogan's considerate nature proven that?

As much as she wanted to return home, she was glad that it would be at least two weeks before they left the village. It would give her time to come to terms with her own misgivings. When she stood before Tarr and Fiona, she wanted to speak from her heart and tell them how much Rogan meant to her.

She wanted no doubts in her marriage. It was important they remain truthful with each other, for without truth, there could not be trust, and that she wanted from him. If not, how could she be certain he would ever mean what he claimed?

Aliss smiled as she watched him whip off his shirt.

"It is hot," he said, tossing the shirt to the blanket.

Her hands went to the ties of her blouse. "My feelings exactly. A dip in the river?"

Rogan laughed, his hands already freeing his plaid. "And here I thought I would need to convince you."

Aliss shed her blouse, slipped out of her skirt, kicked off her sandals, and ran to the river. "I'll beat you."

Her laughter slowed her down and she was not surprised when Rogan rushed up behind her, scooped her up, kicking and giggling, and in they went together.

They came up sputtering and laughing and hugging each other.

"The cool water feels so good," she said, holding his shoulders as they bobbed along with the easy flow of the river.

He stared at her and after a few moments, she grew uneasy.

"Is something wrong?"

He shook his head. "No, I am just amazed with the remarkable woman I wed."

Aliss felt his forehead. "Are you sure you do not have a fever?"

He laughed. "I have a perpetual fever for you."

She slid her hands around his neck and pressed her breasts to his chest. "I think I have the cure for that."

"I warn you," he said, tugging her closer to him. "This is a recurring fever."

"With me having the cure, what does it matter?"

"You will forever tend me?" he asked with a whispered kiss.

"I will always make certain to tend your fever."

"I think my fever is quite high right now."

Her hand moved beneath the water to grasp hold of him. "Higher than I have ever felt it."

"We must do something immediately."

"Here?" Aliss asked, uncertain.

"A perfect spot," he insisted. "It is cool and the water offers privacy."

Suddenly a rapid current caught their feet, tearing them apart.

Aliss nearly panicked when she could not right herself and struggled to gain control.

She was grabbed around the waist and drawn up out of the water so quickly her breath caught.

"Breathe!"

His shout frightened her and it took several moments before she was breathing normally.

"We drifted too far from shore, where the current is sometimes unpredictable," Rogan explained while her breathing calmed.

She looked past his shoulder to see that he was moving them closer to the river's edge. She held tightly to him.

She rested her cheek to his. "I feared for you."

"Never fear that," he whispered in her ear. "Know that I will never let nature, beast, or man take you from me. You are mine forever and always."

Her breath caught and held. Was he about to claim his love for her? His strong declaration certainly seemed a prelude to declaring his love. She waited, her breath suspended.

He cupped her face in his large hands and kissed her lips ever so gently. "The reason I married you—" He stopped and kissed her again.

She welcomed his kiss but ached to hear his words.

"I love you. God help me, I love you."

Her heart felt near to bursting. "Then God help us both for I love you."

He rested his forehead to hers with a shake of his head.

"Do not worry, all will turn out well," she comforted, and reached out for his lips.

Their lips locked firmly together, chasing away doubt and fear and enflaming their passion. Before she knew it, she hungered for him like a woman who has just discovered she loved and was loved.

Her soft sighs soon turned to gentle whimpers as his fingers teased, touched, and tempted her beyond reason.

"I want you," she heard herself beg.

"And I you," he said, nibbling down her neck to take larger, more playful bites along her shoulders.

His hands went to her waist and he lifted her over him, easing them together in a perfect fit.

Her eyes rounded in delight when Rogan set the tempo to their joining, and with her hands grasping his arms, she threw back her head and reveled in the pure pleasure he created for them.

He did not rush them and she was glad. It felt too wonderful for it to end too quickly. She wanted to enjoy every thrust and every sensation until she could not stand it another minute and then, only then, did she want to surrender in climax.

He obliged her without a word being exchanged and she knew then that he understood her much better than she ever thought any man possibly could, and she felt grateful he was her husband.

Her sighs spilled into his mouth, he having captured her lips as she burst with a shivering climax. He followed soon after, tossing his head back and with a rumbling groan released into her.

They clung to each other until both their stomachs rumbled in unison.

They laughed.

"Time to eat," Rogan declared and scooped her up as they neared the water's edge.

Rogan offered her his shirt to dry off, insisting he did not need it. Besides, the day's heat would dry it in no time.

She took it and when she finished dressing, she hung his shirt from a tree branch to dry, then joined him on the blanket. His plaid was damp from his wet body though his naked chest was near dry from the hot sun.

He sat amid the food he had unwrapped, munching on a piece of cheese.

"You must have worried we would starve." She laughed, lowering herself to sit beside him.

He handed her a piece of cheese and tore a chunk of bread from a crusty loaf. "I have a large appetite."

"My sister claims the same."

"You would too if you gave yourself time to eat."

"You sound like Fiona," Aliss said. "She always argued that I would eat just as much as her if I took the time." She tore off a piece of bread. "I am looking forward to seeing my sister again. I have missed her."

"Be prepared for not so warm a welcome," he warned.

"Perhaps at first, but you are returning me home and once it is known you abducted me to heal your people and that I chose to wed you, all will be well."

"That easily, you think?"

She rested her hand on his. "What else can they do? Tarr advised me time and again that the choice of a husband was mine. I made that choice and he will honor it as he has promised."

"What if—"

She put her hands to her ears. "No more. What is done cannot be undone. We meet our fate together."

He grabbed hold of her hands. "Together. Always together." He handed her another piece of cheese. "Eat, you have the time."

Aliss took the cheese, noticing his eyes narrow in concern. "Do you think me too thin?"

He leaned over and nibbled along her ear. "I think you are a perfect morsel that I cannot get enough of."

She giggled and scrunched her shoulder. "That tickles."

"Aha, I have found a weak spot." He grabbed her around the waist and tossed her back on the blanket to attack her ear and neck.

They laughed, ate, talked, and walked the day away.

Aliss learned a lot about her new husband, even the hurt he had suffered when he lost his first wife, Kendra. What surprised her was that their love was the catalyst that made him realize he wished to love again.

In so doing, he claimed, his love for Kendra would always remain strong, and strange as it seemed, Aliss understood his reasoning. If he could not love again or refused to love again, it spoke poorly of his first love.

If he loved with his heart and soul, then he honored his first love. Aliss respected and admired his convictions; they made her care for him even more.

By late afternoon Aliss's thoughts drifted to Daniel and she had a hard time focusing on their conversation.

"You have had enough of me, haven't you?" Rogan asked, sitting beside her on the blanket.

She rested her palm to his cheek. "No, I feel as if I can never get enough of you. However, I cannot help but think of how Daniel is doing."

"You lasted much longer than I had expected, so that tells me something."

"What does it tell you?"

"That you really do love me," he said, kissed her quickly, stood and held out his hand to her. "Come, it is time to visit with Daniel."

She grabbed his hand and jumped to her feet. "I really do love you and I am grateful you understand my need to see how the lad fares."

"Daniel gets to have you for a while." He nibbled at her neck. "I get to have you all night."

She giggled. "I look forward to it."

They packed the basket with the food that was left, folded the blanket on top, and strolled back to the village arm in arm.

"Go see to the lad," Rogan ordered with a smile once they reached the cottage.

"I won't be long," Aliss said, already hurrying off.

"If you are, I will come and get you."

She laughed and ran off.

She noticed a rushed scurrying around the village as if the people seemed unsettled, nervous. She slowed her pace and turned to see Derek hurrying over to Rogan. The two men quickly disappeared inside the cottage with two more men entering after them; the basket lay forgotten on the ground.

Anna and Tara both jumped when she entered.

"Is something wrong?" Aliss asked. "Everyone in the village seems upset."

"A ship approaches shore," Tara said.

"An attack?" Aliss was quick to ask.

"It is not certain, but preparations are being made either way."

"What can I do?"

"Pray," Anna and Tara said in unison.

Aliss could focus on nothing but her husband. She worried for his safety and their future. It was strange thinking of something other than her healing work. She normally thought of nothing but that. Rarely did her mind wander to anything else and here she was unable to think about anything but her husband.

She wanted to run to him and beg him to be cautious now that he had a wife who loved him to consider. And what of children?

Her hand rested on her stomach as she walked out of the cottage, needing fresh air, needing to see her husband. She could be with child and not know it. Lord, how her life had changed in such a short time.

A change she welcomed?

Her heart raced and her stomach fluttered, signs that while pleased she was also anxious. There were no guarantees that the decision she had made had been a good one, but with their love declared she now felt it had been the right one. She would not betray her own faith, she would honor that which was joined before God and witnessed by man and sealed with love.

Her pace turned rapid as she approached the cottage, and she was disappointed to see that Rogan was not inside. Her heart kept pace with her frantic steps as she made her way through the village. All the men were gone and the women with children in tow were headed to the woods.

Battle preparations.

Anna followed behind Tara, who held a sleeping Daniel cradled in her arms.

"Join us," Anna said.

Aliss shook her head. "I cannot. There may be wounded."

"Then I will join you," Anna said.

"You do not—"

"I must," Anna said. "If I am to be a healer, I must."

"Godspeed," Tara said and hurried to the sanctuary of the woods.

"We gather what we need and wait on the edge of the battlefield," Aliss explained.

Anna nodded and they quickly gathered the necessary items before heading for the shore.

"Do you think the ship has landed by now?" Aliss asked.

"I hear no signs of battle."

"Perhaps they come in peace."

"We can only pray they do," Anna said.

They both grew quiet as they approached the end of the woods, not wanting to alert anyone to their presence. They were careful where they walked, treading as soundlessly as possible.

An unimpressive but sturdy ship had been pulled ashore, and from the sound of it the passengers were now disembarking. No swords looked to be drawn, but then no words of welcome rang out either.

Aliss edged closer, the distance too far for her to see anything clearly. The closer she got the more she strained to see since she was certain her eyes played tricks on her. She thought she recognized a few of the men, but it couldn't be.

Could it?

Anna grabbed her arm. "Do not go any closer."

"I must," Aliss said, and inched her way out of the woods to hide behind a large boulder.

"Fiona?" Aliss whispered. "Tarr?"

She smiled and dashed from behind the boulder to sprint across the uneven terrain straight for her sister.

"Fiona!" Aliss yelled, and everyone turned at her approach.

Aliss beamed with joy as her sister ran to meet her. They hugged, laughed, shed a tear or two then hugged again.

"Look at you," Aliss said, her hand patting her sister's rounded stomach. "You and the babe are well?"

"Fine now that we have found you," Fiona said, and took firm hold of her sister's hand.

Aliss felt the same. Her sister's sturdy grip let her know she did not intend to let her go, but things were different now. Adjustments would need to be made, lives would change as Fiona's had when she wed Tarr.

"Fiona, Aliss, come here."

The command echoed in the air and the two women turned to see Tarr, his hand extended to them.

Aliss was eager to say hello and eager to ease the tension that divided the two clans. Once they knew the circumstances of her abduction, her choice to wed Rogan and her love for him, she was certain the unease would dissipate, though slowly, like the early morning mist rising off the shore.

Aliss had no choice but to walk with Fiona, her sister refusing to release her hand. When they neared Rogan, Aliss broke free of her sister's hold and hurried to her husband's side.

She smiled when he wrapped his arm around her waist and tugged her close against him, his fingers digging into her as an added protective measure.

Aliss wanted this done immediately so that the repercussions could be dealt with swiftly and the healing between the clans could begin.

"Tarr, Fiona," Aliss said, her smile growing generous. "I would like you to meet my husband, Rogan of the clan Wolf."

There was such a heavy collective gasp that Rogan's men laid hands on the hilts of their swords.

"We wed by my choice," Aliss added quickly. "I was not forced or coerced into it. I actually proposed to Rogan. And remember, Tarr, you had told me the choice would be mine to make, besides—" She beamed with joy. "I love him and he loves me."

Tarr looked to Fiona and she stepped forward.

"Are the vows sealed?" Fiona asked her sister.

"This was *my choice*," Aliss repeated.

"Are they sealed?" Fiona asked again, more firmly.

Aliss took hold of Rogan's hand to confirm her commitment. "Yes, we are husband and wife and there is nothing anyone can do about it. I had hoped you would be happy for us. I know you consider him an enemy but he is not."

"He is an enemy," Fiona said, her green eyes blazing.

"Rogan has treated me well and he loves me,"

Aliss insisted, attempting to make them see reason.

Fiona stared at Rogan. "Of course he treated you well and claims to love you. You are his bargaining chip."

"What do you mean?" Aliss asked and felt Rogan tighten his grip on her.

"He did not think to see us until winter's freeze, our clan not equipped with ships. However, he failed to consider our parents' capabilities. As soon as their ships returned from voyage, we came for you, ready to meet his demand."

"Demand?" Aliss asked, and stared up at her husband.

He remained silent while Fiona answered.

"The Wolf captured you with intention of ransom—"

Aliss shook her head. "No, his people were sick, he needed my help—"

"A ruse," Fiona said.

"That is not possible—"

"Then why does he demand the Isle of Non in exchange for you?" Fiona spat.

Stunned silent for a moment, Aliss found her voice and declared adamantly, "No, it is not true."

Fiona reached into the pouch at her waist and took out a folded paper. She handed it to her sister.

Aliss almost didn't reach out for it and then slowly she stepped forward, away from Rogan, and stretched out a trembling hand to grasp hold, open and read it.

She read it once then twice and then three times. Each time the words stabbed more painfully at her heart. She fought her tears bravely but they gathered in force, threatening to burst forth in an uncontrollable torrent.

She swallowed several times, fighting with every bit of strength she had not to break down and sob. "You used me," she said, raising her trembling hand and crushing the offending message.

"No—"

"You deny this?" Aliss asked with a harsh laugh.

"I sent the message, but I never—"

"Expected it to be so easy to play me for a fool?"

Rogan stepped forward.

Aliss jumped back. "Do not dare come near me."

"I want to explain."

She shook the crumpled letter in his face. "This explains it all."

"It is different now."

Aliss laughed in his face. "Oh, I forgot, now you love me and that makes all the difference."

"It does."

"Do not think I will continue to play the fool," she shouted at him, and turned to Fiona. "I want to go home."

Chapter 20

~~~~~⚬⚬⚬~~~~~

Fiona wrapped her arms around her sister and directed her toward the ship.

"No!"

Rogan's shout stopped the two women and caused Tarr to move swiftly to their side.

"I am her husband now. Aliss goes nowhere without my permission," Rogan commanded.

"Like hell she does," Fiona challenged. "You have hurt her enough. The Isle of Non is yours. You will surrender my sister as we agreed."

"I will not."

Fiona lunged for Rogan. Tarr stopped her with a powerful grip to her arm.

Rogan glared at Aliss. "We are wed and the union is of Aliss's choice. We remain husband

and wife and there is nothing anyone can do about it."

Fiona snarled at Rogan. "If you think I will let my sister remain with—"

"The choice is not yours," Rogan reminded her with a firm calmness. "Aliss is my wife and will obey my command."

"If you think you will get the Isle of Non now—"

Tarr yanked Fiona gently to his side and spoke directly to Rogan. "The Isle of Non is yours and I hope you take up residence there with your wife and clan as soon as possible."

"We will see," Rogan said. "You are welcome to visit for a few days. My men will show you the way to the village. Right now I wish to speak with my wife alone." He held his hand out to Aliss.

She stared at him, shook her head, and sprinted past him toward the village.

He turned and followed.

"Why did—"

"Hush," Tarr said and forced Fiona to walk with him, putting distance between them and the Wolf clan. "We need time to consider this matter. Obviously they are wed as claimed or Aliss would have spoken up, which means Rogan is right—Aliss belongs to him. Until this can be resolved I would prefer Aliss close by."

Fiona's eyes sprang wide. "In my rage, I did not think. The Isle of Non is not far from us."

"And I am sure Aliss will want you close by."

"She will need me," Fiona said with a firm nod. "She thinks herself in love with the Wolf."

"I doubt she feels that way anymore," Tarr

said. "Now come and let us be civil with our new family so that we may help Aliss."

Rogan found Aliss sitting at the table in the cottage, her head bent and her hands clasped. He had wondered how to approach her on his walk back to the village. How could he make her understand that he laid claim to what was rightfully his? And that he had never imagined falling in love with her. She had been a means to an end. Now she was the woman he loved and wished to spend the rest of his life with, though she would never believe him.

He slid along the bench opposite her at the table, hesitated to reach out to her then finally he laid his hand over hers.

She pulled away as if his touch scorched her skin.

"Will you hear me out?" he asked, praying she would give him a chance to explain, although even then he was not sure she would understand and forgive him.

She did not raise her head. "You lied to me. All this time you *lied* to me."

"No, I did not."

Her head shot up and her blazing green eyes disagreed.

"My people were ill and I needed a healer."

"That was not the case at first, was it?" she asked but answered for him. "The two times you attacked the Hellewyk village you were looking for me to abduct and ransom. When your people grew ill my abduction served a twofold purpose." She shook her head. "I am such a fool for trusting you. I played right into your trap."

"I did not plan on falling in love and wedding you."

"Please spare me the lies," Aliss said with a dismissive wave of her hand.

"It was ransom I asked for, not marriage."

She choked on her laughter. "But marriage to me would guarantee you the Isle of Non. After all, my sister and I would want to be close." She shook her head again. "I had told you that, about wanting to be close. How you must have laughed at me when I proposed. Everything was suddenly in your grasp and all you had to do was—"

"Commit myself to you for the rest of my life?" he asked incredulously. "Do you not think ransom a more sensible choice? Why wed you and be stuck with you?"

"Guarantees. Tarr of Hellewyk would not dare attempt to reclaim the isle if you were wed to his sister-in-law."

"So I saddled myself with you in exchange for the land."

"It would appear the Isle of Non is that important to you."

"Do you not care to know why?" he asked.

She shook her head. "What difference does it make? The isle is what matters to you. I do not and that tells me that you do not—"

"Do not dare say that I do not love you," he said, giving the wooden table one good pound with his fist.

Aliss smacked the table with her hand. "Do not dare insult me by claiming to love me."

He tempered his tone. "I do love you, Aliss."

"No! You love the land more."

Her hurt refused to allow her to listen to him and he could not blame her. Nothing he said right now would make sense to her.

"I want free of our marriage."

"No!" His shout reverberated in the room. "We are husband and wife, joined before God and so shall we remain."

Aliss stood. "We will see about that."

Rogan followed her out of the cottage and over to where Fiona and Tarr stood talking with Anna and John.

"I want out of this marriage, Tarr," she said, coming to stand in front of her brother-in-law.

"I will not release you from our vows," Rogan said with a cold calmness.

"I do not want to be wed to you," Aliss said, her eyes glistening with unshed tears.

"Are you sure?" Rogan asked.

"Yes, I am sure," Aliss said, her voice trembling.

Rogan walked over to her. Her unshed tears tore at his heart and the slight quiver in her chin made his soul ache. He had hurt her terribly, and in so doing, he had hurt himself. He certainly would not forgive himself, why should she?

"A bargain?" he asked.

"Why should I, when you do not honor them?"

He felt the insult like a slap to his face but retained his composure. "I will let you free if . . ."

"I am listening," Aliss said when he grew silent.

"Come with me and my clan to the Isle of Non. Let me prove how very much I love you. At the end of six months' time if you are not convinced of my love, I will free you and take my leave. The Isle of Non will be yours and you need never see me again."

She swallowed hard and he hoped it was because she could not bear the thought of separating from him, hoped that there was a chance for him to redeem himself, hoped she would fall in love with him all over again.

"Three months' time," she bartered to his disappointment.

"Six or you have me for a lifetime."

"All right." She sighed.

Rogan walked over to Tarr. "A fair enough bargain for you?"

"The choice belongs to Aliss, but I feel it a fair deal," Tarr said.

He then turned to Fiona.

She spoke before he could. "I feel as my husband does."

"Then it is settled," Rogan said. He approached John and Derek and yelled out, "Get the people packing. We leave in a few days for a new home."

Aliss stared at her husband's retreating back and felt her legs wobble. They would not hold her up much longer. They would collapse out from under her if she even dared take a single step.

"Aliss, are you all right?" Fiona asked.

She realized then that her whole body trembled. "I am not sure." Before her sister summoned help, Aliss grabbed her arm. "Walk with me. I need to walk."

Fiona hooked arms with her and off they strolled.

"This is such a shock to me," Aliss admitted. "I feel like an idiot. He told me he loved me. I believed him."

"I can kill him for you and settle everything," Fiona said.

"No, you mustn't do that," Aliss insisted, knowing her sister was serious. "Promise me you will not hurt him."

Grudgingly Fiona said, "I promise, but tell me why you do not want me to hurt him. He has hurt you, lied to you, and betrayed your trust. He deserves punishment."

Fiona was right. He had done all that to her and more. He had made her believe he loved her. He had made love to her, told her she was beautiful, and now he wanted time to prove his love— or did he?

Unshed tears choked her, but she refused to acknowledge them. She gave a hard cough to chase them away, and came to a halt by her garden. She took up her hoe to dig in the earth. She had to do something, concentrate on something other than feeling as if her heart were being ripped apart.

"This is my mistake. I must right it."

"You need not do it alone," Fiona said.

"I brought this on myself."

"You most certainly did not," Fiona said, grabbing the hoe from her hands. "He lied to you from the beginning—"

"No, his people were truly ill."

"So he used you twice to serve his own purposes. Isn't he a *wonderful* man?"

"Rogan is a good man."

"Now you defend him?" Fiona asked.

Aliss threw her hands up. "I do not know what to do. I do not know how I feel. I do not know what I want. One minute I cannot bear to look at him and then he goes and claims to love me and intends to prove his love within six months."

"He intends to confuse you and use you all over again. He lied to you once. You do not think he will lie to you again to keep the isle? Need I remind you that he is our enemy?"

"Rogan is a warrior, just like Tarr," Aliss argued. Why she continued to defend him she could not say.

"Tarr has honor, Rogan does not," Fiona said angrily. "Rogan has attacked our village, wounded Tarr, abducted you, lied to you and ransomed you, and now *claims* to love you. Do not be a fool and fall into his trap twice. Send him on his way at the end of six months and be done with the bastard."

Her sister's clear outline of the situation left Aliss numb.

Fiona took hold of her hand. "I do not mean to hurt you, or let anyone else hurt you; Rogan has already done that. Do not let him hurt you again."

"What of love?"

"You will find it one day. There will be no question about it. You will know." Fiona tugged at her to follow. "Now let us get you packed and ready to go. At least you will be close by home and you will have family to help you through the ordeal of the next six months."

Aliss let her sister lead, yet felt the need to escape her good intentions. She had created this mess on her own and she should clean up the mess on her own. She had to settle this matter not only in her mind but also in her heart and only she could do that.

Chapter 21

～∞～

Laughter, chatter, and squeals of excitement filled the air. The village people and the children were thrilled to be moving to a new home and Aliss could not blame them. The land in this area could be difficult to farm, game was not always prevalent, and the winters were harsh and long.

What she knew of the Isle of Non would surely prove to be paradise to them: lush meadows and fields, woods teeming with game, rivers plentiful with fish. It also had once been a home.

Aliss wondered now what clan had occupied the isle and why it had been deserted, its few cottages and keep left to decay. What was Rogan's interest in it? Did he want a good, permanent home for his clan and saw no other way to achieve it? Or did his motive go deeper?

She was curious about this patch of land that had caused so much dissension and now was about to bring joy to a clan who much needed a home that could sustain them.

Aliss walked with unhurried steps on purpose. She was returning to the cottage, where Tarr and Fiona would be supping with her and Rogan, after being summoned by Daniel's mother. She had assumed something was wrong with Daniel, but it had been Tara's concern that her son's injury would worsen with travel. After calming the young mother and assuring her Daniel would do more than well, that he would actually thrive on the adventure, she had taken her leave, but now she hesitated to return home.

It was not a meal she looked forward to and yet it would not be right to leave her husband to face her family alone. That would be a coward's choice, and she was no coward. Her time here with the Wolf clan had taught her that and more.

She had discovered not only her strengths but also her weaknesses and had found the courage to battle them all, though victories were yet to be won. The next six months would be her true battlefield.

Could there be a victor in this encounter or would only losses prevail?

A heavy sigh was extinguished before she entered the house and joined her family, who sat in silence at the table. She slid beside Rogan on the bench.

"Daniel is all right?" he asked.

"He is fine. Tara was concerned about him traveling."

"I had forgotten about his injury. Is he fit to travel or shall we postpone the move until he is well enough?"

"He can travel," Aliss said abruptly. That Rogan should delay the move for a small lad only proved that he was a good man. Did it not?

"That is good," Rogan said, and handed her a piece of meat and bread.

"Aliss does not eat that much," Fiona said, though it sounded as if she scolded him.

"I know my wife's needs," Rogan retaliated.

Aliss took the offered food, not certain how to quell the animosity between the pair and not understanding why she felt the need to. If they disliked each other, what could she do about it? Besides, Rogan would be gone in six months.

The thought made her stomach churn and she could only take a small bite of the food.

To her relief, Tarr managed to direct the conversation to safer territory.

"Raynor says he misses you and hopes to visit with you soon. He had wanted to join us but a few skirmishes on the outskirts of Hellewyk land needed his attention."

"How are Mother and Father?" Aliss asked.

Fiona answered. "They do well and they miss you."

Aliss relaxed as the conversation turned to

family and friends and all the news she had missed during her absence.

By the time the meal was finished, Aliss was relieved that it had gone relatively well under the circumstances. Fiona, however, looked to be killing Rogan with her glaring green stares.

That she disliked the man was obvious and Aliss understood that she was protecting her as she had done since they were young, but they were not young girls anymore. They were young women with lives of their own to live. How did she make her sister understand that? How did she even understand it herself?

They were twins and had relied on each other for so long that it was a given. Aliss had not even considered a life on her own and yet she had been living one. While she had missed her sister, she had enjoyed her freedom of sorts.

"See, I told you," Fiona accused. "Too much food, she cannot eat it."

Rogan did not glance at the food; he focused on Fiona. "Your sister's thoughts are heavy. That is why she has not eaten."

"Of course her thoughts disturb her. How could they not when she has wed a lying foe."

"That is between Aliss and me and does not concern you," Rogan said in a respectable tone, to Aliss's relief.

Fiona, however, did not grant him the same consideration. "It damn well concerns me. I am her sister—"

"I am her *husband*."

"Not for long."

"That is up to Aliss—"

"Who knows what she needs to do," Fiona finished.

"The choice remains hers and you should not forget that."

Fiona looked ready to lunge.

"Enough!" Aliss shouted. "This day has been difficult enough without you two bickering. Rogan is right, Fiona. The choice is mine and I wish to make it without interference or opinions from anyone."

"And so you shall," Tarr said. "We will keep our visits infrequent and brief."

"But—"

Aliss allowed no room for her sister's protest. "I thank *both* of you for understanding."

"What of the babe?" Fiona asked, upset. "You will not be there to deliver him?"

"Of course she will," Rogan said adamantly. "Aliss would never abandon you in your time of need. Besides, she has looked forward to the birth, reminding me often enough she had to return in time to deliver him."

Fiona smiled at her sister and Aliss felt swamped with guilt. Fiona was bold and she loved with a boldness that could devour a person. She had devoured Tarr that way and he loved her for it.

"We can come stay with you at Hellewyk for the birth," Rogan suggested. "So you need not worry."

Aliss could tell by the way Fiona looked suspiciously at Rogan that she was uncertain what to make of him. That was good, for then maybe she could change her sister's opinion of him.

But could she herself do the same?

Would she find a way to make sense of this mess and take a chance that he did not lie about loving her?

The evening meal was finished soon enough, and Fiona yawned repeatedly until Tarr suggested to a protesting Fiona that she needed to sleep. It was not until Aliss advised her that the baby required rest that Fiona capitulated and the pair retired to a cottage that had been prepared for them.

Rogan left the cottage without a word to Aliss shortly after Tarr and Fiona had taken their leave. Aliss was glad for the solitude and packed a couple of baskets with her healing paraphernalia. She had debated about taking the clothes Rogan had given her that had belonged to his wife. He had been generous in giving them to her and she would not insult him by leaving them behind, though she would return them to him when they separated.

Separated.

She shivered at the thought; she had become attached to Rogan and his considerate ways. But had they been part of a well-executed ruse?

A yawn reminded her that the day had been long and emotionally tiring. It would be a relief to have sleep claim her body and mind. She sat on the narrow bed she had slept in when she had first arrived. She could not bring herself to climb into her husband's bed. She did not know where his lies began and where they ended and that left her feeling vulnerable.

She now felt more than naked in front of him even though she was clothed.

"What are you doing?"

Aliss jumped at his booming accusation. "Going to sleep."

"You are in the wrong bed."

His glaring green eyes and his predatory stance reminded her of a wolf, and she suddenly felt intimidated. He stepped to the side, a silent demand that she seek her sleep in his bed, but she remained firm.

"I prefer to sleep here."

"You are my wife."

"The circumstances have changed," she said, attempting to keep the quiver out of her voice.

"The fact that you are my wife has not."

"It is better that I—"

"Tend to your wifely duties."

Her chin shot up. "You intend to enforce my wifely duties? Should I cook for you, sew for you, and disregard everything and everyone except my husband?"

"I did not ask you to be someone you are not. I simply want you in my bed where you belong."

She had enjoyed making love with him when she thought he loved her—but now? She could not share such an intimate act with him knowing he had lied. She would not feel the same.

"I would not be comfortable."

"Why?"

She bunched the blanket between her fingers and searched frantically for an answer that would appease him while keeping her worry to herself.

"Why?" he repeated.

"There is strife between us."

"Sleeping in separate beds will not improve that," he said.

"Sleeping together when I doubt your love will not help, either."

"I want you in my bed."

It was an adamant plea and she almost felt the need to surrender to him. She took a breath, gathered her wits, and said, "I want to sleep alone."

"I am not giving you a choice."

She could not make love with him. She could not, she would surely get pregnant. Then what? He would not abandon his child and she would not relinquish her babe. Was that his plan? Get her with child so he would have to remain with her.

She bolted off the bed. "I will not make love with you."

"I do not recall asking that of you."

"You said you wanted me in your bed," she reminded.

"Sleep was what I said and what I meant."

"And my other duties?"

"I want us to make love, Aliss, but only if you want to make love with me. I want you in my bed, sleeping beside me, but I will leave the choice of making love up to you."

Relief and disappointment flooded her all at once and confused her even more. What was she to make of this? Was he setting another plan in motion? Did he think she would surrender easily to him once she lay beside him?

Her yawn sounded more like a cry of help.

"You are tired."

She had no sooner plopped back down on the bed than he scooped her up and carried her into his room and laid her in his bed.

He turned his back to undress, and knowing it was useless to fight him, Aliss shed her sandals but left her clothes on.

"You will be too warm in those clothes."

"I will not sleep naked beside you."

Rogan went to the chest near the door.

Aliss stared at his naked body, admiring every inch of muscle and tanned flesh and remembering the feel of him against her and inside her. Her body heated quickly and she silently cursed herself.

He grabbed something from inside and returned to the bed to toss a white garment at her. "This will be more comfortable."

It was a white linen shift, soft and trimmed at the round neck with ribbon. He was right, it would definitely be more comfortable, and most probably had belonged to his wife. But then she was now his wife, meant to sleep beside her husband.

He climbed into bed and turned his back to her.

She hopped off the bed and swiftly exchanged her garments for the shift, then climbed under the covers, turning on her side to keep a safe distance between them. She lay stiff waiting for Rogan to move toward her, but he remained where he was and she remained hugging the edge of the bed.

Exhaustion finally claimed her, her body relaxed, her eyes fluttered closed and Rogan turned and draped his warm body over her.

She was too tired to object, and besides, his warmth chased the chill from her flesh and he made no move to touch her. He simply held her.

"I love the feel of you in my arms," he whispered in her ear.

She refused to admit the same.

"And the scent of you—" He breathed in deeply along her neck. "Intoxicates."

Her flesh betrayed her, gooseflesh popped up all over her.

He settled his hand over her stomach and she thought for a moment he would—

Light snoring told her otherwise. He had remained true to his word, and while it pleased her, a pesky disappointment assaulted her once again and sleepiness had suddenly vanished.

Her body was alive with passion for him.

She wanted him. She ached to be kissed, touched, and—

She nearly groaned at the thought of him hard and thick and ready to enter her. She chased the seductive thought away, but it refused to go and sprang back into her mind more vividly than before.

No. No, she scolded. *Do not think about it*.

She shifted and her bottom landed against him. Even soft, his member was impressive.

Stop!

What was wrong with her? She should not be having these thoughts, not after what she had learned. He had lied to her. She could not trust him. She was better off without him.

I will miss sleeping with him.

Damn her wandering mind.

Aliss fought her feelings, fought her desire, fought her own body, until the battle drained her and she finally fell into an exhausted sleep cuddled in her foe's arms.

Chapter 22

❦❦

"**Y**ou have changed."

Aliss looked up from where she kneeled in her garden, shading her eyes from the sun with her hand to see her sister standing there.

"I was angry at first," Fiona continued.

Aliss dusted her hands free of soil and sat back on her haunches. The urgency in her sister's voice meant Fiona had something she needed to say so Aliss remained silent and listened.

"I thought that you did not need me anymore."

"I do not need you to *look after* me anymore." Aliss thought she heard a sniffle and went to her sister's side. "I missed you. I missed our morning walks together and talking with you."

"What did you not miss?"

Aliss hooked arms with her. "Your constant concern. You constantly protecting me. This time on my own has given me a chance to learn about myself. No one was there to pick me up and brush me off or shield me from harm. There was only me."

Fiona grabbed hold of her hand. "You are not alone anymore. Tarr and I will go with you to the Isle of Non. Raynor, Mother, and Father can join us and we will all help you so that at the end of six months you—"

"No!" Aliss took a step away from her sister. "I want to finish this on my own."

"You intend to spend the next six months alone with—with—"

"My husband." Aliss said what Fiona refused to admit. "This is for me to do."

"Nonsense—"

"No, it is not nonsense. Have you not listened to what I have said?"

"I heard, but what is wrong with your family helping you?"

"Aliss *has* family to help her."

Both women turned to face Rogan.

"Tarr and I have spoken. Tomorrow you and he sail home, and *my wife*, I, and the clan sail to the Isle of Non," he said, and walked over to Aliss.

"We will see about that," Fiona said and walked off, her steps turning to a hasty run.

"Tarr will handle her," Rogan said.

"In only two days' time you have come to know my brother-in-law, but then you are similar, both patient, cunning, and understanding when necessary."

Rogan turned away from her. "Do you need help in collecting the plants from your garden?"

She had meant to compliment not insult, but he seemed annoyed, and rather than question him, she ignored it. She had argued enough with her sister over issues that she had already decided upon. This matter was for her to handle, whether anyone liked it or not, and that included her husband.

"I need no help," she said, annoyed. "Do I appear fragile?"

He looked her up and down and grinned. "Not at all."

Her cheeks flared red.

His grin grew wider.

"I do not need you. I do not need my sister. I do not need anyone. Go away and leave me be." She dropped down on her knees and went to work in the soil.

A moment later she was startled to find herself abruptly and unexpectedly hoisted to her feet. Rogan gripped her arm and brought her nose to nose with him.

"Need me or not, I am your husband and I am here for you and I will remind you of that often. I want you to know—nay, I want to you to *feel*— how much I love you."

He kissed her then, like a man trying to prove something—and he did. He proved that no matter what doubts she might harbor concerning their love, she could not doubt her desire for him.

He ended the kiss abruptly, to her regret, and rested his forehead to hers. Their breathing was labored and their passion tittered on the edge, about to tumble over.

Rogan released her gently, stepped away from her, and not saying a word, he turned and walked away.

Aliss collapsed slowly to the ground, her chore forgotten, her mind ruled only by passion. How could she desire a man who had betrayed her? It made no sense. She should hate him, not want him.

He had used her for his own benefit then claimed to love her.

She shook her head. No matter how much she attempted to rationalize the situation it made no sense to her and she was exhausted by the thought of it. It occupied her mind to the point where she had barely considered anything else in the last two days, and that troubled her. She had made a bargain with him as she had done when they had first met and she had set to work healing his people.

Six months was their bargain this time and so be it. The time would serve a good purpose. She would use it to heal herself and build her future on the Isle of Non, no matter how difficult and painful a task it turned out to be.

"Aliss."

She looked up and smiled. "Anna. What is wrong?" she asked, seeing the distress on the young girl's face.

"I have tended the ill as best I could these last couple of days, but there are many who prefer to see you."

Aliss stood in a flash. "You should have come to me sooner."

"You have been preoccupied with all that is going on and neither I nor anyone in the village wished to disturb you."

"Nonsense," she declared. "I am a healer and that comes before anything. Tell anyone who wishes to see me to come right away. I am here for them."

Aliss was glad to see a broad smile chase away the young woman's worry.

"I will tell them right away." She turned to leave. "Oh, Hellewyk warriors, too?"

"There are those in the Hellewyk clan who require a healer?"

Anna nodded vigorously. "One man told me he insisted on coming to rescue you just so that he could seek your help."

Aliss dusted her hands off, reminded of her duties as a healer to both clans. Besides, busy hands kept a mind occupied, and right now, she needed a reprieve from her troubled thoughts. "I will clean up while you go tell them all that I am ready to see them."

"I will help," Anna said.

"If you are busy, I can tend some of them."

After seeing over a dozen ailing people with a dozen more waiting for her, Aliss was grateful that Anna had remained to assist her. The ailments and complaints were mostly minor and could easily be remedied, but it took until just before the evening meal to finish treating them all.

Fiona had stopped by to help but looked annoyed when she saw Anna and left with a frown. Aliss realized her sister felt as if she had been replaced. She had often assisted her when necessary. Aliss laughed as she recalled how William, one of the Hellewyk warriors Fiona had treated before, had commented that Anna had a gentler touch than Fiona. He had whispered it as if afraid Fiona would hear, though she had been nowhere in sight.

Yet she had seen that same man show respect and admiration for Fiona's courage in fighting beside Tarr and his men in battle.

When she finally finished, she went in search of her sister. They needed to talk before they parted.

"Where are you going?" Rogan asked, startling her as she rushed out of the cottage.

"To see my sister."

"I will wait to sup until you return."

She nodded and hurried off, wondering if she had agreed out of habit. At the moment, spending any time with him rankled her. Her hurt was too new, too painful, and yet so was the thought of not seeing him. Lord, but love was difficult.

Fiona sat by a small fire, a rabbit on a spit cooked almost black.

"It is too close to the flame," Aliss said, sitting down beside her.

"You were the one good at cooking, not me."

"You were the one good at defending, not me."

Fiona shrugged. "We balance each other. The young woman Anna is a good helper."

"Not as good as my sister."

Fiona turned and smiled. "You seem to have made a life here, to my surprise."

"To my surprise as well," Aliss confessed. "At first I was so very frightened, but I could hear you in my head guiding me, encouraging me, insisting I could survive until you came for me."

"You never doubted I would come for you?"

"Never!"

"I really helped you?" Fiona asked.

"Endless times. I would hear you in my head especially when I was most frightened or when I questioned my own decisions." She smiled. "I could hear you tell me that I should kiss Rogan if I were ever to know how I felt about him."

"I guess the kiss worked. He does look after you," Fiona admitted grudgingly. "I heard him talking to a woman about food for you when you finished with your healing."

"You know me when I am healing. I do not think of sleep or food or anything."

"Do you love Rogan?" Fiona asked.

Aliss gazed down at the flames searing the meat. "I don't know. I thought I did; he was so kind and thoughtful. But now?"

Fiona reached for her sister's hand. "What do you want?"

"I want to keep my bargain with my husband

and see what comes of it." She paused. Did she dare hope that he would prove his love? "And I want you to encourage my efforts to do so."

"I want you to be happy and safe, though I wish the Isle of Non were closer than several hours away."

"There will only be a distance between us if we let there be," Aliss said.

Fiona squeezed her hand. "Then there will never be a distance between us."

"Never," Aliss agreed.

Fiona jumped then quickly placed Aliss's hand on her stomach. "The babe is surely a warrior. He seems to forever battle in my stomach."

They laughed and began to talk about the babe, the birth, and much more, while feasting on the burned rabbit. The sun had settled and the village had quieted when Aliss gave her sister a hug and returned to the cottage.

When she was a short distance away, she realized that Rogan waited supper for her. She had forgotten—or had she not wanted to return to the cottage?

It was difficult to continue as his wife when so much was uncertain. She would have preferred to be done with it all, and yet that would mean losing him, or would it? Did she actually harbor a spark of hope that the mighty warrior would battle to save their love?

She sighed, frustrated by the barrage of thoughts that refused to allow her some peace, and entered the cottage, stopping short when she heard voices. She proceeded down the hall to the end and turned, entering the room, surprised to see Tarr and Rogan sitting at the table.

Tarr raised his tankard. "Finally, the women are finished."

"Tarr informed me you feasted with your sister," Rogan said. "So I invited him to feast with me."

While the two seemed amicable Aliss knew the two men were doing what any good chieftains would do—getting to know their enemy.

"Join us?" Rogan asked.

A yawn gave her the excuse to decline his offer; she felt the men were better left to themselves. She bade them good night, and after changing into the soft linen shift she climbed into bed ready for sleep.

Her mind intended to torment her with issues that would find no solutions this night and she tossed and turned until, frustrated, she kicked off the covers and let out an exasperated moan.

"Trouble sleeping?" Rogan asked, slipping out of his shirt as he entered the room.

She had hoped to be asleep before he came to bed, and feeling the coward for hiding, she quickly diverted the conversation. "No, did you and Tarr fare well?"

He slipped naked in bed beside her. "We waged no battles."

"But formed no friendship?"

"Be grateful we played our parts as chieftains well."

"Could you call him friend one day?" she asked.

"Does it matter to you?"

"Yes."

"Why?" he asked and turned on his side to face her.

"It is better to have many friends than many enemies."

"You worry about me?"

His query caught her off guard. "I do not wish you harm."

"What do you wish me?"

She stared at him, unable to answer.

"You do not know?"

Finally, she found words. "I thought I had known. I thought I had known you. I believed you."

"You can still believe me."

"After you lied to me?"

"In time you will—"

"Will learn the truth and hate you even more?" Her words were harsh to her own ears, and distraught by her outburst, she jumped out of bed and ran to the other room, tossing herself down on the narrow bed.

Rogan gave her barely a minute before he appeared in the doorway. She stared at him. He stood there like a proud warrior ready to do battle, his nakedness his armor, his determination his weapon.

He walked over to her, grabbed her around the waist, and flung her over his shoulder. He returned her to his bed, tossing her down and coming to rest over her. He locked his fingers with hers, spreading her arms above her head.

" 'Hate' is a strong word, Aliss. Are you sure you hate me?"

"Don't!" she warned, realizing his intentions.

"Let us see how much you hate me."

"Rogan, no," she cried out, too late.

He captured her mouth though she tried to avoid his lips. It was a savage kiss that meant to prove her a liar, and it did. It fired the blood of both to a feverish pitch that soon had her writhing beneath him.

Rogan moved to nibble at her ear. "I told you the choice is yours. Do you want to make love with me?"

Damn him and damn herself for responding to him. Of course she wanted to make love. *Love!* Not make lust with him.

"No," she spat.

He released her hands and grabbed her chin. "Be careful that your stubbornness does not lose you something you will regret."

He rolled off her and turned on his side away from her.

Aliss lay there, her body aching for him, her mind admonishing her for her stupidity and her heart hurting as she had never known it could.

Chapter 23

Rogan stood on the bow of the ship that rose and fell with the swelling waves and stared at the approaching isle. A white sandy shore greeted them and a rocky terrain followed behind, attached to lush green land dotted with trees that thickened to woods.

Hills speared the gray sky, capped by a fine mist that would probably grow thicker with the approaching storm. Rogan had wasted no time this morning; the scent of a squall was strong in the air. The ships were ready and the people willing. They set sail soon after sunrise knowing it would take, weather permitting, until evening to reach the isle.

He had dreamed and planned for this day for years. Unfortunately, his victory tasted bittersweet. He had known a strong love with Kendra, but his love for Aliss was nothing less than profound. He had not even known when he had fallen in love with her. He could not say it had been sudden, though it had been unexpected.

He only knew now that he did not wish to live without her. He had six months to prove his love to her. Six months to speak the truth and wonder if she would hate him even more because of it.

He cringed at the idea that Aliss could hate him. He had known she had spoken with anger last night but her words still cut deep. He had hoped she would understand, but then she did not know the whole of it. He was not sure he wanted her to know all of it. Some secrets were better left buried.

He had wanted so badly to make love with her last night, show her how much they truly loved each other. She had wanted to just as badly, but he had given her a choice and he would honor his word, no matter how difficult. He hoped with time her hurt would pass and she would see that their love had survived, had always been there and would never go away.

If not?

He pushed the painful thought from his mind. He would not visit it again. He was a warrior who had claimed victory in many battles. He would claim victory in this battle or die trying, but he would not—would not let Aliss go.

"We land soon?"

He turned to Aliss, her face pale and her body trembling.

He reached out and drew her into his arms, resting her face to his chest.

"I am not a good sailor."

"The sea is not pleasant today even for a seasoned sailor," he said, feeling her arms slip around his waist and hold on tight. He hugged her to him, wanting to ease her discomfort yet knowing only land beneath her feet could do that. "We will touch land soon."

She moaned. "I am so grateful and jealous."

He chuckled. "I heard your sister, as you bade each other good-bye this morning, tell you how much she enjoyed sailing."

"And she is with child. It is not—" She pulled away from him.

Her face was deathly pale and he knew she was about to be sick. He grabbed her around the waist and hauled her to the side of the ship, gently bending her head over the side.

Waves rocked the ship and sea mist sprayed her face and dampened her garments but he held her firm. He did not intend to let the sea claim her. She belonged to him.

She fell into his arms when she finished, drained from her ordeal. He wrapped his arms around her and carried her to where Anna sat with a few other women. They moved to make space for her.

"I will be back to get her once we reach shore," he told Anna. "Make her stay here. The landing will not be an easy one."

Anna nodded, looking pallid herself.

"It will be over soon," he assured Anna and

looked over to Aliss, who had yet to open her eyes. "Keep watch on her."

Rogan walked off, directing the men to make ready to land. He had hoped they would beat the swelling waves but they were rising fast. It was a tricky feat to land the ship in such hazardous conditions. Sometimes men were lost, ships damaged.

He yelled out instructions and the men obeyed knowing their lives depended on it.

The sea seemed impressed with their well-orchestrated maneuvers and the swells eased enough for the men to jump into the rough waters, ropes attached, and make preparations to get the ship on shore.

With time and effort, poles were made ready, the men took their places, and they heaved in unison to pull the ship onto the waiting poles and roll it onto shore away from the angry sea.

Rogan went directly to Aliss, who was sitting up, color still drained from her face. "Time to touch land."

She reached out to him like a child who was being rescued and he grabbed her, scooping her up into his arms.

"You can rest on shore while everyone disembarks," he said, walking to the side. With ease, he jumped off to land with a solid thud on the sand. That she had not flinched at his actions pleased him. Whether she believed it or not she trusted him, at least to a point.

He settled her on shore away from the frenzy of unloading a complete clan from two ships and warned her to stay put. Did he think she would?

He shook his head. She had not responded but once she began to feel better, he had no doubt she would pitch in and help. And damn if he did not admire her tenacity.

Rogan formed groups to see to the unloading. The women and children would rest while the men cut a path through the woods to the village, then the moving would begin, if they could beat the impending storm.

Rogan and his men were ready for the trek, while a few of the men had been designated to find game for tonight's meal.

He was not surprised to see Aliss join his troop that would slash a path through the wilderness, a satchel slung over her shoulder and her healing basket on her arm.

"I suppose I cannot dissuade you from joining us," he said, pride for his wife's stamina beaming in his smile.

"Your observation is keen and allows us not to waste time," Aliss said with a glance to the foreboding sky. "I would say we have little time before the storm hits."

"Are you certain you do not wish to remain with the women and children and follow once the path is cleared? Our pace will be quick."

"Then you will keep match with mine."

The men around her laughed and Rogan signaled to begin the journey, with Aliss and he trailing behind several of the men whose swords swiftly saw to opening a pathway.

"You will tell me if you grow tired."

"Is the village that far inland?"

"No, but your cheeks have yet to regain their color."

"Do not worry," she said. "I have land beneath me now." With that, she picked up her pace and Rogan followed.

The village was not far, no more than a twenty-minute walk once they entered the woods. The woods had reclaimed remnants of a path over time. The men cut away brush and branches and any debris that would hamper the people, carts, and animals that would make their way to their new home.

Decay had claimed several of the cottages and part of the keep, but it was the lush meadow on the outskirts of the village and the fields that meandered around the cottages and the bright green hill the keep sat upon that stole the breath.

It looked as if the fairies had laid claim to it and blessed it with beauty and grace. Even on this cloudy day, the place looked as if it radiated welcome and Rogan knew, *felt*, that he had finally come home.

"Get the clansmen moving," he ordered. "I want everyone sheltered and provided with food before the storm hits." He looked to Aliss. "We need to see to the condition of the keep. Most will probably rest there tonight."

To their surprise, the keep had decayed little. The massive wooden door needed its hinges repaired and the rooms required intense cleaning. The furniture needed repairs and the kitchen required at least several days' worth of heavy work.

Aliss shivered. "I think we should get fires started."

Rogan went to her and touched her blouse. "You need to shed these damp garments." He took her hand. "Come let us find a suitable bed-chamber. I will get a fire going in the hearth and you can change into dry clothes."

They found an impressive one that connected with a smaller one. It held a large bed and four thick, tall posts anchored each corner. The head-board's design had been scorched into the wood in an intricate pattern. The mattress needed stuffing and was devoid of bed linens, and a lone chair, its arm broken, sat next to the cold fireplace.

"Stand over by the bed," Rogan ordered, and after Aliss moved away, he picked the chair up and smashed it to pieces against the floor. He then used the splintered wood to start a fire in the hearth.

He turned as Aliss slipped out of her skirt, having already discarded her blouse. Her body shivered as she attempted to slip on dry clothes. Rogan hurried to her side and helped her dress, then he took her over by the fire and, standing behind her, he vigorously rubbed her arms and shoulders with his hands to warm her.

He tried not to think of her as she had stood there naked in nothing but her sandals, but the vision refused to leave his mind. Her nipples had puckered from the dampness and her breasts sat round and firm.

Damn, but he wanted to suckle the rosy buds and run his hands over the gooseflesh that had popped out all over her. And where she kept her legs tight together, he would tease with his fingers, or better, with his lips. Then he would—

Rogan silently cursed himself.

How the hell he would make it through six months without making love to her, he did not know. What other choice did he have? He had given his word.

That did not mean he couldn't tempt her every chance he got. Was that fair to her?

Anything was fair if he did not want to lose her.

He hugged her back against him and rubbed her midriff, his fingertips brushing beneath her breasts. "Warm enough?"

She eased away from him. "Much better, thank you. We better see to lighting other fires and I will start with cleaning up the great hall so that there will be a place to eat and sleep for everyone."

He nodded and kept his smile at bay. "Good idea."

His smile broke free after she rushed from the room. His touch had affected her, as he knew it would. He would be patient and seduce his wife slowly while making certain she knew he loved her with all his heart.

The rain began just as the last cart was rolled into the village. The women had joined with Aliss in cleaning the hall, scrubbing the tables and floor and cleaning the hearth before a new fire was lit.

Two cauldrons were hung from hooks over the flames and soon the scent of rabbit stew permeated the air. Chatter and laughter resonated in the room along with the squeals of playing children.

Aliss took a moment to watch the joyous scene from the shadowed corner. These people of varied origins had worked their way into her heart in a very short time. They were family to her and she was proud to be part of them.

"Hiding?"

Aliss jumped, startled by her husband's silent approach and his arms slipping around her waist. "Admiring," she said, and stepped to the side out of his embrace. "Don't you agree?"

He was smiling as he drifted out of the shadows. "Definitely."

"Come," he said, holding his hand out to her. "It is time to address the clan."

"You do not need me for that."

"You are my wife. They expect it."

She wanted to argue that they all knew of the bargain between their chieftain and her so why bother to pretend otherwise. But then this was a joyous occasion and she did not wish to ruin it for anyone, not even herself.

She took his hand.

"Clansmen!" Rogan yelled as they walked out of the shadows.

The room broke into a resounding cheer.

A tankard of ale was shoved into Rogan's hand and one into Aliss's hand.

Rogan raised his tankard. "To the new and *permanent* home of the Wolf clan."

Cheers, hollers, and whistles sounded for several minutes.

Rogan raised his tankard again and all turned quiet. "To peace with our neighbors."

More cheers and whistles.

A tankard went up in the crowd and all turned as Ivan stepped forward.

"In honor of our chieftain and his wife, without whose courage, strengths, and skills we would not be here."

The cheers were deafening, the foot-stomping made the rafters shake, and tears filled the women's and old men's eyes.

"Time to celebrate," Rogan cried out above the roar.

Soon everyone was enjoying the delicious hot stew and fresh bread.

Thunder roared, lightning split the sky, and the rain poured down, but no one cared. They were safe and happy.

The celebration ended early, everyone exhausted from the day's journey and everyone excited about starting their new lives tomorrow. Rogan would decide who got which cottage; the clansmen were confident that their leader knew them well enough to make wise choices. Land needed clearing and planting; though it was late they could get at least one crop in and harvested in time to see them through the winter.

All of it, however, would be a labor of love so it was with grateful hearts the Wolf clan sought their makeshift beds and the keep finally turned silent, the only sound the fire crackling in the hearth.

Aliss had changed into her night shift and stood by the window watching the rain.

"Come to bed. It has been a long day," Rogan said.

She turned. Her husband lay naked beneath the fresh bed linens she had dressed the bed with. The soft green wool blanket rested just below his waist and he held his hand out to her.

She had tried to stop admiring his nakedness, but it was no use. She enjoyed seeing him nude, his body ever so appealing to her eyes and her senses. And she feared if she climbed in bed with him at this moment, she would attack him and demand he make love to her.

Tired as she was, she still wanted him. It made no sense but there it was and she refused to surrender to her traitorous feelings. She had to remain aware of his betrayal. How he ever thought to convince her that his love for her was real, she didn't know.

"I am enjoying the rain." She hugged herself.

"You are cold."

"No!" she shouted as he threw the covers back. "I am fine, stay where you are."

Had she heard a laugh? She was not certain.

"Go to sleep," she ordered. "I will be to bed soon."

"Do not be long. I miss you."

Aliss was glad when he blew out the candle on the small table beside the bed. The only light now was from the fire in the hearth, which granted her a modicum of solitude in her dark little niche at the window.

She stared out at the dark night, letting the steady pounding of the rain fill her mind. No thoughts, no wishes, no wondering what tomorrow would bring, just here and now with the rain.

She took a deep breath, when suddenly she thought she saw a greenish glow. She squinted, searching the darkness again.

Aliss strained her eyes some more, gasped and made a dash for the bed. She jumped in, pulling the covers nearly over her head and pressing her body against her husband.

He turned and draped an arm over her, his light snores telling her he was sound asleep. She did not care as long as he was there beside her.

She tried to close her eyes, but she popped them open as soon as they closed. She continued in that fashion until finally sleep claimed her and filled her dreams with two blazing green eyes staring at her from the woods.

Chapter 24

Aliss had been thrilled to find the remnants of a garden just outside the cottage. Wild onions grew between the weeds and she had even found fairy ring mushrooms. Of course, she would leave them undisturbed, not wanting to upset the wee forest people.

After the heavy rain, she intended to give the rich soil another day to dry. Besides, there was much to keep her busy.

The kitchen in the keep was being cleaned by a bevy of women. All would make use of it until the cottages could be fully repaired and their hearths made ready for cooking.

Aliss along with Anna located a cottage suitable to serve her healing needs and set to cleaning it. Presently, she used a corner in the great hall to see to minor ills and injuries.

She and Anna had been working since early morning at cleaning out the place and had taken a rest to enjoy the food the women had brought to them from the kitchen. A long bench in the shade of the front yard served as their table and chairs.

"It is beautiful here," Anna said, taking a deep breath of the warm fresh air.

"It is heaven on earth," Aliss said and watched Anna nibble at her food. Something was on her mind. She only nibbled when she needed to express her thoughts.

"What troubles you in this paradise?" Aliss asked.

Anna knitted her brow, chewed her lip, until Aliss wanted to pull the words from her mouth. Instead, she encouraged her to voice her concerns.

"Share with me what troubles you."

Anna's head went up and her shoulders pulled back as if a weight had been lifted off them, and words rushed forth. "Many of us worry we will need to leave here."

"Why?"

"Rogan will leave in the allotted time if you and he do not mend the rift between you."

"No one need leave with Rogan. The isle belongs to us all."

Anna shook her head. "Do not misunderstand me, Aliss. The clan cares for you. You are one of us, and we do not want to lose you either. We all believe you and Rogan love each other and that is what we hope you will consider. But we would never abandon our chieftain. He has seen us through many difficult times."

Aliss had known there would be talk and she had not doubted the clan would take their leader's side. He had, after all, saved them from a ravaging illness and had found a new home for them. Unfortunately, she had been the key to achieving his goals. Did they not care at all about her feelings?

She barely touched what remained of her food and wished she could spend the rest of the afternoon cleaning out the cottage alone. She had thought herself a part of them and yet they sided with their chieftain. She really was foolish.

She had been duped by everyone, even herself. She should have been more vigilant. She had been too busy dealing with the ill. Rogan probably had counted on her deep involvement in keeping her from seeing the truth. She had been cautious at first with Rogan, even wondering if this isle had anything to do with her abduction. Then she had grown absorbed with treating the ill and finding the cause of the sickness and Rogan had been so kind, attentive, and helpful . . .

Damn, she had fallen easily into his trap.

Aliss was relieved when John came to fetch Anna, and Aliss insisted she go with her husband. Finally, she had the solitude she craved. Rogan did what was best for his clan and would he not continue to do so? She was merely a pawn in this game and she would do well to remember that.

"Are you all right?"

Startled, Aliss bumped into the edge of the table and shot her husband a surprised look, though it changed quickly enough to one of concern when she saw a bloody cloth wrapped around his hand.

"What happened?" she asked, rushing over to him.

"You answer me first."

She looked perplexed.

"Are you all right?" he repeated.

"Of course I am," she said, annoyed that he knew she was upset. She reached for his wounded hand.

He yanked it away. "I called to you twice from the doorway and you did not hear me."

"Are you going to give me your hand or bleed all over my clean floor?" she snapped and held out her hand.

He placed his hand in hers. "I am as concerned for you."

"Don't be."

"You are never curt when treating someone. Something is wrong. What is it?"

"None of your concern," she said and removed the cloth, resting his hand on it.

Her eyes spread wide. "This is a knife wound. How did you get it?"

"Tell me what troubles you and I will tell you about the wound," he bargained.

"No," she said, and shoved him to the table. "Sit."

She went to work as soon as he sat. She cleansed the wound, which she was relieved to see was not deep. More of a surface cut that had bled out and would now heal with proper attention.

"Your gentle touch belies your anger."

"I am not angry," she snapped, and almost winced at her own biting tone.

"Did someone upset you?"

"I need to concentrate. No more questions," she ordered, and to her relief he remained silent.

She spread a generous amount of salve on the wound then bandaged it with a strip of white cloth, tying a secure knot to hold it in place.

"Keep it dry and clean," she said, and turned only to be spun back around and drawn between his spread legs to rest close to him.

His hands held her hips firmly, letting her know he did not intend to release her. She thought otherwise and wiggled to free herself of his grasp.

"Stay put!"

His demand surprised her. It was not like him to command her. He had always been respectful and considerate with her, but then she had always granted him the same courtesy.

"I want to know what troubles you."

"Why?"

His brow wrinkled. "You are my wife and I—"

She yanked herself free and moved away from him. "We are no longer truly husband and wife."

She took a step back when he stood, the

strength of him filling the room, his sleek movements reminding her of a wolf that prowled his territory.

"I disagree."

Even his voice resembled a low growl.

She placed her hand on the rough wood mantel for support. "You deceived me. Now you expect me to trust that you speak the truth about your love for me?"

He marched over to her, grabbed a finger and placed her hand to his chest. "Feel my love for you. Know that my heart beats wildly when I see you and when you are out of my sight too long I miss you."

Aliss dismissed the heavy beat beneath her hand. Surely, it was her imagination.

"I love when I wake before you in the morning and feel your warm body snuggled next to mine. I love holding you, hearing you breathe, watching you sleep, waiting for your eyes to flutter open and for you to smile. You always smile when you wake and look at me."

How could she deny her own similar feelings? She felt safe and comfortable in his arms as if she belonged in them. And she couldn't deny the smile that came so easily to her lips when she woke to see his face.

That she loved him was obvious, but she could not reconcile his betrayal. It tore at her heart.

She shook her head. "I do not wish to discuss this."

"I do."

"We don't always get what we want."

"No, we don't," he said. "Sometimes we have to take it."

"Such as this isle that is more important to you than I am?"

He turned his head and stepped away from her.

She reached out and grabbed his arm. "Deny it."

"I will relinquish the land according to our bargain. Does that not answer your question?"

"Do you really expect me to believe you will keep your part of the bargain?"

He took hold of her wrist, yanking her hand off his arm. "Are you too afraid to give me a fair chance to prove my love for you?"

He didn't wait for an answer. He walked out.

Aliss threw the cloth down on the table and squeezed her head with her hands. She wasn't afraid. She was strong. It had taken all her strength to agree to his bargain and remain with him. Didn't he realize how badly he had hurt her? Didn't he know how much she loved him and wished that he truly loved her? Didn't he know how frightened she was he would betray her again?

He had played her for a fool once. She could not allow him to do the same again. She would remain strong.

She plopped down on a chair, fighting tears.

Aliss turned at the sound of sniffles.

"I fell," said five-year-old Joseph and held out his scratched and bleeding arm.

Aliss went to him, bending down to his short height and gently taking hold of his skinny arm.

"It hurts." Joseph wiped his nose on the sleeve of his free arm.

"It doesn't look bad. I think we can fix it," she assured him.

"It won't hurt, will it?"

"It may sting a little."

Joseph shook his head and took a step back. "Like a bee?"

"No, no, nothing like a bee sting."

Joseph stopped, wiped at his nose again then stepped forward. "Okay, fix it."

Aliss talked with Joseph as she cleansed the abrasion and gently rubbed salve on it. In no time, she had him giggling and laughing and forgetting all about his injury.

Before he left, he looked around the cottage then called her to him with a crook of his little finger.

Aliss went to where he stood by the open door and bent down.

"I am glad you have magic hands," he whispered.

"Magic hands?"

He nodded. "Everybody says so and I'm sure glad you're our healer. You'll always be with us, right?"

"Why do you ask that?"

He shrugged. "I heard some people say you might leave us."

"Aliss is not going anywhere, Joseph."

Joseph smiled and giggled as he was scooped up in Rogan's arms. Rogan then placed him back on the ground and ordered him to go play and have fun. He turned to Aliss and said, "You are needed in the kitchen. There has been an accident."

She retrieved her basket. "The choice is mine whether I go or stay."

Rogan snatched the basket out of her hands. "I'm confident that I can convince you to stay."

They hurried to the kitchen, Aliss aware that her heart beat much too fast for her hurried pace and aware that she would need to remain vigilant this time. She might be the Wolf's prey but this time she wouldn't be caught.

A deep cut that refused to stop bleeding had everyone frantic and the injured young woman crying in fear of losing her arm.

Anna showed up shortly after Aliss, and while they worked on Teresa, Rogan calmed everyone down and herded them outside to wait.

The wound would require several stitches and there was fever to worry about, but Aliss was sure that Teresa would be fine and continued to tell the young woman so.

What concerned her more was Anna's pale complexion. It had started when Aliss had begun to tend the wound and had grown worse by the minute.

"Are you all right?" Aliss asked, as she prepared the arm for stitching.

"My stomach is upset."

"Something you ate?"

Anna shook her head. "I don't know. I have been feeling this way since traveling on the ship."

Aliss frowned. "It cannot still be seasickness."

"The illness has not returned, has it?" Teresa asked anxiously.

"No," Aliss assured her. "We got rid of that for good."

The young girl sighed with relief then smiled. "Perhaps you are with babe."

Anna's hand rushed to her stomach. "I never thought of that."

Aliss smiled. "Could it be so?"

Anna laughed with glee. "Yes. Yes, it could be so. Actually, now that I think about it, it most definitely could be so."

"How wonderful!" Teresa said. "You will have the first babe to be born in our new home."

Chapter 25

❧━━━∽◯◯∽━━━❧

Rogan sat under the shade of a large oak tree watching his wife chat with two other women. Once they had learned that Anna was with child it was all the entire village could talk about.

Two days later and the gossip continued; most claimed the impending birth was a blessing from heaven, a sign that assured them this was the perfect place to settle and call home.

Kendra and he had hoped for a slew of children, since both were only children while most families had more than they could feed. Fate, however, had different plans for them, but Kendra wanted him happy and, before she died, had insisted that he find love again.

She had taught him how unselfish true love

was and only recently had he begun to realize the wisdom of her legacy.

"Admiring your wife from afar?" Derek asked, joining him under the shade of the tree.

"She is a beauty," Rogan said with a smile.

"You are a lucky man."

"So you're the one who was elected to speak with me?"

Derek looked affronted.

"Do not bother to deny it. I know the clan has gotten together with the intention of trying to keep Aliss and me together."

"Good, then I can speak my mind."

Rogan coughed though it sounded like a laugh.

"All right, so I always speak my mind," Derek said. "You are an idiot."

Rogan grabbed his shoulder. "That was a hit."

"It is your heart that is going to suffer the damage."

"It already has," Rogan admitted reluctantly.

"Then do something."

"I intend to."

"The clan is content here and—" Derek shook his head. "You do?"

"A plan has bubbled and stewed in my head since we've landed here."

Derek rubbed his hands together. "Has it finished brewing?"

"Just about."

"Tell me," Derek urged in a whisper.

"No!"

Derek fell back, affronted. "Why not?"

"Because you will tell another then he will tell another and another until—" He threw his hands up. "It will be common knowledge to the whole clan."

"You accuse me of gossiping?"

"I most certainly do," Rogan said with a laugh.

"At least you intend to take care of it or else I would have to—" Derek smiled and shook a fist at him.

"Is that a threat?" Rogan asked.

"You threaten your chieftain, Derek?"

Derek spun around and Rogan jumped to his feet. Neither man had heard Aliss approach.

"He needs it now and again." Derek grinned.

"Perhaps he does," Aliss said.

"A woman who knows her husband. You would do well to remember that, Rogan." Derek grinned again and with a nod bade them good day.

"Why do you rub your shoulder?" Aliss asked as Derek drifted off.

"Is that what brought you over here? Concern for my shoulder?"

"Is something wrong with it?"

He thought to lie but then that was what had got him into this mess in the first place. He was better off with the truth.

"No. There is nothing wrong with it."

She turned to go as he expected she would. He reached out and took hold of her hand. "Sit with me for a moment."

"I have work to do."

He tugged her gently under the tree. "Just for a moment."

Aliss obliged reluctantly.

They settled in the shade of the towering oak in tense silence. Rogan knew she would jump up any second and be off. He knew she was afraid to open her heart to him again. After all, he had damaged it once; why would she take another chance? So he intended to court her, treat her extra special, and let her know how very much he admired, respected, and loved her. He would do anything and everything to repair the damage to her heart and help her to love again.

"It is wonderful news about Anna and John."

She beamed with delight. "I couldn't be happier for them."

"It is always good when another babe joins the clan."

"A birth is a joy everyone can share in."

"And this birth has the distinction of being the first in our new home," he said, holding her glance with his. "Or is there a chance that you could be first?" He had to know. Ever since he had heard of Anna, he had wondered if Aliss was with child. Surely, she would know by now.

Her silence made him even more curious. "Is there something you want to tell me?"

"There is nothing for me to tell you."

"While I am sorry to hear that, I am also relieved," Rogan rushed to explain, seeing her startled expression. "I am eager for you to have my child, for I have no doubt you will be an excellent mother. First, however, I want to make certain you are secure with my love and know that you are my life, my breath, my being. Then I will get you with child."

Aliss stared at him speechless then simply turned and walked away.

He watched her go and knew that there was no way he could watch her walk out of his life. His heart already ached from the distance that had been forged between them even though every night she slept in his arms.

His plan was set and placed into action. He would advance forward as an army of one and conquer her. He jumped to his feet, gave a quick look around, and spied what he wanted. He gave it a swift pluck and followed Aliss until he caught up with her. There in front of the cottage where she did her healing, he attempted to begin to heal her heart.

"For you."

Aliss turned around.

He held out a yellow wildflower and cringed when he saw that in his rush he had yanked out root and all.

She smiled, laughed, and took it from him. "Thank you."

That she was gracious in accepting his mistake made his heart soar even more with love for her and he stepped forward. "One kiss," he murmured. "I have missed kissing you. Just one—please?"

She looked from him to the flower then to him again and with a tender smile stepped close and kissed his cheek then stepped away.

"I had more than that in mind."

"You asked for a kiss and I gave it. You gave me a flower and I accepted it."

She was right. She had accepted his gift freely and gladly, root and all. He owed her the same.

"No root next time."

"No cheek next time."

She entered her cottage sniffing the flower, her green eyes sparkling, and Rogan smiled as he turned and walked away.

The night brought with it a thunderstorm and a fever to Teresa.

Rogan knew his wife would remain by Teresa's side until the fever no longer threatened her. Anna would not be there to assist; Aliss had insisted it was not necessary.

He brought supper to his wife but she was too busy to eat. She gently cooled the young woman's body with wet cloths while assuring her in a soft voice that she would be all right, and she meant it.

Rogan had watched her carefully when he had first brought her to his clan. He had heard of her unique healing abilities, but he had not been certain if they were tale or truth. Her talent seemed almost too mythical to be true, but he had learned differently.

He had learned that she possessed the heart and touch of an angel and the determination and strength of a warrior. Her presence alone had the capability of bringing relief to the ailing. Even now as the young woman's fever raged, Teresa lay calmly in bed, relaxed by Aliss's tender touch.

There was no point in disturbing the two, so he took his leave quietly, hoping Aliss would find time to eat when Teresa slept.

He returned to the keep and spoke with the few men and women in the great hall whose cottages were not yet ready for occupancy. Then as the night grew late he made his way to his bedchamber and climbed into an empty bed.

He lay there thinking of Aliss as he did most of the day. She forever invaded his thoughts, and without her here beside him she continued to haunt his mind. He forced his eyes closed and before long they drifted open and he found himself staring wide-eyed at the ceiling.

A strange thought came to him. He would spend many nights here staring at the ceiling and it would be a good idea to have it painted with an interesting scene. Then he would have something to gaze at while waiting for his wife's return.

He laughed to himself. He was planning a future with Aliss and it felt so very right. He turned on his side and looked at the pillow where Aliss rested her head. In a very short time, he had grown accustomed to having her there beside him. He would not want to sleep without her and would not want to wake without her there.

He threw off the blanket, pulled on his shirt, his plaid, and his sandals, and hurried out of the room. He would go to Aliss and wait for her no matter how long it took.

Rogan entered the cottage quietly though Aliss turned her head and acknowledged him with a nod as he closed the door. He took a seat in a wooden chair near the fireplace and settled in to wait for his wife.

He was snoring in no time.

Aliss heard the familiar sound and smiled as she bathed Teresa's forehead with a cool cloth. The fever lingered though it raged no more and she was certain that in a couple of hours it would be gone completely.

She dipped the cloth in the bowl of water to rinse the heat from it and caught the sight of her husband, legs stretched out, arms folded across his chest and his head lolled to the side, sound asleep.

She smiled as she recalled his earlier gift. In his haste to offer her a token to prove his love, he had plucked a flower out by the roots. His thoughtfulness had touched her heart and the exposed roots made her think of their own love that had been carelessly uprooted and discarded without care.

Should she give him a chance in his quest to prove his love? Or was he simply doing it to keep what meant more to him—the isle.

Aliss returned her attention to Teresa. Finally, three hours before dawn, her fever vanished and she rested comfortably.

Anna's entrance stirred Rogan awake but did not surprise Aliss. She knew her helper would arrive early to relieve her even though she had insisted Anna's help was not necessary.

"I could not sleep any longer," Anna said once at Aliss's side. "How is Teresa?"

"The fever is finally gone and she sleeps."

"Then I will stay with her while you go sleep yourself."

Aliss did not argue. She was tired. She stood and stretched and winced at the ache in her neck and shoulders.

Her husband's strong hands were suddenly there massaging the sore muscles.

"Let's go home to bed so that I can tend your aches," he whispered.

He eased her into the crook of his arm and she went willingly, her tense muscles insisting she capitulate and her body warning her she was headed for trouble. Even worn out from the long night, she felt the flutter of passion beginning to stir. It always did when he touched her.

They walked in silence to the keep and up to their bedchamber.

She changed into her night shift and slipped into bed beside him, thinking she should tell him she was tired and wanted to sleep.

But as soon as she stretched out, he gently turned her on her stomach, straddled her hips, and went to work on her sore neck and shoulder muscles. His fingers worked magic, kneading, squeezing, forcing her aches away, and she did not protest.

She let him have his way.

His thumbs worked in circles at the base of her neck and she moaned from the relief he brought her. He expanded to her shoulders, urging the taut muscles to relax with strong manipulation. They surrendered one by one and he moved down her back, attacking every tight muscle he discovered.

His hips swayed along with his movements and she found her passion stirring little by little as he eased himself down over her bottom, his hands massaging up and down her spine.

He nestled between her legs fully aroused and yet he made not a move to make love to her. He simply continued massaging her with his powerful hands until her body was completely limp and pliable and thoroughly aroused.

She was ready for him.

It would be easy once she turned over to guide him into her. She was more than moist, she was saturated with desire for him. He would claim her nipples with his mouth and send her into a fast and furious climax then bring her to climax again along with himself.

But while her body ached with desire, her heart ached for love.

He slipped off her.

She quickly turned on her side, curling her legs up, fisting her hands to her chest in an effort to protect her aching heart. Her breath caught for a moment, anticipating he would turn and wrap his arms around her.

When he didn't she relaxed enough to finally drift off to sleep, though not before a single tear slipped down from the corner of her eye.

Chapter 26

"**A**liss!"

"You sound anxious, Anna, is something wrong?" Aliss asked, stepping out of her cottage.

"You are needed on the shore."

"Let me get my basket."

"No, you must hurry," Anna said, shoving her away from the cottage door. "I will bring your basket to you."

Aliss turned and wound her way through the woods, her pace swift. A scenario of possible accidents played in her mind while doubts nudged their way in. The more thought she gave to it, the more she felt she had been duped.

Anna normally would have followed her, healing basket in hand. But she had all but chased her away from the cottage.

Curiosity kept her going, and once out of the woods and onto the shore she stopped short.

Rogan paced beside a blanket spread out a few feet from the water's edge. A basket overflowed with bread and cheese, goblets and a small cask of wine, and colorful wildflowers minus their roots lay mingled among them.

He stopped once he caught sight of her and waved her to him with a smile.

A tickle of delight stirred her heart. He had prepared a secret rendezvous for them and she eagerly joined him.

He held his hand out to her and helped her to sit. "The last few days have been busy for us both and I haven't gotten to spend time with you. I thought I should remedy that."

That he made the time for her, even though there was so much to be done, pleased her. Of course, there was that little voice, possibly Fiona's, reminding her that his actions were all a ruse to make her believe he loved her.

But a bargain was a bargain. He had six months to prove his love, and at this rate, there might be a good chance he would be victorious.

Again, she heard her sister's warning ring clear in her head. Ultimately, however, the choice remained hers.

He poured them wine and she stretched her legs out in front of her and drank not only the wine but the beauty of the sea rolling lazily onto

shore. The sky could not have been any brighter, •
the water any bluer, the sun any brighter, and the
feeling of peace any more profound in her heart.
This was a perfect day, a perfect setting, and she
intended to enjoy it.

"I am glad you whisked me away," she said.

"We both needed it. I miss being with you and
you alone."

"You attempt to woo me?"

"Is it working?"

She laughed. "A wolf that woos."

"I can howl." He grinned and she blushed.

They feasted on bread, cheese, wine, and conversation.

He impressed her with his attentiveness and
his leisurely nature. He was not in a hurry to end
their interlude. On the contrary, he seemed to
want the afternoon to lazily roll by.

She saw no reason to object. It gave her the opportunity to discover if her husband's motive
was sincere—to prove his love for her.

"I should alert you that Giann is in the area,"
he said.

"Is she? Why?"

"She feels safe with the clan and goes where
we go. She has helped us several times. She actually was the one who advised me that you would
heal my people."

Her mouth fell open. "You never told me that."

Rogan placed his goblet aside and reached for
her hand.

She snatched it away.

"I want to be honest with you—"

"That would be a change. You told me you had heard of my skills as a healer."

"From Giann."

Her eyes suddenly rounded. "Did you also know of the prophecy?"

"I learned of it only recently."

"How recently?"

"After we wed," he said adamantly.

"You spoke with Giann after we wed? Why?"

"Is that a cloud in the distance?" he asked, shading his eyes from the blazing sun.

"There is not a cloud in the sky and even if a thunderstorm burst overhead we would remain here until you answered me."

He reluctantly obliged her. "I wanted to know if you were my destiny."

"Her answer?"

"She told me that your destiny was written before your birth."

"I want to speak with her."

"You already have," he said.

Her brow knitted. "I have never spoken with her."

"The day we found you in the forest. Giann had summoned you."

Aliss jumped to her feet. "I have had enough of this woman's interference in my life. Her prediction has caused my sister and me nothing but grief since we were born."

"What happened at your birth?"

"Giann arranged for our abduction."

"She must have had a good reason," he said.

"You defend her?"

"She sees the future with an accuracy that astonishes me. Therefore, she must have seen danger for you and your sister."

"So we were told. We were kept safe until the prophecy could be fulfilled, averting the destruction of the clans."

"That was all of it?"

"As far as I know. That is why I want to speak with her, to once and for all settle this nonsense."

"Careful, Aliss," he warned. "Giann is a powerful woman whom you don't wish to offend."

"She has offended me and she owes me answers and I will have them," she insisted. "Where do I find her?"

"She will find you."

"She had best do that or I will make certain I find her."

Aliss made certain to scan the edge of the woods that surrounded the village for the next few days. She looked for the green glow that had frightened her on more than one occasion. Thus far, she had seen nothing, but she would not forsake her vigil. She would keep at it until she finally met with Giann.

It seemed that the truth was beginning to reveal itself, starting with Giann. Now it was time she finally addressed the issue of this isle. It had been a thorn in the side for both her brother Raynor and brother-in-law Tarr, though it was never clearly explained why.

Her impression had been that the abandoned

isle lay unclaimed until Raynor and Tarr came along. Why the interest in it, she did not know. It certainly wasn't a strategic piece of land. The only other possibility was that it actually belonged to one of the clans. If so, why leave it vacant all these years?

Aliss walked through the village in the early afternoon looking for Rogan. She hoped to ask him about the isle. She found him helping to raise freshly cut timbers for the walls of the storehouse.

Her eyes rested on his bare chest, where droplets of perspiration clung to him and glistened in the sun. He was a fine specimen of a man. His muscled arms strained under the weight of the split log he carried with another man. His leg muscles also showed the strain of the tremendous weight but he kept his pace and in no time had the log deposited in place.

He snatched his shirt off the ground and used it to wipe the sweat from his face then drank greedily from the bucket of water provided for the men. He was a chieftain, but when he worked with his clansmen he was one of them. You could see the pride on their faces when they glanced at their leader, and suddenly she also felt pride for her husband.

He was a good man. She had acknowledged that often enough. If only she could reconcile his betrayal; it was not an easy adjustment. The hurt over his deception would rear its ugly head when least expected. Just when she thought she had gotten past the pain, because of his endless and thoughtful attempts to reconcile them, there it was, stabbing at her again. Would she ever get over the hurt?

She took a breath. Was she marching forward into the enemy camp? Or did she march into the arms of love?

"You search for me?" Rogan asked with a smile.

"I thought a stroll might do us good, though you might prefer a spot under a shady tree."

"Do you mind?"

"Not at all."

They made their way to a favorite spot under the large oak tree. Aliss crossed her legs beneath the deep blue skirt she wore and left the ties of her tan blouse open, needing a reprieve from the heat of the day.

"Everyone prospers here," she said. "It is a good place."

Rogan nodded and wiped again at his perspiring brow with his shirt. "That it is. It will provide abundantly for the clan."

"How did you come to know the beauty and bounty of this land?"

Silence greeted her query but she waited with patience.

"My father brought me here as a lad."

"He was familiar with the isle?"

"He knew the area well, because he was always searching for land that would provide adequately for his clan."

A solid answer she could not dispute. Why

then did she believe there was more to what he told her?

She decided bluntness was the best course of attack. "Is that why you wanted the land? Because your father made you familiar with it?"

"It is a good piece of land."

"That doesn't answer my question."

"Why the curiosity?" he asked.

"I want to know the reason why you ransomed me for this land."

"You weren't curious before when I once intended to explain."

"I am now," she said.

He stood. "It doesn't matter anymore."

"It does to me," she said, jumping up.

He grabbed her chin. "What should matter to you is how much I love you."

He kissed her then, hard and quick, a surprise attack that stunned and left her speechless. And with the desire to taste more of him. Why did she continue to desire him when she felt so betrayed? She should have more sense than that and keep her mind focused.

She watched him walk away, shirt in hand, the sweat on his back glistening in the sun, and admired his narrow waist and the confidence of his gait. Her fingers drifted to her pulsating lips and his kiss. It had left her—

"Damn," she whispered. He had never answered her question.

Chapter 27

Aliss woke to the forlorn wailing of a horn. Shaking off sleep, she realized that the horn announced the arrival of a ship. She jumped out of bed and dressed quickly in a blue skirt and white blouse. She twisted her red hair into a knot and fastened it to the back of her head with two bone combs. Loose strands broke free at her neck as she rushed from the room, slipping on her sandals as she went.

Was it friend or foe arriving?

She had mentioned to Fiona that she preferred to have no visits from family for at least a couple of weeks. And since she had lost track of time, she imagined it had been that or possibly more since the Wolf clan had arrived on the Isle of Non.

Aliss looked around in search of her husband. Not finding him in the great hall, she hurried outside where several women were herding the children together.

"Are we in danger of attack?" she asked Tara, who balanced a smiling Daniel on her hip.

"No, we gather the children to see the arriving ship."

"Who visits?" Aliss asked with relief.

"We think your family, since it is the ship that brought your sister to you."

Aliss was not certain how she felt about her family's arrival. She had wanted to handle this matter on her own. She had struck a bargain with Rogan, and it was between them. She needed no interference from anyone.

She marched through the woods, almost ready to tell whoever had arrived to turn around and go home. She exited the woods determined to do so, but then she saw her brother Raynor, so handsome, tall, and proud standing on the shore speaking with Rogan.

She recalled how serendipitous their first meeting had been. Then, she had not known he was her brother or that he searched for his twin sisters. She had healed him back to health after he had temporarily lost his sight during a battle with Tarr and his men.

Through his efforts everyone had been reunited and enemies had become friends. He was a good man and she had missed him.

Once past the rocky terrain, she ran full speed while yelling out his name.

He grinned wide and threw his arms out to welcome her.

He picked her up and swung her around before they hugged.

"I have missed you, Aliss," Raynor said.

"And I you, brother." She looked past his shoulder. "Who else has come with you?"

"No one."

She wrinkled her brow. "Fiona? Mother?"

"They both would have joined me if—"

"Fiona is all right?"

"She is fine, just very large and very cranky. Mother is at her beck and call and refuses to leave her side, and—"

"You ran away," Aliss said, laughing.

Raynor grabbed her hand. "I had to, please forgive me. Fiona told me you wanted no visits for a while but it has been so long, and I was so desperate. Don't make me go back, I beg you."

Aliss laughed at her brother's pleading. "They do not know you came here?"

"Tarr and Father do and they wished, nay they prayed, I would take them with me."

"Just wait until you return," she said, her laughter bubbling over.

"I was hoping I could stay a while, quite a while, perhaps until Fiona delivers the baby?"

"I will be going to deliver her babe."

Raynor nodded. "And if I return with you, she will ignore me—"

"And the fact that you ran away?"

"Exactly."

"You are welcome to stay," she said. She noticed that Raynor looked past her, glaring. She turned to see Rogan watching them from only a few feet away. He looked ever the wolf warrior, his own hair a mane of light and dark, his eyes blazing, his lips more of a snarl than a smile and his stance territorial.

She looked from one man to the other. "Is there a problem between the two of you?" Though a good four feet separated them, she moved to stand between them, prepared for a confrontation.

"Ask your brother," Rogan nearly growled.

"I make no bones about my anger at you for abducting my sister and the consequences that followed. But like Tarr, I respect my sister's decision regarding your bargain, and I will be respectful of her husband—since he will not be around long."

"A matter that does not concern you," Rogan informed him, stepping closer.

"If it concerns my sister it concerns me." Raynor also advanced, his hands fisting at his sides.

Aliss stretched out her arms. "Enough." She turned to Raynor. "This matter is between Rogan and me. I will tolerate no interference. Is that clear enough for you?"

He nodded reluctantly.

She then turned to Rogan. "I expect my brother to be welcomed in *our* home."

Rogan answered with a sharp nod.

"Good, it is settled," she said, though she doubted her own words. The two men obviously were far from being friendly. It didn't seem likely now that she would be able to enjoy her brother's visit.

"Our home," Raynor whispered to her as they walked toward the village. "I thought you planned on ridding yourself of him. Chase him off and claim this land as your own."

"Fiona's words?" she questioned.

"I should have known." Raynor shook his head. "You are twins. You're as stubborn as Fiona."

She hooked her arm in his. "Visit with me and forget about what Fiona has told you. See for yourself and tell me your opinion on the matter. I welcome your opinion. It would mean much to me."

"Maybe you're not as stubborn as Fiona," he said. "I surely have missed you and have thought often of the great lengths you went to, to save my life. You have no idea how you made a very difficult time bearable for me. I want to be there for you as you once were for me. Anything you need, Aliss, just ask."

A table was set outside, the weather far too beautiful for them to stay indoors. Platters and tankards filled with drink and food were placed before the three.

"This land is bountiful and more beautiful than I recall," Raynor said, glancing around with curiosity and awe.

"If I remember correctly, you and Tarr had a dispute over this land," Aliss said, hoping to discover as much as she could about the isle.

"We did."

"Who actually owned the land?" she asked, eager to continue her investigation.

"That is debatable," Raynor said.

"Not really," Rogan corrected. "The land rightfully belongs to me, inherited from my parents."

Aliss almost choked on her wine. Rogan had told her of his father bringing him here as a young lad, but never had he said it was an inheritance. Why had he not confided in her?

"Tarr would object to your claim since the isle belonged to his mother's family," Raynor informed him.

"Then why did you lay claim to it?" Rogan challenged.

"I was told that the land would unite two important clans and bring peace to the area for years to come. I hoped to be one of those clans."

"Who told you that?" Aliss asked, more curious than ever.

Raynor shrugged. "I don't recall."

He obviously lied and Aliss wondered why. Didn't he want Rogan to know? And if so, why not? She would find out when she had the chance to speak with him alone.

"Then peace should reign now, since two important clans, Hellewyk and Wolf, have united," she said, hoping to avert a clash between the two obviously tense men.

"For now," Raynor reminded.

"Forever," Rogan corrected.

"From what Tarr tells me, you two have a bargain, and in six months you will be gone, out of my sister's life."

"But still her husband."

"What do you mean?" Raynor asked.

Aliss watched her brother grow tall in his seat, his shoulders drawn back as if he were on the defensive. She wanted no altercation between them, but her husband's remark also had her inquisitive.

"I will leave if that is Aliss's choice, but I will remain her husband until death separates us. There will be no dissolution of our vows."

Chapter 28

Dusk had settled when Raynor went to join his men, who had set up camp just outside the village.

Aliss had grown weary from the tension that had been palpable between the two men, and while she looked forward to her brother's visit, she could do without the animosity between the two.

Then there was the startling news that Rogan had claimed the isle as his rightful inheritance. She wanted to know more and waited for him to come to bed.

Her eyes were drifting shut when he finally entered their bedchamber. He was exceptionally quiet, attempting not to make a sound. Was it his intention to avoid her?

She would have none of that. As soon as he

slipped gently beneath the covers she asked, "You mentioned that you inherited this isle from your parents."

He jumped. "I thought you were asleep."

"I waited for you. Which parent had it belonged to?"

He rustled uncomfortably in the bed. "It doesn't matter. The isle is rightfully mine and will be passed on to our children."

"Until this is settled between us, you yourself felt a child would only be an interference."

He turned on his side to face her. "Don't you want a child, Aliss?"

"We made a bargain," she snapped, her own doubt annoying her. "A child would keep us together."

"I love you and I want us to spend the rest of our lives together. I want to raise a family." He rested his hand on her flat stomach. "I want to watch you round with my child. Watch our children grow, a fiery redheaded daughter with your smile and a son with my handsome face."

She couldn't help but laugh softly and her mind conjured up the picture he painted.

"I want to grow old together for I know age will never diminish your beauty. Your smile will always light my heart, your green eyes will always entice me. It couldn't be any other way. I love you that much."

His declaration warmed her heart. Someone to laugh with and someone to cry with, someone to love you through the good and the bad times.

Someone you can always count on being there for you even if you haven't done the same for him.

Rogan.

His name reverberated through her mind. He had been there for her even before they had wed. She had never had to seek his help. He offered it generously and genuinely.

"Take your time to answer. That tells me there is hope."

She had a lot to consider.

"I want to hold you, let me hold you."

Did she dare move closer to him? Would he think she forgave him?

"I love you," he said again. "And I plan on telling you that every day for the rest of our lives."

She stared at him.

"You still find it difficult to believe?"

"If you had been truthful with me from the beginning I would not have difficulty now. You told me once you loved me and I believed you with my whole heart, only to discover it was a ruse for you to benefit by."

She shook her head. "Why? Why couldn't you have told me the truth from the start?"

"I did what I thought was best."

"For whom?"

"For all."

"You were wrong," she said.

"No I wasn't. I planned for everything except—"

She waited.

He finally rolled over. He braced his body against her side and took hold of her chin, squeezing lightly. "I never planned to fall in love with you, but I thank God every day that I did."

He leaned over her, bracing his hands on the sides of her head, and lowered his mouth to hers. He brushed his lips with hers and sighed.

"Tasting you is like dusting fire with sweet wine. It fuels the flames. One kiss isn't enough, one touch isn't enough, one coupling will never do."

He made her passion soar, teasing her lips with promised kisses, never tasting deeply, only skimming the surface and causing her to ache with need for him.

She groaned and tossed her head to the side, a mistake. He nibbled along her neck, sending gooseflesh trembling over her entire body before traveling down to suckle at her nipples through the linen night shift until they were so hard they pulsed.

"Tell me to stop, Aliss."

She couldn't find the words. They refused to leave her throat.

He moved down, kissing her midriff, while working her night shift up along her body and exposing her stomach, which he nipped and nibbled on until she squirmed.

"Tell me to stop," he warned again.

"No." She breathed a heavy sigh.

"No, don't stop?"

"Damn you, Rogan."

"You don't want me inside you?"

His husky query sounded like an erotic invitation and quickly she said, "Yes." But changed it just as quickly to, "No."

His fingers found his way gently inside her. "I think you do want me."

She groaned when he flicked her tight little bud with his tongue. Then he did it again and again and again.

"Damn it, Rogan."

His finger deep inside her matched the thrust of his tongue and she thought she would go insane from her uncontrollable mounting passion.

She was lost, completely lost, and he was her only way out.

"Please," she begged.

"I do this because I love you."

He thrust his tongue inside her, and if it were not for his hands grasping her bottom firmly, she would have vaulted off the bed. He made love to her as she had never thought possible, bringing her pleasure after pleasure while ignoring his own needs.

And when he finished he took her in his arms and held her until the ripples of passion faded and she drifted into a restful slumber.

Aliss woke feeling wonderful. She stretched herself awake and smiled.

"You slept well?"

Aliss's cheeks beamed bright red as she turned to face her husband.

He smiled and got up from his chair to walk over to sit on the bed beside her.

She wanted to hide beneath the blanket, not

only recalling the intimacy of last night, but feeling herself grow wet with wanting him yet again.

"I was unfair with you last night."

She shook her head vehemently.

He nodded firmly. "Yes I was. I took advantage, knowing how you would respond when I promised the choice would be yours."

"It was mine."

"You did not initiate it. I forced the issue and you simply responded."

"But you pleased me, not yourself," she said, defending him.

"I may not have climaxed, but I took pleasure in making love to you. The choice remains yours as to when we make love."

Aliss stared at him, speechless. He had yet again proved his honor to her and she continued to think him deceitful? She should put an end to this tormenting situation right here and now. She should forgive him and love him and share her life with him. But she had yet to have all the answers. She had yet to be sure of his intentions. She had to know for sure. She could not be made to feel a fool again.

She moved to the end of the bed, holding the sheet to her chest.

"I am a patient man. I will wait."

She almost winced at the thought that he contained his own desires while seeing to hers. How unselfish of him.

Or wise.

She wanted to slap that pessimistic voice right out of her head. But it was a warning she needed to heed. She had to make certain he loved her without reservation. She wanted no doubts, no barriers in the way of their love. She wanted love pure and simple and unburdened.

She shook her head. Could that ever be?

"Is something wrong?"

"No, my thoughts just drive me crazy."

"I know what you mean."

He smiled and her heart leaped. He was such a handsome man, ruggedly handsome, the kind that makes a woman act foolishly. A fate she could attest to. Or was it her heart that actually found him more handsome than she had realized?

"Your brother grows impatient to visit with you. He insists that you usually rise with the dawn and it is already well past dawn."

She gasped. "You jest."

He laughed. "No, you slept and snored quite soundly."

"I did not," she protested.

"You did, but I will not tell anyone if you wish me not to."

"I cannot believe it. I always rise with the sun."

"Your brother's exact words. I think he thinks I keep you prisoner."

A prisoner of love. She blushed a crimson red.

He laughed, walked over and kissed her. "I love you."

She stared motionless as he shut the door behind him.

Aliss and her brother hibernated beneath the heavy branches of a large oak tree after she had finished a later-than-usual morning meal, while Raynor had enjoyed a second one.

"Rogan treats you much better than I had expected. He is considerate of you, patient with you, and sees to your needs better than you do."

"You sound disappointed," Aliss said, considering her brother's remark. Had she neglected to see the obvious?

"The Wolf has been a nemesis for some time. It isn't easy to go from considering him a foe to a friend when the past keeps rearing its ugly head."

"You think me foolish for wedding him?"

"I never thought you foolish or stubborn, those qualities belong to Fiona."

They both laughed.

"I just want to make certain the Wolf isn't using you to benefit himself."

"Which is why you think he treats me well?"

Raynor shrugged. "I cannot say for sure. I was surprised by his attentiveness toward you. But it could be a ruse to make certain he keeps this land."

"The land is his. Tarr gave it to him freely."

"It was a wedding gift to you both and for a good reason. Tarr knew neither you nor your sister would be happy living too far apart."

"He was right about that, but I'm curious. Did this land hold any special meaning for Tarr?"

"It was an inheritance from his mother's people, as far as I know. I think Tarr mentioned that his mother's father designated it to someone specific, though I don't recall who."

"It does not disturb him to see the land leave his family?"

"The land does not leave his family," Raynor said. "You became part of the Hellewyk clan when your sister wed Tarr. As far as he is concerned the isle remains part of his clan."

"The Wolf clan now being an extension of the Hellewyk clan," Aliss concluded.

"It is the way to become an unequaled force: smaller clans expanding larger ones and the chieftain's power growing when each unite. I am sure Rogan is pleased that his insignificant clan has joined with a powerful clan. After all, a chieftain's duty is to make choices that will benefit his people."

"A good reason to wed me, but then aren't many marriages arranged just for that reason?"

"The differences being that most betrothed women know that before they wed. You made a choice to wed based on lies," Raynor said. "Can you live with that?"

"The very question that haunts me."

"You have time. Do not rush it, make sure it is what you want," he said.

"What would you want, Raynor? An arranged marriage or one conceived in love?"

"I have a duty to my clan."

"Then you would wed a stranger if it was beneficial to your clan?"

"Not through lies or subterfuge."

"If it were the only way?" Her question had him pausing as well as herself. Had Rogan approached his dilemma in the only way possible?

"I see your point, though I grieve to admit it. You are my sister and I want what is best—" He shook his head. "I want you happy."

"And if Rogan should prove to make me happy?"

He threw his hands up in surrender. "What choice would I have?"

"You did learn to get along with Tarr because of Fiona and me," she reminded him.

"It was either that or lose the sisters I had just found."

"So you compromised."

"No, I think I just looked at the situation and saw what I would be losing if I chose to be stubborn instead of sensible."

"Are you finally admitting that stubbornness is a family trait?"

"Shhh," he said with a finger to his grinning lips and a quick scan of the area. "It's a secret."

Aliss laughed and took hold of his hand. "I am glad you came to visit."

Raynor squeezed her hand. "I am here for you, Aliss, no matter what your choice is."

Chapter 29

~~~ ∞ ~~~

Rogan sniffed the handful of dark soil spilling through his fingers. Crops would grow plentiful in this ground and would provide more than enough sustenance for his clan. The woods teemed with game and the sea provided an abundance of fish. The clan would flourish here.

He let the rich soil drain through his fingers as he caught sight of Aliss strolling through the village.

Time was fast running away from him. Raynor had been here a week already, and the clan had been on the isle over a month. Rogan had remained true to his plan, but his efforts weren't enough. Aliss looked for solid proof that his love was real and he wasn't certain how else he could prove it to her.

She was a stubborn one, but he was just as obstinate.

Theirs was a perfect match, if only she would admit it.

She waved to him, the other hand shading her eyes from the bright sun.

He waved for her to join him, suddenly feeling the need to have her by his side, to hold her hand, to kiss her softly and slowly until he was drunk with the taste of her.

She hesitated at first, so he marched through the field demonstrating his willingness to meet her. She responded in kind and made her way toward him.

Her beauty never failed to capture his breath and play havoc with his senses. Her red hair sparkled like a brilliant flame and highlighted her gentle features. And he liked the way her garments fit her curves so nicely, now that Fiona had brought clothes for her.

She also seemed to be forever in motion, going here, going there, tending this one, aiding that one, forever on the move until, exhausted, she dropped into his arms and slept. He liked when she did that, then he could hold her close and know she was safe.

He smiled as she scooped up a handful of dark soil and brought it to him.

"Fertile soil."

He took a small amount and rubbed it between

his fingers. "It will produce an abundant crop next year."

She dusted the soil from her hands and stared at him a moment before she suddenly caught herself and looked away.

"Would you like to take a walk?"

"What do you have in mind?"

"Exploring the woods."

She sighed. "I've been wanting to do that, but I haven't found time with all the work that needs doing."

"Exploring the woods is today's work," he decreed.

She smiled and began edging toward the woods. "I cannot deny an order from my chieftain."

Rogan signaled his intention to Derek on the far side of the field and Derek waved them off with an encouraging smile. From day one on the isle, the clan had persisted in doing everything they could to keep Aliss and him together. Their help was certainly welcome and not at all intrusive, though thus far it had not proved beneficial.

They entered the dense woods, Rogan tempering the pace, though Aliss seemed not to mind. He wanted time alone with her, just the two of them, to talk, to listen, to share the silence, together.

The deeper they went in the woods the thicker the growth of trees and foliage, producing a cool haven from the summer heat. Rogan cleared a path for them as best he could, especially with Aliss warning him not to damage any plants.

"Fern," she said with excitement and ducked under Rogan's arm as he prepared to hold back an intruding branch so that she could pass.

Rogan followed and bent down beside her to investigate her thrilling find.

"Isn't she a beauty?" Aliss asked in a reverent whisper.

Her respect for the lacy plant was obvious in her gentle touch, and the joy in her eyes brought a generous smile to his face.

"Lovely," he said, paying respect to both plant and woman.

"The spores are believed to hold magic."

"What kind of magic?"

"The magic of finding treasure, and it is said—" She lowered her voice. "Swallow the spores and it will render the person invisible."

He reached out.

"No," she said, grabbing his hand. "I don't want you invisible. Besides, it's nothing more than myth."

He stood, taking her along with him. They remained as they were for a moment in silence, their eyes fixed on each other. Both seemed to want to speak and yet they were unable or unwilling.

"Can we walk some more?" she asked softly.

"Whatever you like."

Staunch warrior reflexes kept him from reacting to her hand moving slowly off his arm, where she held it, to drift down to his hand and lock her fingers around his. She waited then for him and he took the lead and led them through the woods.

Her hand felt good in his, warm and snug and *willing*. She had taken hold of him on her own. Was his hard work beginning to pay off? She could have walked ahead of him or waited for him to take the lead and then followed.

Her actions gave him hope that she was starting to believe his love was real. He couldn't allow this chance to slip away. He had to make certain to grasp it and expand on it.

How?

He had tried everything he could think of with no success. What was left to him?

She slipped out of his grasp to investigate another plant and he felt her sudden absence like a blow to his heart. The pain reminded him of when he lost Kendra. Life had been so empty and so very lonely without her beside him. He did not want to hurt that much ever again.

She turned with a smile and rattled on about the plant she had found and how she intended to gather its seeds to add to her garden.

He smiled and held his hand out to her. He wanted to beg her to come to him, hold on and never leave him. But he kept his fears to himself and held his hand extended in a simple offer—that represented so much more.

She rushed back to him and took hold of his hand all the while chatting about how the woods held a variety of plants she intended to examine.

He listened, enjoying the sound of her voice so cheerful and confident, and walked with her until he noticed her pace had slowed.

Rogan stopped, walked over to a fallen tree not

yet ravaged by decay and sat, taking her down with him.

She sighed when her bottom touched the tree.

"Tired?"

"A little," she said.

"We will rest here for a while."

"You seem to know your way around here."

"My father brought me here many times when I was growing up. I know the land well."

"I wondered how you knew the distance to the keep from the shore the day we landed."

"He thought it wise that I become familiar with my future home."

"He wanted this land for you?"

"And the clan," he added.

"He encouraged you to claim it?"

"He encouraged me to fight for it."

"Then he knew a fight would be necessary?"

He nodded. "There was no way the land, though mine by birthright, would be surrendered willingly."

"So he helped prepare you to fight for the isle?"

"He did, though I chose a different way. I did not want to start life on this land with the blood of my clan or my enemies on my hands. I hoped to obtain what was mine with no loss of blood or lives and with a minimum of injuries."

"You succeeded."

"Some suffered," he said. Her in particular, though he had not planned it that way.

"Suffering eventually ends, but deaths are forever. I admire your effort to avoid spilling blood and taking lives to claim this land." She glanced around. "No wonder it is so beautiful. You have brought no bloodshed and death here, so it rejoices and repays your respect with abundance for your clan."

"I always felt I had come home when my father brought me here."

"How did it come to be that the Hellewyk and Wolf clan both lay claim to this land?"

He stood abruptly. "I am not certain."

Aliss pushed herself up off the fallen tree. "Why did you not tell me all of this from the beginning?"

"It really did not concern you."

"It most certainly did. It was the reason for my abduction."

"Part of the reason, and besides, you were to serve your purpose and be returned to your people. I had not anticipated falling in love with you or your proposing marriage to me. It changed everything."

"But not your quest for this isle. That came first, even before love."

"Will you ever forgive me for the hurt I've caused you? Does it make any sense for me to continue to try to make you realize how much I love you? What must I do to make you understand how much I do not want to lose you?" He shook his head. "I should be done with this nonsense and negate our bargain. You are my wife and should remain my wife."

"You told me the choice was mine. You go back on your word?"

"You really think I would not keep our bargain?" he asked.

"I know not what to think anymore. You love me and you love this land. Yet you used me to get this land. Now to prove you love me, you will give up this land? Or do you play me for a fool yet again?"

"What about accepting that I love you and love me in return? What about realizing that my plan never included hurting you. What about giving us a chance to make a life together?"

"You robbed us of that when you lied to me."

"You are obstinate," he said.

"Cautious," she corrected.

"Too cautious. Why not take a chance?"

"I did once. I proposed to you."

He reached out and grabbed her by the shoulders. "I am glad you did."

"Of course, it served your plan well."

He rested his forehead to hers. "I love you, Aliss. I don't know how many times I must say it. I don't know what else to do to prove it. This isle means much to me and I offer to surrender it for your love."

"No, if you loved me you would have surrendered it when my family arrived to ransom me."

Chapter 30

Aliss left Rogan behind in the woods. She had walked a good distance and had been nearing the edge of the woods when her pace finally slowed to a crawl. She was worn out more from her constant doubts than anything else.

"Do not put more of a distance between us." Rogan said, coming up so quietly behind her that he startled her.

"It is not I who have placed the gap there."

"Perhaps, but you can begin to close the gap if only you will let me into your heart. I will not hurt you again, I promise. Forgive me and let us start anew."

She wanted to believe him, Lord, how she wanted to believe him.

He stepped up against her back and wrapped

his arms gently around her then squeezed tight. "I don't want to let you go. I love the feel of you in my arms, your fresh scent in my nostrils, the taste of you on my lips."

"I have work—"

"It can wait," Rogan said, and lovingly stroked her neck.

"You do not know that."

"If the work was that important you would not have accepted my invitation to walk in the woods."

"Let me go, please."

"Are you certain?"

Her heart thudded madly in her chest. His tender touch, his warm breath against her skin, the strength of him wrapped around her, his asking forgiveness made her want to scream. *No, I'm not certain about anything.*

Instead, she nodded.

Rogan released her, his hand slowly drifting off her neck, tickling her skin until gooseflesh rushed down her arm.

She hurried off to her cottage before he could tempt her with another word or touch. The door to her cottage always remained open, an invitation to enter to all those seeking her skills. This time, however, she closed it behind her.

Work was not on her mind, Rogan was. He had penetrated her defenses in more ways than one. The flowers she had grown accustomed to receiving from him, their unplanned escapes, his kindness and the intimacy she longed to once again share with him.

He had made her fall in love more deeply with him without her even realizing it and the thought nearly broke down all her defenses.

He had wooed her and it looked as if he might be on the verge of winning the bargain with time still left to him. And yet, the memory of that day her family arrived to rescue her haunted her. If he loved her so very much, why hadn't he negated his ransom demand?

A gentle rap on the door shattered her musings and she bade the caller enter.

Anna peeked her head in. "With the door closed I thought you might be resting."

"Seeking a bit of solitude."

"I can leave—"

"No," Aliss said and waved her in. "I am sick of my own company."

Anna laughed and opened the door wide. "Then let the sun and the beautiful day visit with you."

The sun's light spilled across her workstation and rushed over her, hugging her with its warmth and making her smile.

"I wanted to make sure you were all right." Anna walked over to the table. "It's not like you to close your door."

"I am fine."

"You're not feeling well?" Raynor asked upon entering.

"I am fine," she repeated more firmly.

"Good, for I wish to visit with my sister."

Anna was quick to take her leave, giving them time alone.

"I have enjoyed my visit with you thus far. I needed to see for myself if you were happy."

"Am I?" She asked the question of her brother but it was a query she needed to answer herself.

Raynor pulled out a chair from the table and straddled it. "In all honesty, I needed to get past my own misconceptions before I could see the truth."

"How so?"

He gave a brief laugh. "I believed I came to rescue you as you once did me. I thought you were a prisoner here."

"Had Fiona helped plant the thought in your head?"

"She might have, but my own thoughts served me well enough. The Wolf had attacked Hellewyk land, injured Tarr, and of course, the worst of his offenses, he had abducted my sister. There was reason enough to hate him."

"Have you now changed your mind?"

"Thanks to Rogan." He nodded and laughed. "The perplexed look on your face tells me I should explain."

"Please do."

"When I learned of the bargain between you two, I, like Fiona, thought it a ruse, a way to keep his precious land by convincing you that he actually loved you. My own plan was to observe Rogan's lies for myself and help you see them as well. Then I would take you home with me."

"It hasn't worked that way?"

"After a couple of days here, I knew the situation wasn't what I had thought. By week's end, having watched Rogan with you, I knew the man was besotted." His laughter filled the room. "Actually, it did my heart good to know that my sister has tamed the mighty Wolf."

"I have not," she protested, not believing him.

"Oh, come now, Aliss, you must see for yourself how much he loves you. Everyone else sees it; even my men do and find it quite humorous. He picks flowers for you, for goodness' sake."

She looked away from her brother. Had she been so lost in the hurt and pain of Rogan's betrayal that she refused to see that he had truly loved her all along? That love had caught him off guard as it had done to her?

"Aliss," Raynor said gently.

She turned back to him. "You *have* rescued me, brother."

"You do not realize how much he loves you, do you?"

"No. I was too busy feeling sorry for myself."

"That does not sound like you."

"I'm afraid I don't know myself anymore."

Raynor grinned. "Love has a way of doing that to people. Besides, you have time left to work through your feelings; after all, a bargain is a bargain. And Rogan does need punishment for betraying you, though I daresay he's probably suffering miserably right now. Let him suffer a bit more. It will do him good, and when you're ready, release the man from his self-inflicted prison."

Raynor stood. "And don't forget, little sister, to forgive yourself. Foolishness didn't get you in this position, love did, and love will get you out of it."

Aliss sprang off her chair and flung her arms around him. "Thank you for rescuing me."

He hugged her back. "You're most welcome, though don't expect me to leave anytime soon. I do not want to see cranky Fiona unless you're standing beside me."

They both laughed and Raynor left, leaving her to think on her newfound knowledge.

Raynor voiced what she had known but was only beginning to acknowledge. Hearing that her husband loved her from her brother somehow validated what she was slowly coming to realize. Rogan had worked hard to demonstrate his love and in a shorter time than she had expected. To know that he had always loved her filled her with a sense of joy and relief. But what of his betrayal?

She wasn't quite ready to forgive Rogan for that. A few things still needed to be made right in her mind, the ransom demand for one and this isle, the other. She had a feeling that the history of this place could reveal much, especially about Rogan.

Her musings were interrupted throughout the afternoon by people needing tending. She then spent the remainder of her time replenishing her stock of salves and potions.

Her neck began to ache from stooping over the table and she rubbed at her tense muscles as she raised her head.

She jumped and gasped at the shadow with

glowing green eyes that filled the open doorway. She blinked, and when she looked again her husband stood there.

She reached out to him and he rushed to her side.

She wrapped her arms around his waist and buried her face in his chest.

"What is wrong?"

"I must be tired. My eyes play tricks on me," she said, keeping her cheek to his chest, his earthy scent a balm to her senses.

"I knew I should have come sooner for you, but the few times I passed by, you appeared so busy I did not wish to disturb you."

"I am finished now," she said, not wanting to remain alone in the cottage.

"Good, then I do not have to take you away from your work."

"No, I go willingly," she admitted, though she was not willing to be torn away from him. She felt safe tucked against him, even more so now that she knew he loved her. Not that she planned to admit it to him; there was time left for that.

"You shiver," he said and wrapped himself more tightly around her.

She trembled, slowly releasing all the barriers she had erected and allowing his love to begin to seep deep into her heart.

"When you are ready, we can go," he said.

She took a deep breath, drinking in his love so that it could nourish her heart and soul. Her body, however, grumbled for substantial nourishment.

"You are hungry."

"So my stomach tells me." She laughed and looked up at him. "And you?"

"Starving."

After blowing out the candles and shutting the door, they walked hand in hand to the keep. The hall was empty; the clan members occupied their own cottages now that the repairs had been finished.

"Where are Raynor and his men?" she asked, turning her head as if to catch them lurking in the dark corners.

"With Derek and some of the other men. We have the keep to ourselves tonight."

The thought suddenly appealed to her. She had so enjoyed making love with him when she believed they loved each other. She had continued to lust for him but it meant nothing without love and so she had denied him her passion. Now she knew he loved her and she had never stopped loving him, so why not—

She smiled softly, feeling the weight of the heaviest of barriers drift away. Her body sprang to life, her skin tingled, and her nipples hardened.

"You are quiet," he said as they climbed the stairs.

"I grow tired," she said, bed suddenly appealing to her.

"We will eat and rest." He pushed the door to their bedchamber open with his shoulder, entered and nudged it closed with his foot. "Then we can go to bed."

Chapter 31

~~~∽◯◯∽~~~

Aliss sat at the table spread with platters of food and found her appetite waning. Her thoughts were on a completely different type of nourishment.

"Is something on your mind, Aliss?" Rogan asked with concern.

"No."

He laughed. "You sit there chewing on your lower lip when there is much more appetizing food on the table."

"I can't decide what I want." That was no lie. Did she start with his appetizing lips or go straight for the main dish?

"I know what you like, I'll choose it for you," he offered and reached out to spear a slice of meat.

He certainly did know what she liked and she

almost shivered with the memories of their lovemaking.

She picked at the food he had piled on her plate, not at all interested in it.

Rogan leaned back in his chair. "What's wrong? You sit silently, moving your food around, not eating a thing. Something is obviously on your mind."

He was right about that.

"Want to share it with me?"

She did, but it would make no sense that all of a sudden she was willing to make love with him. It didn't even make sense to her, but then her desire for him had never waned. Love had been the missing ingredient.

However, she wasn't ready to forgive him so easily. Besides, she liked the way he had courted her and wouldn't mind it continuing for a while.

"You're still upset over our talk in the woods, aren't you?"

She had been, but no more. "I admit it has been on my mind."

"Is there anything I can do to ease those concerns?"

Make love to me.

She shook her head. The thought was crazy. She couldn't just jump into bed with him—and what? Forgive him? Start fresh? Begin to love again?

Or forget everything just for one night and *love*?

She pushed her plate aside and leaned her arms on the table. "Tell me *why* you fell in love with me."

He stared at her a moment, rubbed the back of his neck then shook his head. "I've asked myself the same question over and over, and over and over I get different answers."

"Do you now? Why is that?"

"Because I find more reasons to fall in love with you each day."

Her heart fluttered, her breath caught, and she sighed softly. "You are good at wooing a woman."

"I am good at wooing the woman I love," he corrected.

"Woo me some more," she said, aware that the more he professed his love the more she desired him.

"You are easy to love."

That surprised her. "I sometimes think myself selfish, always involved in my work."

"Your work is important to you. A husband who truly loves his wife would understand and allow her to be who she is. I love *who* you are, and your work makes you even more appealing. I love the way you become excited over the simplest things, like discovering the fern earlier. I will never grow tired of exploring the woods with you."

Her heart melted with every word.

"I also admired tremendously your attempt to escape my men when first they captured you. You dared to take a chance in the dark of night, in unfamiliar terrain, your wrists bound and your mouth gagged."

"I was terrified."

"I would not have known it. When I tossed you over my shoulder I sensed only your resolve to escape and I knew if I let you go, you would attempt to flee again. So I held on to you, as I continue to do."

"You make me think that perhaps that gap between us should be bridged, at least a little."

"I will settle for a little, for now."

"You don't intend to give up, do you?" she asked.

"Never," he said, pounding the table once. "I will make certain you know that I love you every day of my life, now and always."

Her defenses vanished completely.

"You make it easy for a woman to love you," she said, and hurried from the table to stand in front of the cold hearth.

He came up behind her as she hoped he would and slipped his arm around her waist to ease her back against him.

"I know that you love me; believe that I love you, if only for tonight," he whispered near her ear and kissed her temple.

She turned in his arms and brushed her fingers faintly over his lips. "Tonight, I believe," she confessed in a murmur.

She touched his lips again, lingering along the bottom one before she nibbled it gently then pleaded in a whisper, "Love me."

"Always," he said, and captured her lips.

She liked that he took his time tasting and savoring. It seemed forever since they had lingered in a kiss. He teased her bottom lip with nibbles and bites then devoured her lips once again.

"Damn, but I love you," he whispered against her mouth, scooped her up in his arms and carried her to bed.

He deposited her on the bed, and she smiled as she watched him disrobe. He had a splendid body, all taut, sleek muscles, and his movements were like those of a stalking wolf, slow and determined.

But this time she wasn't his prey; she was his mate.

She smiled and stretched her arms out to him.

He returned to the bed, kneeling beside her to undo her leather belt and toss it to the floor. She relished the feel of his warm fingers pulling her blouse free of her skirt and working their way beneath to gently fondle her flesh. He pushed the blouse up to expose her breasts to his eager mouth.

She moaned when he rolled his tongue repeatedly over one nipple then the other, turning them so hard they ached. Then he went back and suckled each one until she panted breathless beneath him.

His hands drifted to her waistband and he inched her skirt down over her hips, his lips nibbling along her tingling flesh. It felt good, so very good, and she didn't want him to stop. She knew his intentions, and when he discarded her skirt, she spread her legs in welcome.

She gasped when his hands captured her bottom and brought her up to meet his mouth. No sooner had he run his tongue intimately over her than she felt her passion soar beyond reason and her senses explode.

She was lost in the labyrinth of their love-making, neither able to find her way out nor wanting to.

She could taste the sweat of her passion thick and salty on her lips. She reached down and stroked the silky length of him and then grabbed hold and squeezed, feeling his desire pulsate in her hand. He was her husband and she wanted him more than she ever thought possible.

She arched up to accept him and guide him into her, but he moved her hand off him. Then he swung her legs up to rest against his chest, grabbed hold of her backside and inched himself slowly inside her.

She sighed when he finally settled fully within her then shocked her when he swiftly withdrew only to begin again. She grasped hold of his taut arms, the muscles bulging from the exertion of his position, but he didn't budge. He held firm and worked his way in and out of her, sending her into a frenzy of mad desire.

She cried out his name, she cried out for him to stop, and then she cried out for him to never stop. Her body was being battered with lovemaking and she ached for every pleasurable plunge.

Her eyes widened when he suddenly stopped, moved them both down in the bed, and with one hand lifted her head to place a pillow beneath it.

She hadn't realized her head had been hitting the wall, but he had.

She reached out to him and urged him down on top of her.

"I am so very lucky to have found you," he whispered.

"I agree," she said, and as she claimed his lips, he claimed her.

She arched and he pulled back and soon the rhythm was set, their tempo fast and furious. Time stood still as Aliss felt the force of first one climax then another hit her and ripple repeatedly throughout her body.

She had barely regained her senses when she felt Rogan groan and knew his pleasure was close at hand. She thrust her hips against him, keeping their rhythm strong, and before she knew it, she felt her own passion return and build uncontrollably deep inside her.

She never expected to—

The climax hit them like a rushing wave, knocking them completely senseless. They held on to each other until the very last ripple of their lovemaking had faded.

Rogan collapsed alongside Aliss and she reached out and took hold of his hand.

Speech wasn't possible—their breathing was still labored from their lovemaking—so silence reigned. That was all right with Aliss. She enjoyed lingering in the afterglow of their passion.

He finally turned on his side and, with a smile, reached out and pushed her damp hair off her face. "I love you."

She sighed. *I know*.

Chapter 32

Aliss had just administered a salve and bandage to Tara's minor burn when Rogan appeared at the open door of the cottage.

"I interrupt?"

Aliss shook her head and waved him in. "All finished."

He wore his dark plaid and tan shirt, the sleeves rolled up to his elbows. The summer sun had lightened the blond strands that ran through his long hair and tanned his skin to a healthy bronze. It delighted her to see that she had such a handsome husband.

Tara stood to leave, drawing her attention. "Daniel does well?"

Her smile spread generously across her pretty face. "He runs around without a limp or complaint. He tires me out just watching him."

"Good, I am glad that his broken bone healed so well."

Tara hugged her. "Thanks to you and your skills. I do not know what we would do without you. The clan is so very grateful to you." She hurried out the door with a wave.

"The chieftain is also grateful for your skills."

Aliss laughed and walked around the table to step into his open arms.

"I've missed you," he said.

"You just saw me at breakfast a couple of hours ago."

"Much too long, don't you agree?"

She did, actually, having thought of him all morning. Soon they would need to talk and settle things between them, but not just yet. For now, she needed time to heal her wounds and love him.

"Aye, I do agree, perhaps we can find time today and slip away together."

"I already have it planned," he whispered.

A gruff cough at the door had them both turning around.

"Sorry to interrupt," John said apologetically. "You are needed at the keep. A foolish dispute."

Aliss sighed and whispered, "When and where?"

He bent and nibbled at her ear. "You'll find out soon enough."

Gooseflesh ran over her skin and she shivered as she watched him walk off.

"A brisk walk," she ordered, needing to stem

her passion. She left the cottage and headed for the woods. She wanted to be alone, solitude her only companion for now. She wanted to find a place to sit, relax, and enjoy the beauty of the last days of summer. Soon she would journey with Rogan to await the birth of Fiona's babe. She looked forward to seeing her sister. She missed her and wished to talk with her.

It had been too long since they had shared walks together, talking and laughing and offering each other advice. Aliss's advice had always been the more logical of the two.

She heard a rustle and looked around, hoping to spy friendly animals at play. She loved to watch their antics. They always made her laugh.

She saw nothing and assumed they were scurrying about out of sight.

She continued walking. A cloud slowly sneaked across the sky and covered the late afternoon sun, robbing the woods of sunlight. A chill breeze rustled the trees, shedding leaves and sending a shiver through Aliss.

She had not thought to bring a shawl. The last days of summer lingered, with only the occasional hint of autumn in the air.

With a rough rubbing of her arms, Aliss kept up her unhurried pace.

A noise that sounded like rushing footsteps had her swerving around.

She stared at the dense woods and heard nothing but her rapid heartbeat. Was she being followed? Was someone playing a trick on her?

"Rogan?" she called out, her own voice returning in an echo.

She suddenly felt uneasy. It seemed as if the forest had grown darker, though the cloud covering had not grown heavier. The urge to flee took hold of her and she tried to calm herself.

It did not work and finally she decided her best course of action was to satisfy her irrationality and return home.

Aliss turned, and staring at her through a grove of trees was a pair of brilliant green eyes.

Rogan listened to the two squabbling women from his perch atop the long table that sat in front of the cold fireplace in the great hall. The two were bickering over the ownership of a fine piece of a recently woven plaid.

He knew it was an important matter for both women, but he would have much preferred to be with Aliss. Last night he had realized that he loved his wife even more than he thought possible and he knew she loved him. He hoped soon, very soon, he would hear her say "I love you" to him as easily as he said it to her.

For now his attention was needed here in the hall, but as soon as he finished he intended to return to Aliss and whisk her away to a very special place, and share a part of his past with her.

Both women claimed their skilled hands had weaved the cloth, and they expected him to settle the dispute. But it was impossible to settle. He would have to designate one of them as the better weaver and thereby animosity would grow between friends.

"Let me see the cloth," Rogan said.

John handed it to him while the two women looked on and several other women watched from the surrounding tables. No men took interest in the debate, though Raynor had wandered in and sat to the side watching with interest.

Rogan weighed the cloth in his hand and saw that it was a fine weave made by skilled hands. He also knew that one of the women would suffer because of his verdict. He gave it thought, studying the cloth, bringing it up to examine it closely.

"You both claim to have weaved this, you say?"

Both women nodded and affirmed, "Yes!"

"There is a knot here in the weave."

Both women stepped forward and stopped when Rogan turned the cloth over and back again.

"A loose weave in spots," he said, once again bringing it up for a closer look.

One woman took a step back.

The other noticed and joined her.

"This looks to be the work of a beginner," he said.

Both women gasped at the insult.

"You both teach the young ones to weave, do you not?"

"Yes, yes, we do," said one.

"Could you have made a mistake and this cloth may be the work of one of the young women you have taught?" he asked.

"I think he is right, Agnes," one said.

"I believe you are right, Cara," the other agreed.

"The cloth?" he asked, holding it out to them.

"Keep it," both said, and turned and walked off together.

The other women followed, smiling broadly. There would be no hard feelings this day.

Raynor walked over to him, shaking his head. "You handled that well."

"What choice did I have?" Rogan asked with a laugh. "The other women would have had my head if I had caused a rift between the two women who weaved the cloth for the clan."

Raynor grinned and slapped him on the back. "Your meals may have also suffered. I spied one of the women who cook for you lurking in the shadows."

Rogan gave a quick glance around the hall.

"Don't worry, she left with a smile."

"I tell you, settling disputes between women is worse than going into battle without a weapon," Rogan said.

"Amen to that."

"Did something bring you to the hall?" Rogan asked. "Since I do not think a woman's quarrel would bring you here."

"I wondered if Giann was visiting you. She visits with my family on occasion and I thought I saw her wandering the woods," Raynor said.

"She has made her presence known."

"Does she intend to speak with Aliss?"

"She has not made mention of it," Rogan said. "Why?"

"I saw Aliss walk into the woods and wondered."

"Wondered what?"

"If Giann had summoned her?"

Aliss stood perfectly still, not sure who the glaring green eyes belonged to, animal or human. Her urge to flee dissipated and her heartbeat calmed. She instinctively realized she had nothing to fear, though much to say.

"I am glad we finally meet."

Aliss stared as sunlight spotlighted the woman who emerged from the woods, the cloud having drifted away from the sun. She was stunning, with blond hair and green eyes that claimed the color of the forest. Her garments blended with nature's own colors so that her tall, graceful body could move within the woods undetected. She carried a gnarled walking stick that was topped with a claw that held a clear stone.

"You are Giann," Aliss said.

"And you are Aliss, one of the twins."

She drifted closer to Aliss, and that is exactly how it appeared—as if she drifted, not walked, toward her.

"Whose life you have interfered with much too long."

"Not I, fate," Giann said gently, and led her to a thick, flat stone.

Aliss had been anticipating their meeting and she eagerly sat beside the woman. "Are you telling me fate was responsible for my sister's and my abduction? You had nothing at all to do with it?"

"You both were meant to fulfill a destiny. I was meant to help and guide you along the way."

"You talk of the prophecy."

Giann nodded.

"My sister and I suffered because doom was predicted for the clan and in order to avoid it our uncle thought to sacrifice us. Not to mention the untold suffering of my parents and brother, wondering all those years what had happened to us. And you tell me all that was due to fate?"

"Fate must be appeased."

"At any expense?"

"What expense have you suffered?" Giann asked gently. "Your sister has wed a man she loves. Raynor, your brother, thrives on reuniting with you both. Your parents will greet a new granddaughter soon and watch her grow into a fine young woman—and you?"

Giann looked her over with a loving glance. "You will help fulfill the final part of the prophecy so that peace may finally be achieved."

"How so?"

"You will discover that in time. Fate has yet to be completely appeased with the current situation."

"Why isn't fate appeased?"

"What was once done wrong must be made right."

"I do not understand."

"You will when the time comes," Giann said.

"Fiona and I both wed as the prophecy predicted we must. Does that not settle it?"

"The prophecy was not only about you both marrying."

"How can you say that?" Aliss asked, perplexed. She then recited, "On a full moon twin babes are born, with their birth sounds the horn, eyes of green, hair of red, destruction comes unless both wed."

"That is not the prophecy."

"It isn't?" Aliss asked incredulously.

Giann smiled, raised her hands to the heavens as if drawing down the light to her, and recited, "On a full moon twin babes are born, with their birth sounds the horn, eyes of green, hair of red, destruction comes if for love the twins do not wed, for true love will open the door for peace to reign forever more."

"The prophecy was always about love?"

"For many, not merely the few."

"You talk in riddles," Aliss accused.

Giann smiled like a patient teacher. "Open your heart and you will understand."

"So we're back to love again."

"Love is what connects us all. Understand that and fate will be appeased."

"Another prediction?" Aliss asked.

Giann reached out and touched her cheek. "No, my child, a gift."

Chapter 33

Rogan reached the edge of the woods and stopped abruptly. He knew the time would come for Aliss to meet Giann face-to-face. It was what Aliss wanted, and a meeting that was necessary. He had no right to interfere.

He stepped back, grabbed a large stick off the ground and snapped it in two as he paced impatiently. He would give Aliss time. How much, he wasn't certain, but for now he would wait.

He snapped the now smaller stick again and continued to pace.

A pile of broken sticks covered the ground before he saw Aliss in the distance making her way around the trees. He snapped the last stick he held and tossed it away then stepped forward, eager to greet her.

She stopped in front of him.

"Are you all right?" he asked, not certain why her green eyes glared so brightly.

"I met with Giann."

"Did the meeting go well?"

"Do you think it is possible for me to be more confused now than I was before?"

He shrugged, realizing it would be better for him to listen.

"Love. It all comes down to love. For the many not just the few." She began to pace in front of him. "Love is a gift, she says, but who gives the gift?" She stopped pacing and poked him in the chest. "And what if I don't want the gift? Can I give it back? And is the gift even for me?" She threw up her hands and continued pacing.

"It makes no sense," he said. He had hoped this meeting would settle unanswered questions for Aliss. It definitely had confused her even more. He had caused her enough concern. He didn't wish any more problems heaped on her.

"That is not all that doesn't make sense. She tells me that love connects us all. Who is us?" She shook her head. "It is all too much for me. I never wanted to deal with love in the first place. See where it has gotten me." She halted abruptly and pointed a finger at him. "Probably because I knew it would be nothing but trouble. Now here I am smack in the middle of a riddle."

Her hands went up in the air again. "I even rhyme as Giann does."

That he found humorous and attempted to hide his laughter.

"It is not funny," she said, shaking a finger at him. "This prediction of hers—" She waved her hand at the woods. "It has brought much heartache to many and I do not wish to see it cause any more."

"As difficult as it may be to believe, Giann is wise in ways we know nothing of. Perhaps we should trust her."

"I do not want my life in the hands of another."

He stepped closer to her and took her hands in his. "Your life is in my hands and mine is in yours. I would never let any harm come to you. I would die first."

"Hush," she said, her hand rushing to cover his mouth. "Do not speak nonsense. I would not see you die for me."

"The choice is not yours."

Her eyes rounded wide. "Promise me you would never do something so foolish."

"I cannot," he said honestly, for if a time came when it was necessary to forfeit his life for hers, he would do it gladly.

She slapped his chest repeatedly. "You will not lay down your life for me."

He grabbed her hand and kissed her reddened palm. "I would."

She rested her forehead to his chest. "I would not want to lose you."

He grabbed her chin. "I *will not* lose you. Have faith and trust that I will always keep us safe."

She raised her head. "But I am the one who is to fulfill the last of the prophecy and appease fate."

He grabbed hold of her arms. "You are my fate. The prophecy is fulfilled."

"Then what wrong is to be made right?"

"Worry not, it is done." He realized then that the prophecy involved much more than just the twins. Fate had cast a wide web over the many not just the few.

"I don't understand—"

"You don't need to. Leave it to me. Now come with me. It is time for us to escape." He felt the need to run away, leave all behind and go, just Aliss and him, and that was what he intended if only for an hour or two.

He did not give her a chance to object. He grabbed hold of her hand and tugged her along with him. They would not run far, just far enough to be alone. He intended to take her to his favorite spot, a place he had found when he was a young lad and his father brought him to the isle.

"Where do you take me?' she asked, rushing to match his hurried pace.

"You will see."

He stopped suddenly. Aliss would have collided with him if he had not grabbed hold of her and swung her around in front of him.

"My secret place," he whispered in her ear.

He gazed along with her at the towering weeping willow tree whose flourishing branches brushed the ground. Its many roots drank from the nearby stream and its thick trunk told of its advanced age, though its leaves shone a healthy green.

"Let me show you," he said, and walked over to part the weeping branches for her to enter.

She stepped forward, peeked in, and entered.

He stepped in behind her, releasing the branches.

"It is like a hideaway," Aliss said.

"The very reason I liked it when I was young." He pointed at the walls of willow branches. "No one can see in. It shelters its occupants. It sheltered me as a child. I wanted to share it with you."

She turned in circles with a smile. "What did it shelter you from?"

She would ask that of him, the healer who always wanted to heal. She would realize that a child who sought shelter from the world hid from something. But perhaps that was why he had brought her here, to share the pain of the past with her, to help her better understand him.

"From my anger," he said.

"This land belonged to your mother's clan?"

He nodded.

"She wanted you to have it?"

"My legacy, she told my father. Her firstborn son was entitled to the isle, and she wanted to make certain her firstborn received what rightfully belonged to him."

She walked over to him and placed her hand on his arm. "I understand. Your mother wanted this for you."

"Her legacy to me. How could I deny it?"

"Why didn't you bring me here sooner?"

He stepped away from her. "I couldn't. Not right away. Not until—"

"You believed I loved you."

He nodded and walked over to her, taking her hands in his, bringing them to his lips and kissing them gently. "This place was where I felt closest to my mother. To me it is a place of love and I wanted to share it with the woman who loves me."

He kissed her then, a soft whispery kiss, and they drifted closer together, his arms circling her waist, her arms going around him, closing tight, protecting, sheltering, just like the willow branches that surrounded them.

"Much could have been avoided if you had been honest with me from the start," Aliss said.

He stepped away from her and spread his arms. "An angry young boy planned his revenge here. It smoldered in his heart for years and nothing was going to stop him. Love threw him a curve and he didn't know what to do. He was foolish and made a mistake, which he now regrets and probably will for the rest of his life." He held his hand out to her. "But he doesn't regret falling in love with the most beautiful, understanding woman in the world."

Aliss smiled and took his hand. "There you go, wooing again."

"I'm glad it works." He tugged her into his arms. "Forgive me for being a fool and not telling you the truth from the start."

"You have told me everything now?"

He rested his cheek to hers. He had abandoned the last of his plan. There was no need for anyone to know of it. It would do no good and serve no purpose. It would bring only pain and he had lived with the pain far too long. He wanted his past buried now, and his future to begin with Aliss.

"Everything," he whispered in her ear.

They lingered, sharing stories of their youth, until they both grew hungry and hurried back to the village.

There was excitement in the air; everyone was running in the same direction.

Rogan spied Derek, Tara beside him and Daniel straddling his shoulders. He and Aliss caught up with the couple.

"What goes on here?" Rogan asked.

Derek laughed. "A fight over a woman."

Rogan shook his head. The worst kind, since pride would allow neither man to surrender until one was left near lifeless.

"You must stop this," Aliss insisted.

"It is between the men," Derek said.

"What of the woman?" Aliss asked. "Does she have a say in it?"

"No," Derek said. "When a man wants to fight, he'll fight."

Aliss looked to her husband. "Stop this senselessness or I will." She marched off ahead of them.

Derek grinned. "I think I'd rather break up the fight than face my wife if I didn't."

"A wise choice," Tara agreed.

"Thanks for the advice," Rogan said, and marched forward. He would settle this to please his wife, and besides, he didn't want her spending the rest of the day tending to avoidable wounds.

"Stop!" Rogan commanded, once on the scene. His voice reverberated across the field where the men fought, both bloody and bruised from a battle that looked to have gone on far too long.

The men were far too engrossed in beating the hell out of each other to hear their chieftain's shout. The clan members surrounding them heard and parted when Rogan marched toward the circle.

Rogan shouted twice more to no avail. He'd had enough. He ran forward with a fierce growl, grabbed one man by the back of the shirt and tossed him aside to tumble in the dirt. He then reached for the other fool and gave him a good toss, sending him sprawling to the ground. He stood with hands on hips, his feet spread apart and his handsome face contorted by fury.

"This fight is over."

Peter, tall and lanky, spat blood from his bleeding mouth before standing. "He stole my woman."

"She's my woman," Robert said, his one eye nearly shut closed by bruising as he rose on shaky legs.

"She is not," Peter shouted, and lunged for Robert.

Rogan's hand shot out and caught the young man in the chest. He stumbled but remained on his feet. "I'll not see another fist thrown or there'll be hell to pay."

"I have a right to fight for the woman I love," Peter asserted, blood covering his chin.

"She doesn't love you," Robert spat, shaking a raised fist.

Rogan shot a warning glance at Robert and the man quickly lowered his clenched hand.

"A fight will settle it," Peter claimed bravely.

The crowd agreed with a cheer.

While Rogan didn't agree with their method of settling this dispute, he could not fault it either. Any man worth his honor would fight for the woman he loved, and most in the village would agree, except his wife. And he was much more concerned about pleasing her right now.

"What of the woman? Does she want either man?"

The shout came from the back of the crowd.

Rogan recognized his wife's voice, distinct and determined, and nearly grinned. Had he really expected her to stay out of this?

The crowd made way for her and she came to stand just at the edge of the circle.

"Shouldn't the woman be heard?" Aliss asked, both hands set firmly on her hips.

The women cheered in unison.

The men attempted to drown them out with their own protests.

Rogan raised his hand and shouted, "Enough!" While he admired his wife's audacity, he needed to keep order in his clan.

"We fight and settle this," Peter said once it turned quiet.

"Aye, it's the way of things," Robert agreed.

Before Rogan could address the issue, Aliss turned to the crowd.

"Who claims to love one of these men?"

Both men craned their necks to eye the crowd.

Silence followed, everyone looking at everyone else.

"Sheila, speak up," Peter cried out.

"Yes, Sheila, set this to rest once and for all," Robert urged, his one eye wide and searching.

A young woman finally emerged reluctantly from the crowd, her head bent and her hands clasped together. Whispers and murmurs trailed her every step.

Rogan wasn't surprised to see his wife walk over and offer her hand to the young woman, or that she took hold of Aliss with a nervous tremble.

Both men began to speak but Rogan quickly silenced them with a raised hand.

"What say you, Sheila?" Rogan asked. "Do you favor either man?"

Both men puffed their chests out and stood tall, though both looked a fright covered in dirt, blood, and bruises.

He noticed her hand tighten around Aliss's, her slim knuckles turning white. His wife placed a comforting arm around her shoulders.

"You have nothing to fear," he heard Aliss whisper to her.

Sheila raised her head and kept her eyes on Rogan.

He thought that a telling sign since if she loved one of them, her gaze would immediately go to him. He waited, as did the silent crowd.

"I favor neither man, my lord."

A mingle of gasps and cheers circled the crowd.

Rogan recognized the young woman by the

way she had addressed him. None in the clan called him "my lord." He wasn't one nor did he fancy himself one, he was Rogan to them all. But she had only joined their clan a short time before Aliss's arrival, and she had kept much to herself like many did when they first arrived.

The women had befriended her and informed him that she had been badly abused by the lord she had served and was fearful of men.

"I bring you game for your table," Peter said.

"I bring you flowers," Robert said more gently.

Rogan caught the promise of a smile when Robert spoke. She liked the young lad but feared him at the same time.

"Do you wish them to stop?" Rogan asked.

Aliss whispered something in her ear.

"I like the flowers," Sheila said.

Robert grinned.

The crowd cheered.

Peter grew red with fury and lunged for Robert.

Rogan stepped in quickly and Peter's fist connected with his jaw.

Chapter 34

❦

Silence pierced the earth; not even a bird sang or a leaf rustled. All stilled following the accidental assault on the chieftain that had left him standing and his jaw swelling.

"You idiot," Aliss yelled and stomped over to Peter, who stood pale and speechless. With a wagging finger in his face, she let him have it. "Have you no brain in that thick head of yours? You use fists to settle a problem instead of using common sense." She jabbed at his head. "Your own stupidity will see that you remain unwed, since no woman would want such a dumb man. You are—"

"Aliss." A hand on her shoulder had her spinning around. "I think you have chastised him enough."

She almost sagged with relief when she saw

that Rogan's jaw was not as swollen as she had first suspected. It was red and could possibly bruise but the swelling was not serious and would probably vanish in no time.

"He got what he deserved for hurting you," she said, and turned to see Peter sulking off in defeat and humiliation. "Oh, dear."

"You really gave it to him," Raynor said with a laugh, as he approached through the dispersing crowd.

"I did not mean—" She shook her head, reminded of the young man's injuries and her own fury at seeing her husband attacked. She had wanted to pummel the young man. She took a deep breath. "Raynor, go and bring Peter to my cottage so I may see to his wounds."

"He doesn't need a nursemaid."

"No, but he could use a friend just now," Aliss said. With a few mumblings and sputtered oaths Raynor complied.

She took Rogan's hand and looked around for the other injured man. Spying him sulking away, she stopped him by shouting out, "Robert, to my cottage so that I may tend your wounds."

"I—"

"Now!"

The young man scurried off, stopped near Sheila and with cautious steps approached the young woman. Within minutes, She began to smile while Robert's swelling made his grin appear distorted. They walked off together.

Aliss and Rogan were left standing alone in the field.

She raised her hand to his swollen jaw, hoping her loving touch would help ease his pain. She didn't want him to hurt, to suffer, but then hadn't he wanted the same for her? The truth would set both of them free. Would it take long for her to be truthful with him and let him know her feelings? Hadn't he finally been truthful with her?

He kissed her palm.

"I did not think before I spoke," she said by way of apology.

"I noticed."

"I became furious when I saw Peter hit you. How dare he strike my husband. I could only think of—"

"Coming to my rescue?"

She winced. "I usurped your authority."

He kissed her palm again. "You did me a great honor."

"I did?" she asked, doubtful.

He nodded. "As Peter and Robert fought for the woman they love, you defended the man you love. And in front of the whole clan. That certainly will be fodder for wagging tongues for at least a month."

Aliss winced again. "I did not think. I did the very thing I accused Peter of doing, only I attacked with my tongue."

"A strong weapon for you."

"I am no better than the two men who battled over Shelia."

Rogan took hold of both her hands. "Love is instinctive, which causes people to react, even irrationally."

"Love is completely chaotic."

He kissed her lips gently before whispering, "Drown with me in the chaos."

"I must tend the injured men," she murmured regretfully, and stepped away from him.

"Will you tend me afterward?"

"Only if we can get lost in the chaos and forget all else."

"I will make it so," he said.

"Then I will see you soon." She hurried off, though she really didn't want to leave him. They were healing, the two of them. He had finally been completely honest with her. Their love had been too new, too fresh, for him to ignore the debt he felt he owed to his mother. It had festered for a lifetime inside him. She could not expect him to toss it aside for a love he had newly discovered. He had a right to claim what was his and trust that his new love would survive.

Love certainly wasn't simple.

It was complex and torturous and made you feel the fool more times than you cared to remember. Yet everyone wished to find love, claim it, hold on to it, and never let it go.

Peter and Robert certainly acted foolishly over love, but then so had she. She shook her head as she walked. She was not proud of her actions. She should have handled it differently, but at that moment when Peter connected with Rogan's jaw, fury reared its ugly head and possessed her like the devil himself. All she could think of was *attack*.

Now she felt shameful for humiliating the young man.

"Stop beating yourself up," Raynor said.

Aliss looked up. Raynor sat in front of her cottage on the bench, legs stretched out.

"The two are inside right now talking like old friends. Peter is probably glad you gave him a tongue-lashing. It was a lesser punishment than he would have received from Rogan."

"I never thought of that," she said, sitting down beside him. "What would Rogan have done?"

"A chieftain getting punched in the face, accident or not?" Raynor shook his head slowly. "It would not have been pretty. You are most likely everyone's hero today."

"I'm no hero."

"Of course you are, and Rogan knows it and should be proud of you. You saved Peter, the idiot, from punishment, you spoke up in defense of a fearful young woman and helped her speak up for herself, and you helped Robert discover that there just might be a chance for him to win Sheila's heart. But most of all, you defended your husband in front of the whole clan. You are certainly a hero."

"I attacked—"

"You defended."

"I spoke before—"

"Anyone else could, saving the day," Raynor confirmed.

Aliss laughed. "I like your version better than mine. It makes me appear a powerful warrior fighting for justice."

"That's because you are." He sat up. "I was proud of you today. You've changed. You need no one to defend you and no one to hide behind."

"You insinuate that I hid behind my sister?" She needn't ask the question; she knew it was true. She had depended on Fiona far too long. Her abduction had allowed her to grow into an independent woman and for that she was grateful.

"Let's say that Fiona overpowered anyone in her presence."

They both laughed.

"She has a demanding way about her, but a loving heart," Aliss said.

"True, but time away from each other has given you a chance to discover your own strength, to become independent."

"It has and I must admit I like it."

"Fiona will adjust to her new sister and be proud of her," Raynor said then stretched to a stand. ˙

Aliss popped off the bench with a smile. "Not without protest."

Raynor agreed with a nod and a grin. "See to the injured idiots and then I will see you later at supper."

"I may be occupied," Aliss said without thinking, and turned bright red.

Raynor laughed. "I'll be an uncle soon enough again."

Her hand went to her stomach after Raynor turned and walked away. He was right, he just might be an uncle soon.

* * *

Clouds drifted overhead and gathered in number as Rogan walked to the keep. A storm approached, he could smell it, and it wasn't far off. He hoped Aliss would finish soon so she wouldn't get caught in the rain, but then he actually hoped she'd finish soon so that they could get lost in a couple of hours of endless lovemaking.

She stirred his passion, refused to leave his thoughts, and was forever a part of his soul, and it felt wonderful.

Margaret acknowledged him with a smile and a nod when he entered the hall. She was busy instructing a couple of young girls at a table. His decision to place Margaret in charge of the keep had been a logical one. She was alone, with time on her hands, and she loved to cook. She had been honored and thrilled when he had asked her and had not hesitated to accept.

He was pleased that it had proven to be a good choice for all concerned. Meals were excellent, the keep was kept clean, his wife was free to heal, and Margaret was happy.

He climbed the wooden steps, noticing that the weak and broken steps had finally been replaced. There was much yet to be done in the keep and the village itself, but day by day more repairs and improvements were being made.

The Wolf clan finally had a home they took pride in, and he had finally settled into a life with a wife he loved dearly. Of course, there was the bargain to consider. Aliss had not let him free of it yet, but all indications assured him that she would. He longed to hear her tell him that she loved him. He had heard it too few times before he was robbed of the pleasure. Soon, if he remained hopeful, he would hear her say "I love you" again and again.

He shut the bedchamber door closed behind him and stopped for a moment to look out the window. He had dreamed of this day, of looking out over his land, and now that it was here it was not how he had imagined it.

What had once been of first importance to him now took second place to his feelings for Aliss. She mattered more to him now than anything else in his life, and he did not even try to make sense of it all. He did not want to. He simply wanted to share his life with his wife, have a slew of children with her, and grow old with her.

He walked to the bed, stripping off his shirt and tossing it to the chair as he went. Then he took off his sandals and stretched out on the bed. He recalled how lonely his father had been through the years, missing his wife more and more as the years passed.

He didn't know how his father had managed. He had hurt so badly when Kendra died, but then death had claimed her; he had no say in the matter. Not so with his mother. She chose to leave to protect him and his father. She had been alive all those years but they had never gotten to see her.

He could not live like that again. Those years had been difficult, and he could not imagine walking away from Aliss never to see her again, yet knowing she was alive and well.

He shook his head.

There was no way that would happen. He and Aliss were meant to be together, and in time, she would understand that and realize how much they truly loved each other. All would go well for them, he was sure of it.

And the rest of his plan?

Again, he shook his head.

If he chose to proceed with it, it would surely cause a rift between his wife and him that might never be mended. He could not take that chance, and he truly believed his mother would not have wanted revenge that would hurt so many. He was finally in possession of his inheritance and now his mother would want him to be happy with the woman he loved.

Thunder shook the heavens, lightning struck the ground and sent it smoldering while rain pounded the earth. Rogan listened to the downpour nourish nature.

Nature's melody soon lulled him to sleep.

Something tickled his lips and he wrinkled his nose and shook his head in an attempt to chase it away. It persisted and he swatted at it. The stubborn little bugger returned, but this time he waited, let it alight and grow comfortable.

The faint strokes danced across his lips as light as a fairy steps. He let it have its way, enjoying the enticing little dance until finally—he attacked. His tongue rushed out to capture it and connected briefly with the faint sweet taste of wine.

Then the same sensation came with a waltzlike dance along his naked chest, before floating down across his bare stomach and suddenly changing to sensuous nibbles and nips as it retraced its path up again.

Had he heard a faint sigh?

Or was that him?

Was this a dream?

He felt his kilt being ever so slowly spread apart and thought to open his eyes, but if this was a dream, he'd wake up and he didn't want to wake up just yet.

Chapter 35

❧

Rogan almost vaulted off the bed when moist lips began to sample him. Tentative, shy licks as if uncertain if she should taste or if she would savor the taste. The licks turned robust, and when she took him in her mouth his eyes flew open.

"Aliss?"

Her head popped up. "You were expecting someone else?"

"No, no, I never expected you to—"

"Pleasure you as you do me?" She laughed. "You can't have all the fun."

"Have all the fun you want," he encouraged. "But then it's my turn."

He felt her shiver between his legs, then her hand moved to cup him gently and her mouth descended with care over him. In her inexperience and total desire, she became masterful. But more importantly, she was doing this of her own accord. She had wanted him and had claimed him as her own and that brought his passion to heights he had never thought to experience again.

Damn, but he loved this woman.

He lost himself in the sheer exquisite pleasure of her generosity. She taunted and tempted and drove him nearly insane. He swelled with desire and felt ready to burst but that wouldn't be enough for him. He wanted to be inside her, feeling her clamp tightly around him.

He reached down and to her surprise lifted her to nest on his groin.

She gasped, smiled, then quickly stripped her blouse and skirt off, tossing them carelessly to the floor.

He ran his hands over her round hips, her skin as smooth as silk, then rested them at her waist. "I will guide you."

She shoved his hands away. "I need no help."

He watched as she stretched her arms to the ceiling, running her fingers through her mass of red curls, her breasts round and full, the nipples hard. Then with a roll of her neck and arch of her back she raised herself up and with sensuous grace lowered herself over his engorged manhood.

Little by little, she slid down over him and when he thought she would finally take all of him, she started all over again, a wicked little

smile on her face. She enjoyed teasing him and
he would let her have her fun for a time, since it
gave her pleasure and outrageously stimulated
his senses.

Then he would take command.

She moved over him like an experienced cour-
tesan, but then she lost herself in pleasure and
that was all it took. He groaned like a dying man
when she bounced with agility, stimulating him
to new unimaginable heights.

It felt so good. He could let her go on and
on . . .

Thought vanished and sensations raced
through him, his heart pounding, his blood rushing, and his desire hot and heavy.

He heard the faint laughter as if from a distance and he glanced at her. She smiled,
laughed, stretched her arms, sighed and bent
over him, her hands resting on his chest. Her
grin was victorious.

It took a mere second for him to flip her on her
back. Her round shocked eyes glared at him, her
mouth hung open, and he drove his tongue in as
his manhood swiftly penetrated her moisture.

He captured her gasp in his mouth as she
arched up and welcomed the length of him.

He released her mouth. "My turn."

She ran her hands up his chest. "Have you the
stamina to satisfy my hunger tonight?"

"Don't challenge me," he warned teasingly.

But she did, she ground her pelvis against him
and groaned. "I could come all night long."

He drew back out of her, though not all the way, and returned slowly. "We'll see about that."

They taunted each other, Aliss reaching climax several times and Rogan asking if she had had enough. He was surprised when she answered with a laugh and encouraged him to continue.

The night turned long and memorable until finally Aliss begged Rogan to join her and he did, both of them reaching dizzying heights of pleasure and erupting like bursting stars that rained to earth and settled contentedly.

They lay apart, their bodies moist with perspiration, their breathing calmed and their hearts no longer racing.

Rogan reached out to join pinkies with her. She took firm hold and they lay comfortably beside each other.

He turned his head to face her. "I am a lucky man to have found you."

"But I brought chaos to your life." She angled her head to look at him.

"Thank the Lord. I was getting bored."

She laughed. "You fib."

"That I do," he said gently. "I wasn't bored, I was lonely."

She turned on her side, their fingers parting, and she rested her hand on his chest. "Do you not still find yourself lonely? My work often keeps me from you."

"It may separate us at times, but you always return to me and I can always find you if I feel the need for your presence. Don't you know that is why you find me popping up at the healing cottage so often or tracking you down wherever you may be?"

She shook her head, her expression sad. "I never gave it a thought."

He pressed his hand over hers. "You wound me, woman."

"I am sorr—"

Rogan halted her words with a finger to her lips. "There is no need to apologize."

Aliss attempted to speak.

His finger remained firm. "You came to me tonight filled with a loving passion. That tells me more strongly than words how you feel."

She moved his finger away. "And it is enough?"

He stroked her cheek. "It goes beyond enough. You gave more of yourself to me tonight than you have ever given and that proves to me how much you love me and perhaps forgive me. You are a good wife and—" His hand rested on her stomach. "Someday you will make an excellent mother."

"You have such confidence."

"As should you. You have a gentle touch with the ill. How can you not help but have a tender touch with your own child?"

"You want children."

"A slew of them, if you agree," he said eagerly, then poked her. "Have you even given it thought?"

"Now and again I have."

"We are making headway," he teased.

"Do you think we are?" she asked seriously.

He moved to stroke her face again. "I know we are."

She yawned. "I should trust the Wolf."

"With your life."

She laughed. "Place my life in the hands of a wolf? That would take trust."

"A wolf is trustworthy."

"To whom?" she asked.

"His pack. He guards them with his life."

"You do that. You guard your clan, and I believe you would give your life to protect them, though I would not want to see you do that."

"If necessary I would."

She touched his face like a young child exploring, and with a sad smile she said, "I would give my life for you."

"No, you would not," he said adamantly. "I forbid it."

She shook her head. "You cannot. I have already made it known. Besides, you told me I could not stop you from forfeiting your life for mine. What you can do, so can I."

"You will take it back."

"I will not," she said, as if insulted that he demanded she do so.

He took firm hold of her arm. "Never even think that, promise me . . . please?"

She scooted closer to him and gave him a gentle kiss. "I did not mean to upset you."

"Then promise me," he said, stroking her lips with his.

"You tingle my senses when you do that." She

held up her gooseflesh-covered arm for his inspection.

He kissed the raised bumps on her flesh. "Promise me."

"Remind me of this promise."

"My kisses titillate you so much you do not recall?" He kissed her some more.

She licked her lips. "How can I think when passion races through me?"

"Promise me," he urged, running his fingers slowly over her naked flesh.

She sighed.

"Promise and I will stroke you to sleep."

"What if I don't want to sleep?"

"Then I will love you to sleep."

She laughed. "I promise. I promise. I promise."

Before the sun could greet them the next morning, Aliss was summoned to Margaret's cottage with a strange request. It was imperative that she come alone. Aliss was relieved when Rogan made no fuss. His only request was that she confide in him as to why all the mystery.

She had agreed and hurried off in the predawn morning, healing basket in hand.

Margaret stood outside waiting and opened the door just enough for them to enter.

"Whatever is—" Aliss turned speechless when she spotted Ivan on all fours in Margaret's bed, a blanket draped over him, though his hands and feet stuck out.

"We were having ourselves a little fun when Ivan went to move over—"

Aliss held up her hand. "No need for details."

"I heard something crack in his back."

"Hurts like the devil if I move," Ivan said. "And feeling the fool doesn't help."

"Nonsense," Margaret chastised. "We were having a wonderful time—" She looked to Aliss. "Ivan has the stamina of a young man."

Ivan grinned.

Aliss smiled. She couldn't wait to tell Rogan.

"I heard a crack," Margaret said. "His back, I think."

"Let's have a look," Aliss said, and walked over to Ivan.

"I'm naked," he warned.

"I tried to at least get his kilt on but—"

"It's all right," Aliss assured the couple. "I don't need to remove the blanket."

Ivan sighed with relief.

Margaret smiled. "Good. I don't want another woman seeing how well endowed my man is. It might give her ideas."

Ivan grinned again.

Aliss saved her laughter for when she spoke with Rogan.

After a thorough examination along his back, she explained, "I am going to blend a poultice that Margaret will apply to your back, Ivan. While the towels soak, I'm going to work on your back with my fingers. I think we can get you to where you will be able to move enough to lie flat and rest until it heals."

By the time the sun had risen a good distance in the sky, Ivan was sitting on the edge of the bed, not completely pain free but feeling better.

"You won't go telling anyone, will you?" Margaret asked.

"She'll tell Rogan, you can count on it," Ivan said.

"Well, of course, she loves him. I would tell you if it were them I saw."

Ivan grinned. "That would be a sight."

The two of them laughed.

Aliss shook her head. "I won't say a word."

"Except to Rogan," Margaret corrected.

"Except to Rogan," Aliss confirmed.

"Good," Ivan said, with a pound of his fist to his thigh and a wince. "My chieftain will know that the old warrior still has stamina."

Margaret sauntered over to him. "That you have, deary, that you have."

"None of that for a while," Aliss ordered.

They both looked devastated.

"How long?" Ivan asked. Margaret held his hand tightly.

"A week at least, then we'll see how your back is."

They both looked as if they'd been handed a death sentence.

"It's either that or a month."

"A week, a week," they both said in unison.

Aliss left Margaret fussing over Ivan. She smiled on her way to the keep. They made a good couple. You could see how much they cared for each other by the way they looked at each other. It was there in their eyes; they sparkled.

Love seemed to be in the air along with autumn's first crisp bite. Besides Ivan and Margaret, she spied Robert carefully placing a freshly picked bouquet of heather in front of Sheila's door. To his surprise, she opened the door before he could make his escape.

She picked up the bouquet and smiled at him. He returned the smile and they were soon talking.

She even spied Derek chatting with Tara while little Daniel ran around his legs. Now there would be a good match. Tara had arrived at the Wolf clan seeking sanctuary from a brutal lord who had killed her husband.

Perhaps there would be a wedding or two, maybe three, this winter or spring. She couldn't wait to tell Rogan. She hurried into the keep and spotted her husband sitting at a table by the fire's hearth, the table prepared for breakfast.

"I waited," he said, standing to greet her with a kiss.

"But I've been a while. You must be starving."

"I nibbled," he said, and demonstrated on her neck.

She giggled and hurried to sit. "I have gossip to share, though some of it you must not share with anyone."

They were soon deep in laughter.

"Ivan's right. I am proud of him," Rogan said with a grin.

Raynor entered the hall and hesitated to join them, but a wave from both had him sitting down just in time to hear about Derek and Tara.

"I thought those two had eyes for each other," Raynor said, piling his plate with food.

"What about you?" Rogan asked. "Aren't you interested in finding a wife?"

The piece of thick bread stopped before entering Raynor's mouth. "In due time I will find a suitable wife."

"Suitable?" Aliss asked.

Rogan rolled his eyes.

Raynor shook his head. "I will not have you or Fiona interfering with my future plans."

"You have plans?" Aliss asked accusingly. "And you haven't shared them with us?"

"I have no plans yet," Raynor said. "You and Fiona will be the first to know when I do."

Suddenly the horn sounded throughout the village, the sorrowful wail penetrating the windows of the keep.

Rogan stood. "A ship approaches."

"No reason for alarm," Raynor said, and finished his piece of bread before he stood.

Aliss was already at her husband's side. "You know who comes?"

Raynor nodded after taking a drink of ale.

Aliss glared at her brother. "Do not tell me that you sent a message to—"

Raynor shook his head. "She's probably come searching for me."

Chapter 36

Aliss watched Tarr and Fiona disembark. Her sister looked wonderful, round with child and a healthy glow to her cheeks. Her red hair was piled high on her head, but not all the fiery strands remained contained. Several fell free, framing her face.

A deep blue wool cloak clung to her shoulders but didn't hide her protruding stomach. Her sure-footed steps made Aliss jealous; Fiona showed no signs of having been sick at sea and she was heavy with child.

Aliss approached her sister with a smile, ready to greet her with a hug.

"Where is Raynor?" Fiona asked on her approach, and stopped in front of her sister. "He sneaked off to visit you without telling me. I finally discovered where he went." She paused for a breath. "And please tell me you have come to your senses and have chosen not to remain with the Wolf."

"Good day to you too," Aliss said with a gentle laugh.

"It would be if you tell me you're returning with us."

"You should not have traveled this distance with your time drawing near," Aliss chastised, determined to ignore her sister's persistent nature.

"There was no convincing her of that, once she learned where Raynor went," Tarr said, looking accusingly in his brother-in-law's direction.

"I didn't tell her because I knew this would happen," Raynor protested vehemently.

Fiona shot him a heated glance.

"He wanted to rescue me," Aliss said in her brother's defense.

"Tell me he did," Fiona said, her hands folded in prayer.

"It wasn't necessary. I realized how well suited they are for each other," Raynor admitted.

"What?" Fiona snapped. "You cannot be serious? Aliss deserves someone better."

"Aliss deserves someone to love her and Rogan loves her," Raynor argued.

Tarr stepped into the middle of the dispute. "Neither matters, as I have decreed that the choice belongs to Aliss. So there is no sense in you two bickering."

"Nor was there any sense in you making this

trip," Aliss said. "Rogan and I had plans to come and stay with you within the next two weeks so that I would be there in plenty of time to deliver the babe."

"She refused to listen to reason," Tarr said with a shrug.

"My sister is making the mistake of her life and I'm to sit back and watch? I do not think so."

"It is my mistake to make," Aliss argued.

"So you admit it is a mistake?" Fiona asked hopefully.

"That's the point, Fiona, it doesn't matter. It is mine to make. Just like you chose Tarr of your own accord."

"He is a good choice," Fiona said, hooking her arm in her husband's.

Aliss turned to her husband who stood a step behind her. She had known he had quietly taken a spot behind her, yet he had remained silent, allowing her to speak for herself. She was grateful for his understanding and confidence in her.

She placed her hand on Rogan's arm. "My husband is a good choice for me."

"You are stubborn," Fiona spat.

Tarr and Raynor laughed.

"This is not funny," Fiona scolded. Then she suddenly doubled over, grabbing her stomach.

Tarr had his arms around her in an instant. "What's wrong?"

Fiona's eyes clouded with tears, her tone worried. "A sharp pain."

Aliss was already at her side. "This voyage was too taxing. You need to rest."

"The babe?" Fiona asked, concern making her words tremble.

"Will be fine. You're here with me now," Aliss assured her with confidence that brought a smile of relief to her sister's face. "Let's get you back to the keep and in bed so that you can rest for the remainder of the day."

Tarr lifted his wife in his arms.

"It is too far for you to carry her all the way," Rogan said. "We will take turns."

"He's right," Raynor said. "We will help."

Tarr nodded and hugged his wife to him.

Aliss watched for her husband to catch up with them, since he had lagged behind to issue orders for his men to help Tarr's men secure the ship and unload whatever was necessary. It didn't take him long, though it did take Tarr some time before his wife grew burdensome in his arms.

Aliss wasn't surprised to see Rogan offer to relieve him.

"Raynor can carry me," Fiona protested.

"Let Rogan carry you for a while, then I will carry you the remainder of the way," Raynor said and walked ahead slowly.

Aliss was glad he had refused their sister. Fiona would have to get used to Rogan sooner or later and she preferred it be sooner.

They spoke not a word to each other and Fiona kept her arms crossed over her chest, refusing to take hold of Rogan. Aliss could only shake her head and walk alongside her husband in support of him.

Another pain had Fiona grabbing Rogan's shirt. "Stop. Stop."

Rogan stopped dead and Tarr reached out to take his wife. She buried her head in his chest, while he looked to Aliss with fear-filled eyes.

Aliss went to her sister and spoke softly to her while she ran her hand over her stomach. She felt no hardness, as some women get just before they go into labor.

"Tell me the truth," Fiona pleaded.

"You would get nothing but that from me," Aliss said.

"Then what is it? Have I harmed the babe by traveling here?"

"You may have disturbed him and he simply protests, or he may be getting ready to birth sooner than expected. Either way, I would suggest you do not return home. It would be safer for you to remain here until the babe is born."

Fiona looked to her husband. "I am sorry. I know you would have liked for your child to be born on your land and in the bosom of your clan."

"As long as you and he are all right, it matters not," Tarr assured her with a sweet kiss. "Now let's get you into bed so you may rest as Aliss ordered."

"She suggested. She didn't order me," Fiona corrected.

"Do I need to order you?" Aliss asked firmly.

Fiona shook her head. "No, you are right."

"What did I hear?" Raynor said, hurrying over to them. "Did you say Aliss was right?"

"Enough from you," Fiona said. "It is your fault that I am here in the first place."

"Your stubbornness brought you here," Raynor said, walking alongside her.

"*Our* concern for *our* sister brought me here."

"Not another word!" Aliss ordered. "Fiona, you need to rest and not worry."

"You heard her," Tarr said firmly.

Raynor drifted off, Tarr marched forward with his wife in his arms, and Aliss turned to her husband.

"You have remained silent through this all."

"This is between you and your sister," he said, reaching out for her hand and curling his fingers around hers. "And as Tarr reminded us all, the choice is yours."

She drifted up close to him. "It is an easy choice and you helped make it so."

"Aliss!" Tarr called out.

"Go see to your sister," Rogan said. "We can talk later if you like."

She stared at him a moment and tentatively touched his cheek. He was good to her, patient and understanding. She did love him and want to remain his wife, and soon, very soon, she would tell him.

He took her hand and kissed the palm. "Go and worry not about us. It is your sister who matters now."

Aliss kissed his cheek. "Until later." She hurried off, a sudden feeling of happiness attacking her without provocation. Rogan made her happy in so many different ways. The realization startled her and yet brought a smile to her face. His courting had worked much better than he ever imagined and he had topped it with the truth when he had taken her to his secret boyhood haunt and confessed his past anger.

She would choose to stay with Rogan, be his wife, the mother of his children. He had been truthful with her and she would remain with him.

Fiona was settled with a modicum of problems and complaints in the bedchamber across the hall from Aliss and Rogan. Tarr reluctantly took his leave, promising his wife he would remain close, while she insisted he go tend to whatever was necessary and not worry about her.

As soon as the door shut Fiona whispered, "You can speak freely now that we're alone."

Aliss sat beside her sister on the edge of the bed. Fiona was sitting up, resting against several pillows, dressed in a comfortable night shift.

"You think I have not spoken freely to you?"

"With so many about, it would not be easy to say what you wish."

"I have nothing to hide," Aliss said.

"Then you will remain with the Wolf?"

"*Rogan*. His name is *Rogan*," Aliss emphasized.

"Do you love *Rogan*?"

Aliss hesitated.

"You love him or you don't."

"I do," Aliss insisted. "I just suddenly wondered if I could offer him even a small amount of the love he offers me."

"Then you do question your love for him?"

"No! I question whether I can love him with the same fervor as he does me!"

"That is foolish," Fiona scolded. "Love is love."

Aliss stood. "Not to me. Rest—you need it. I will see you later." She left the room, leaving the door ajar behind her and Fiona with her mouth hanging open.

She didn't expect anyone to understand. They would have to understand the depths of her commitment to her healing work to understand her issues with love. She loved healing. It fulfilled her, made her feel worthwhile, and she gave it all she had.

Did she truly have room left to love?

At least love properly? While Rogan filled her mind daily, healing occupied her mind a good portion of the day, so that she often forgot about sharing meals with him. If she loved him as strongly as he did her, wouldn't she be more thoughtful of him?

He had made it clear that he did not mind her absentmindedness. However, she did. She did not think it fair, especially since he was so attentive to her.

"You look worried."

Aliss jumped in fright, her hand flying to her chest.

Tarr reached out, placing a hand on her shoulder. "I am sorry. I did not mean to frighten you. Your expression had me concerned about Fiona."

She took a breath to calm her racing heart and walked with Tarr to a table in the empty hall. "Fiona is fine; she rests."

"The babe—"

"From what I can tell he seems fine, just fussy," Aliss said, and attempted to move his worries off the babe. "I am surprised that Mother and Father didn't come with you."

"Your father suffered a sprained ankle—"

"Is he all right?" she asked, concerned, then realized Tarr was grinning. "He didn't sprain his ankle?"

"Let's just say your sister has been a bit difficult to deal with lately."

"Mother remained behind willingly?"

Tarr nodded. "Insisted that she needed to look after her husband, though she secretly informed me she would be rested and ready to resume care of her daughter upon our return."

"She will be upset and worried when you don't return home soon."

"I will send a message so they do not worry, though the clan had looked forward to your return. Wagging tongues had it that Fiona would not be half as difficult to contend with if you were there." Tarr paused, clearing his throat. "Your sister misses you, especially now."

Guilt squeezed at Aliss's heart. "I should have been there all along for her. We have always been there for each other. I have been selfish."

"It wasn't your fault you were abducted."

"But what followed is my fault."

"I would say love should take the blame," Tarr said. "And we certainly can't argue with love, and I don't think you're selfish. It is good we are here now with you in Fiona's time of need."

"I would swim the sea if need be to help my sister."

"Fiona would have done the same if I had not

talked sense into her the day we discovered you were abducted and a ransom demanded."

"We think alike," Aliss said, and then asked, "Who occupied this isle?"

"The land belonged to my mother's people. An older brother of hers occupied it for years until he died. My grandfather bequeathed the isle, then uninhabited, to my mother when she wed with the stipulation that her firstborn son inherit it.

"My father reminded me often enough that this isle belonged to me and should pass to my son and that I was to allow no one to take it from me."

"Yet you surrendered it to Rogan?"

"My mother told me one day that this land would bring peace to many. She was right. This land has brought clans together and will keep sisters close. It has served its purpose."

Chapter 37

◦◦◦

"I am feeling better," Fiona said the next morning, when Aliss checked on her. "I slept soundly and I have had not a pain or ache."

"Which means you want permission to get out of bed," Aliss said.

"I beg you," Fiona said with clasped hands. "I promise I will take it easy, rest, do nothing, worry not, just please, please let me out of bed."

Aliss pulled back the covers. "After breakfast you can come with me to my healing cottage and rest there, then we can talk when I'm not tending someone."

"Wonderful," Fiona said. "I have missed talking with you."

"And I with you, Fiona," Aliss said, extending

her hand to help her sister. "Though I talk with you often in my head."

"I do the same, I must confess . . ." Fiona said, pausing to slip out of her night shift and into her day shift and tunic. "You mentioned when first we found you how you spoke with me often in your head after the abduction. I did the same, encouraging you to be strong and reminding you every day that I would come for you."

"I heard every word." Aliss hugged her sister. "You kept me strong."

"I think you kept yourself strong and I admire your courage."

"You taught me."

"Nonsense," Fiona said. "We learned from each other."

They hugged each other tightly.

"Let's go," Fiona said, grabbing her sister's hand. "I am starving."

Rogan and Raynor stood when the twins entered the hall. Tarr hurried to his wife's side, his arm going around her.

"You are well enough to be up?"

"So says Aliss," Fiona said, giving her husband a peck on the cheek. "After we eat, I am going to spend the day with her at her healing cottage, so you needn't worry. If I deliver, she will have everything at hand."

Tarr paled.

"She jests," Aliss assured him, and walked to sit beside her husband at the table while Tarr seated his wife.

Raynor stood to assist.

"Everything looks delicious," Fiona said, licking her lips while her husband piled her plate with food.

"Rogan has worked wonders with the isle," Raynor said. "A field is ripe for harvesting, the storehouse is near full for the winter, logs and peat have been gathered and stocked by each cottage. Shelter has been constructed for the animals and the cottages fortified against the cold."

"You turned a foe into a friend?" Tarr asked with no malice.

"It would seem that way," Raynor admitted.

"That is good since we are family now," Tarr said. "Though I am curious, why did you insist on ownership of the Isle of Non?"

Rogan shrugged. "It is a good place. My clan can thrive here."

"There are other areas where your clan could have thrived; why this particular isle?"

"My father brought me here when I was young and I took a liking to it."

"It must have made quite an impression on you to remember it after all those years," Fiona said in between bites.

Rogan stood. "It did. Please enjoy the meal, I have things I must attend to."

"I offended him?" Fiona asked once he was gone.

Aliss slipped off the bench. "No, he has much to look after. Excuse me, I'll be right back."

The sun was bright, the air cool, as Aliss hurried after her husband. She had to keep a quick pace to catch up with him, as his steps were determined.

"Do you run away?" she called out when nearly on top of him.

He spun around. "Go back to your family."

"What upset you?"

"Nothing. Go to your sister, she needs you."

"*You* need me right now," she said, refusing to be ignored.

"I need no one."

His words pierced her heart like a sharp blade, but she maintained her courage. He had worked hard to win her and she would work hard to keep their love strong. "I think that you do."

"You care?"

"Yes, I care or I wouldn't have come after you."

He grabbed hold of her, to her surprise, and buried his face in her hair. "I'm glad you care. I'm glad you came after me."

She hugged him tightly to her. "Tell me what troubles you."

"Aliss," Anna yelled from the cottage door, and waved. "You're needed."

"Go," he said, and pushed her away.

"No!" She turned and shouted to Anna, "Take care of it!" Then she turned her attention back to her husband, who stood with a look of shock on his face. "Are you all right?"

"I cannot believe you just did that." He reached out, grabbed her around the waist, and swung her up against him. "God, but I love you so much."

"Then tell me what is wrong. You worry me."

He smiled. "Nothing is wrong. Everything is fine now. We're all at peace."

He lowered her and they hugged.

" 'Peace.' I have heard that word often of late, starting with Giann and her prediction. Tarr recently mentioned that his mother had told him this land, which he inherited from her, would bring peace to many. He generously gave of his inheritance so that—"

Aliss gasped and turned wide eyes on her husband. "Oh, my God. Your mother bequeathed this isle to you, as your birthright. Tarr's mother bequeathed this land to him, as his birthright. Your mother left you in order to protect you and your father. She returned to wed a man of her father's choosing. That man was Tarr's father, wasn't he? Tarr is your half brother."

He took her hand and tugged her along after him, and she realized that he wanted privacy. They walked to the side of the keep, out of earshot and away from prying eyes.

"Tarr is my half brother."

"Why didn't you tell me? I asked if there was anything else—"

"What purpose would it serve? It would only hurt others if they knew and what right did I have to ask you to keep my secret? It is better left buried."

"Doesn't Tarr have a right to know?" she asked. "That his mother had a first husband and son she loved dearly, was forced to desert them, and was then forced to wed another man and bear him a child?"

"I would want to know that."

They both turned to see Tarr standing there.

DONNA FLETCHER

"Fiona isn't feeling well. I came out to get you, Aliss, and saw you both hurry off. I followed just in time to hear the news—*brother*."

"I saw no reason to tell you," Rogan said defensively.

"I have a right to know."

"Let's take this inside so that I may tend to Fiona," Aliss said.

"You go in, Rogan and I have things to discuss," Tarr said.

She did not like the way the two men regarded each other. "No, either we all go in, or I remain out here with you both."

That persuaded Tarr to leave. As they entered the hall Tarr called out.

"Meet my half brother." He stretched his arm out to Rogan.

"What?" Fiona asked, rubbing her stomach.

Raynor shook his head. "What are you talking about?"

Aliss went over to Fiona.

"Tarr need not have summoned you. It is just an upset stomach, which I seem to suffer often of late. I am more concerned with this news." Fiona looked to her husband.

Aliss returned to Rogan's side and took his hand.

"Explain," Tarr said, bracing himself against the edge of the table near his wife.

"It's simple. My mother is also your mother," Rogan said.

"I am to believe this?"

"Believe what you wish. It is the truth and the reason why I wanted the Isle of Non. It belongs to me. You acknowledged that yourself when you said that your mother's firstborn son was to inherit the isle."

"And you claim to be her firstborn?" Tarr asked.

"*I am* her firstborn."

"Then tell me about mother," Tarr challenged.

"You wish to discuss this in front of everyone?"

"We are all family here. And dare I say we are curious?" Tarr said.

Aliss wisely remained silent, as did Fiona and Raynor, though none would dare leave.

"She was loving, kind, and generous, thinking always of others before herself."

"Many women are like that," Tarr said. "Besides, how old were you when you say your mother was forced to desert you and your father?"

"A small lad—"

"With few memories," Tarr argued.

"My father's memories served well enough, which is why he brought me here to the Isle of Non again and again, telling me of its importance to my mother. She told my father this isle was all she had to give me to remember her by. She loved this place, having spent time here with an uncle and aunt she adored and wished were her parents. She hated her father, and her mother had died when she was young."

It was obvious to all that his words affected Tarr, who remained silent, his arms crossed over his chest and his fists clenched.

"My father spoke often of how she had told him that whenever I watched a flower bloom on this land, an animal at play, a fruitful harvest, that I was to know that she was with me and would always be."

Tarr shoved away from the table. "My mother said no such thing."

"Maybe not to you."

"You imply my mother did not love me?"

"No, you were her *second* son and she would love you with all her heart, even while her heart broke for a son she had been forced to abandon."

"If you believe she loved so strongly, how could you truly believe she would willingly abandon you? Would she not have fought to remain with you and your father?"

Rogan gave a guttural laugh. "Did you know our mother's father?"

"A brave warrior."

"A bastard," Rogan spat. "He outlined in detail to my mother what he would do to me and my father if she did not return and serve her clan."

"Your father should have fought for the woman he loved."

"He wanted to, though he had barely twenty men who were willing to fight with him."

"The rest of your clan refused their chieftain?"

"Those twenty men were his clan and would have gladly died with him defending my mother and me, and then what? *Your* grandfather would have killed me anyway and Mother knew it. She wanted to prevent senseless slaughter and made the only choice she felt would serve the greater good."

"So she loved *you* so much she sacrificed for you?"

"Jealous?"

"Of what?" Tarr snickered. "A tale fueled over the years by a bitter man who probably kidnapped a woman from a clan, forced himself on her until she was finally rescued by her family."

Rogan stepped forward, his fists restrained at his sides. "My father did no such thing."

"Really, then how do you explain your similar actions, if not learning it from your father?"

Aliss rushed between the two men, reaching them before her sister, who had wobbled at a good speed to reach her husband's side.

"Enough," Aliss warned. "This needs to be discussed, not argued over."

"He implies I was conceived out of forced lust and not love," Rogan said. "He is jealous that he witnessed no love between his father and mother, while as young as I was I recall them always in each other's arms."

"She was probably trying to get away from him," Tarr said.

"Stop," Fiona snapped. "Aliss is right, verbal warfare will settle little. This matter needs to be discussed sensibly."

"There is nothing to discuss," Tarr said with a dismissive wave at Rogan. "He can believe as he wishes, I know the truth."

"You refuse to see the truth," Rogan said with a jab of his finger in Tarr's direction.

"You think me an idiot to accept what you say as fact and not challenge your claim?" Tarr argued.

Aliss had a hand braced against each man's chest. "Shouting and arguing will not get this settled."

"It needs no settling," Tarr said, and jabbed at his own chest. "I know the truth."

"You fool yourself into believing lies because to face the truth would mean that your mother *hated* your father and grandfather for robbing her of the man and child she loved."

"You cannot face the fact that your father forced your mother, never wanting you in the first place."

Rogan lunged.

"Raynor," Aliss screamed, knowing she was no match for the two towering giants she was sandwiched between.

Raynor jumped in and did his best to keep the two heated men apart, while Aliss tugged at her husband's arm to pull him away. Fiona did the same with her husband.

"None of this matters now," Rogan shouted. "I got what Mother wanted for me. The Isle of Non is mine."

"That can be remedied," Tarr warned.

"You renege on your gift?"

"It was no gift," Tarr corrected snidely. "It was ransom for return of my sister-in-law."

"Enough, Tarr," Fiona warned.

The reminder, however, had done its damage, though not to the intended target. It hit Aliss where it could do the most damage, in her heart. She stood firm, though, and let no one see the pain it caused her, except her sister who knew and shared her hurt.

"This stops now!" Fiona ordered with a strength that shocked both men silent. "You two are behaving like spoiled children who want their own way. You are grown men, warriors who have faced difficult battles and yet emerged victorious. You both should be ashamed of your actions. This matter is not about the two of you. It is about a woman who after all these years and from beyond the grave wishes to be heard. When do you both intend to listen to her?"

Aliss wanted to applaud her sister's words. She had put the problem in proper prospective for them. Would they realize it and handle it as Fiona advised, with the dignity it deserved?

Aliss nudged her husband. "Fiona is right. Your mother does not deserve being argued over. I suspect she would want you both to act like . . . brothers, long lost and recently united."

Fiona continued to encourage them along with her sister. "Think of it as a door opened to you both where—"

Aliss gasped. "That is what Giann meant."

"You met Giann?" Fiona asked, excited.

"Yes, and she recited the prophecy, which was different from what we were told."

"What is it?" Tarr asked.

Aliss recited the words she heard in her head. " 'On a full moon twin babes are born, with their birth sounds the horn, eyes of green, hair of red, destruction comes if for love they do not wed, for true love will open the door, for peace to reign forever more.' "

They stared at her and she shook her head.

"Don't you understand? Fiona and I must love the men we wed, our love brings you both together, opening the door for peace to reign among all our clans forever more."

Raynor shook his head. "I don't understand. You both were kidnapped to bring you to this point in time and reunite two brothers?"

"Destiny takes many twists and turns until it is appeased," Aliss said.

"You sound like Giann," Rogan said.

"I think I finally understand what she attempted to tell me. What is decided here this day between you and Tarr does not only determine our destinies—" She paused and gave thought to the babe she finally was certain she carried inside her. "But future destinies as well, and for some reason that is important."

"You two better make amends," Fiona threatened.

"Is that an order?" Tarr snapped.

Fiona poked her husband in the chest. "It certainly is."

"Give me a good reason why I should be intimidated by your threat."

"You're going to argue with me about this, here and now?"

"Unless you can give me a good reason why I shouldn't."

Fiona bit at her bottom lip, grimaced for a moment, took a deep breath then said, "Because I think I am about to give birth to your child."

Chapter 38

◦—◦◦—◦

Chaos took hold and everyone attempted to do something while actually nothing got done, until Aliss finally took charge.

"I have all I need at my cottage. It is best to take Fiona there," she said, offering her sister comfort with a squeeze of her hand.

"Whatever you say," Tarr said, and lifted his wife in his arms.

"I'll go ahead and see that Anna has the bed prepared," Rogan said, and rushed out of the hall.

Tarr was close behind him, while Raynor appeared lost and turned to Aliss.

"What can I do?"

Aliss grabbed his arm. "You have the most important chore of all."

"I do?"

Aliss nodded. "You must keep peace between Tarr and Rogan."

"You ask a lot," Raynor admitted. "They are both ready to throw fists, though I cannot blame them. The news of them being half brothers is startling."

"See that they don't, please, for your sisters' sake. There will be time later for the two to dispute the finding; for now Fiona must be considered."

"I'll do my best."

"Then I won't worry," Aliss said, kissed his cheek and rushed out of the hall. Raynor followed close behind.

Fiona was settled comfortably in the bed, her husband by her side, holding on to her hand as if he dared not let her go.

Aliss looked from one to the other. "It is better if Tarr leaves."

"No, I'm staying," he insisted.

Aliss shook her head, grabbed his arm, and yanked him away from Fiona. "No, you are leaving." She pushed him to the door. "I will summon you as soon as the babe arrives."

He looked lost and helpless, his eyes resting on his wife.

"I'll be fine," Fiona assured him. "Do as Aliss says."

He nodded, hesitated, then reluctantly left the cottage.

Aliss turned to see her sister crying and hurried over to her. "Everything will be fine."

"Will it?" Fiona asked, as if she expected a promise.

Aliss leaned over and combed her sister's hair with her fingers, gathering it in the back to tie with a ribbon. "You and Tarr will be the parents of a fine babe this day. Do not worry."

"If our husbands don't kill each other first." She sniffled.

"I ordered Raynor to keep watch over them."

"That is good," Fiona said with a modicum of relief.

"Now relax, you will need your strength as the pains increase."

Rogan sat, with Raynor to his right, beneath the tree that shaded the cottage, watching Tarr pace in front of the closed door.

"Aliss is an excellent healer," Rogan said, hoping to ease his concern.

"Don't you think I know that," Tarr snapped, never missing a step.

"Then there is no need for you to worry," Rogan said.

Tarr spun around. "Tell me you would not worry if it were Aliss giving birth."

"She is a healer who—" The sudden clarity of his remark made him think. There would be no one as experienced as Aliss to deliver a babe when she eventually gave birth. He would need to remind Aliss to teach Anna all she could about birthing.

"Worry all you like," Rogan finally said.

Tarr nodded. "I plan to."

"You don't give your wife enough credit,"

Raynor said. "Fiona is stubborn and strong. She will do fine."

A couple of hours later all three men weren't so sure about that when piercing screams resonated from the cottage.

"You did not warn me that it would hurt this much," Fiona accused, dropping back against the pillow exhausted after several hours of labor.

"It would not have mattered if I did. You would do what you wanted anyway," Aliss said in jest.

"And you don't? You jumped into marriage with a man you love, to discover he loved you only to be betrayed by him. You then enter a bargain with him giving the idiot time to prove his love, which evidently he's done. But still you continue to worry if it's all real."

Aliss stared dumbfounded at her. Where had that come from? Her sister's mind should be on her delivery and here she was pointing out Aliss's problems.

"I know the way you think," Fiona said with a shake of her finger.

"You seem to," Aliss answered calmly, knowing this was not the time to discuss her and Rogan's relationship.

"Why afraid to speak up?"

"This isn't a conversation we should be having now," Aliss warned.

"Why not? We have nothing else to do but wait for the babe, who will come in his own good time. Your words, not mine. If it were up to me, he would have been here weeks ago. Now tell me if I am right."

Her sister would harp and harp if she didn't speak, and besides, she ached to talk with Fiona. They might argue, but in the end, problems would be hashed out and decisions made. "Rogan has proven he loves me time and again. He confided much in me over the time we have been here . . ."

"But?"

Aliss knew she should not let it bother her, but it had been such a shock to find out, and even more of a shock that he had not told her about it before anyone else. "Rogan did not confide in me about Tarr being his half brother."

"Understandably. It would have only caused more friction at a time Rogan was focused on getting you to realize how much he loved you. You came first to him. Damn, I hate taking his side, but the truth is—" A sharp pain robbed her of her words.

"No more talk, save your strength," Aliss ordered, wiping her sister's perspiring brow with a cool, moist cloth.

"No, this needs to be said," Fiona insisted on a rolling breath. "The truth is, the man has put you first."

"How so?" Aliss argued.

"Don't sound like a spoiled child," Fiona scolded. "He could have spilled his guts from day one and made everything worse."

"He would have made it better."

"That's a laugh," Fiona said. "Think of it. It would have sounded like you meant nothing to him and he did everything to get revenge. I imagine the idiot figured his only chance was to prove his love before he enlightened you to the truth. He actually put you first, thought of your feelings. Isn't that what you wanted?"

That her sister made sense stunned Aliss to silence.

"My advice to you, dear sister? Feel love, accept love, live love, and stop worrying about all the extra nonsense."

"I didn't know you were such an authority on love."

"I didn't either, but I learned that you need to respect and honor love even if it doesn't turn out exactly as you wanted it to. I'll get used to the idiot, and the only reason why is because he loves you and will keep you safe. He's—" She cleared her throat and rushed to add, "He's a good man."

"You've changed your mind about him?'

"A little, *just* a little."

Aliss sat beside her. "Why?"

"I didn't realize until today how much you both loved each other."

"What do you mean?" Aliss asked.

"When Rogan explained what this land meant to him and that he was willing to give it up for you, that spoke volumes. He would sacrifice all he had planned and held dear, for you." She shook her head. "That takes real love. And the way you rushed after him, the hurt in your eyes over his suffering and wanting to comfort him—" She shook her head again and swatted away a fat teardrop. "You two love each other, plain and simple."

Another pain attacked and had Fiona mumbling several oaths beneath her breath as she grabbed her stomach.

"How much longer?" she pleaded.

"A couple of hours at least."

Fiona groaned and dropped her head back on the pillow. "Enough talk. Tell your husband you forgive him and love him and get it over with. I can guarantee it will be much less painful than what I am going through."

"Did you hear that?" Tarr asked, springing away from the tree trunk he sat braced against.

The other two men cringed as they shook their heads.

"I don't know how much more I can take," Tarr admitted.

"I think it should be Fiona considering that," Raynor said.

Tarr groaned and dropped back against the tree trunk.

That evening, as the sun set, Elizabeth entered the world, to her mother and father's relief. The two very proud parents cuddled her close while the whole village celebrated the first birth of a child in their new home.

"Mother would be proud that her first grandchild was born on this land," Rogan said, his arms around his wife's waist, her head resting back against his chest.

"She was a loving and unselfish woman," Tarr said.

"That she was," Rogan agreed.

Aliss was pleased by the exchange for it signified a truce of sorts and the willingness of them both to eventually settle their differences.

"Then it is only fitting that you provide her with her first grandson on the Isle of Non," Tarr said, touching his daughter's wrinkled face. "After all, Elizabeth will need someone to protect her."

"If she's anything like her mother that won't be necessary," Raynor said, chuckling, and so did everyone else except Fiona. She glared at him.

Anna peeked her head in the door. "I don't wish to interrupt, but there are many who would like to see the first babe born on the Isle of Non, if that is all right?"

"Your choice, Fiona," Aliss said.

"Tarr and I would be honored."

For the next couple of hours, villagers streamed in and out of the cottage, each one leaving a small token for the babe and for what her birth meant to them all, a new life.

It was well into the evening when Aliss settled mother, father, and babe for the night and took her leave.

She had sent Rogan home an hour ago under protest. He had wanted to wait for her, but she needed time with her thoughts. The walk to the keep would give her that time.

Her mind flooded with memories of the last few months and she allowed them to roll by, dismissing each one. It was easier to do that knowing the whole truth. Everything made much more sense, and she needed to finally let go of her doubts and fears. She now had all the facts. The decision was hers.

Actually, her abduction had proven beneficial to her. It had allowed her to discover her own strength, separate from that of her sister.

Aliss smiled. Giann had been right. She had been given a gift and she would treasure it forever. Now all that was left was to tell her husband how she felt.

She entered their bedchamber and immediately drifted into her husband's arms. Aliss rested her head to his chest, grateful to hear the steady beating of his heart and to know his heart beat with love for her.

"Everyone is fine?"

"Yes."

You must be tired," he said.

"No," she said, lifting her head and taking his hand to lead him to the bed. She nudged him to sit down. "I have something I must say."

He reached out and rested his hands on her hips. "I am listening."

Where should she start? It ought to be easy, and yet standing in front of him now, staring down at his handsome face, his wicked smile and heated eyes, she didn't want to do anything but make love with him.

She shook her head.

"What is wrong?"

"You distract me."

"How do I do that?" he asked innocently, while his hands urged her forward between his legs.

"Just like that," she said, and squirmed away from him, holding out her hand when he stood so that he would not approach her. "I need to say this."

"All right, you have my attention. I promise not to distract you."

She appreciated that he folded his arms across his chest. She'd be safe from his touch, at least until she finished, and then she intended to run into his arms and never leave.

"We have been through much together—"

"And have survived it all."

She laughed softly. "You stole my words."

"We think alike."

"I have come to realize that."

His dark eyes focused intently on her and she was covered with gooseflesh. Lord, but the man could stir her passion.

He waited, and she could see in the depths of his green eyes that he knew what she wanted to say to him. She knew that he wanted to hear it, had patiently waited to hear it, and had been sure that he would hear it.

He had been right.

It had taken her far too long to get to this moment, to forgive him and to let down her defenses and simply love him. All that he had done had

been for love. Love for a mother he had hardly
known and love for a woman he had never expected to find love with.

He drifted over to her.

"Our bargain is no longer necessary," she admitted, her heartbeat rising and her breath
catching.

"Why is that?"

"You proved that you love me."

"You know that for sure now?" Rogan asked.
"You have not a doubt? I don't want you to have a
single doubt."

"Not a smidgen of doubt. You've made certain
of it. Besides, my sister agrees and pointed out
just how much you love me."

His brow wrinkled. "Fiona did that?"

She nodded. "She reminded me how you were
willing to walk away from this isle that meant so
much to you, all for my sake. You could not have
done that if you did not truly love me. And you
could not have wooed me so tenaciously if there
was no love in your heart for me."

"And my betrayal? You have said nothing of
that."

She smiled. "Fiona helped me to understand
the wisdom in your choice. I respect you for it
and I forgive you. After all, love caught us both
off guard and created complete chaos. You have
redeemed yourself quite nicely."

He kissed her. "I have waited patiently and
what seemed like forever to hear you say that."

"There is more. Two more very important
matters."

He wrapped his arms around her. "What are they?"

Aliss took his hand and placed it on her stomach. "I will give birth to your child come spring."

He spun her around, scooped her up in his arms, and hugged her tight. "I thought I could not love you any more than I already do, but I love you much, much, much more than ever before."

Aliss laughed, smiled, and grabbed hold of his face. "My turn, husband." She kissed him gently. " I love you with all my heart. I always have. I always will."

Just before their lips touched in a kiss, they both whispered in unison, "I love you."

No fooling! The best in romance comes from Avon Books...

Promise Me Forever by Lorraine Heath

"Lorraine Heath steals your heart!"
—*New York Times* bestselling author Christina Dodd

A very proper lady rekindles the passion—and love—with the Earl of Sachse, a man she thought she'd lost in this latest by *USA Today* bestselling writer Lorraine Heath.

Sighs Matter by Marianne Stillings

"Marianne Stillings writes fun, sexy suspense!"
—*New York Times* bestselling author Carly Phillips

When Claire finds herself in danger she turns to a sexy detective she had vowed never to see again . . . even if they had engaged in a willing, mutual seduction.

The Viscount's Wicked Ways by Anne Mallory

"A fresh, vibrant talent who cannot be ignored."
—*Romantic Times* BOOKclub

The brooding Viscount Blackfield is a man any well-bred lady would shun. But Patience Harrington has never been a proper lady!

Angel in My Bed by Melody Thomas

"An author to watch!"
—*USA Today* bestselling author Karen Hawkins

Meg Farady believed her former life was behind her—until the man she believed had betrayed her came back into her life. And that man is...her husband!

Avon Romantic Treasures

Unforgettable, enthralling love stories, sparkling with passion and adventure from Romance's bestselling authors

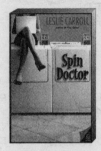